Songbirds

Brought up in London, Christy Lefteri is the child of Cypriot refugees. She is a lecturer in creative writing at Brunel University. Her previous novel, *The Beekeeper of Aleppo*, is an international bestseller, selling over half a million copies worldwide.

Songbirds

CHRISTY LEFTERI

**MANILLA
PRESS**

First published in the UK in 2021 by
MANILLA PRESS
An imprint of Bonnier Books UK
80–81 Wimpole St, London W1G 9RE
Owned by Bonnier Books
Sveavägen 56, Stockholm, Sweden

This is a work of fiction. Names, places, events and
incidents are either the products of the author's
imagination or used fictitiously. Any resemblance to
actual persons, living or dead, or actual
events is purely coincidental.

A CIP catalogue record for this book is
available from the British Library.

Hardback ISBN: 978–1–83877–376–2
Export ISBN: 978–1–78658–082–5
Special edition ISBN: 978–1–78658–125–9

Also available as an ebook and an audiobook

1 3 5 7 9 10 8 6 4 2

Typeset by Palimpsest Book Production Ltd, Falkirk, Stirlingshire
Printed and bound in Great Britain by Clays Ltd, Elcograf S.p.A.

Manilla Press is an imprint of Bonnier Books UK
www.bonnierbooks.co.uk

For Marianne

1

Yiannis

ONE DAY, NISHA VANISHED AND turned to gold. She turned to gold in the eyes of the creature that stood before me. She turned to gold in the morning sky and in the music of the birds. Later, in the shimmering melody of the maid from Vietnam who sang at Theo's restaurant. Later still, in the faces and voices of all the maids that flowed along the streets like a turbulent river of anger, demanding to be seen and heard. This is where Nisha exists. But let's go back. We need to go back.

2

Petra

THE DAY NISHA DISAPPEARED WE went to the mountains. The three of us put on our hiking boots and waited for the bus that goes up to Troodos, which comes just twice a day. Nisha would normally go out on her own on Sundays but this time, for the first time, she decided to come along with Aliki and me.

Oh, it was beautiful up there! The autumn mist mingled with the ferns and pines and twisted oaks. These mountains rose from the sea when the African and European tectonic plates collided. You can even see the Earth's oceanic crust. The rock formations, with their veins and lava pillows, look like they are wearing snake skins.

I love thinking about beginnings. Like that story my aunt used to tell in the back garden: *When the Creator finished his creation of the world – Petra, are you listening?! – he shook the remaining clumps of clay from his hands and they fell to the sea and formed this island.*

Yes, I love thinking about beginnings. I don't like endings, though I suppose I'm like most people in that. An ending can be staring you right in the face without your knowing it. Like the last cup of coffee you have with someone when you thought there would be many more.

Aliki played with leaves as Nisha and I sat beneath the heater at one of the small taverns on the trail we were taking, and drank coffee. I remember the conversation we had.

Nisha had been unusually quiet, stirring her coffee for some time without drinking it. 'Madam,' she said, suddenly, 'I have a question to ask.'

I nodded and waited while she shifted in her seat.

'I would like to take tonight off to—'

'But Nisha, you had the whole day off!'

She didn't speak again for a while. Aliki was gathering armfuls of the leaves and placing them on a bench. We both watched her.

Nisha had decided to spend her free day with us, to join Aliki and me on this trip. I shouldn't be expected to give her more time off.

'Nisha,' I said, 'you have all day off on Sunday. In the evening, you have things to do. You need to help Aliki get her bag ready for school, and then put her to bed.'

'Madam, many of the other women have Sunday night off too.' She said this slowly.

'I know for a fact that other women are not allowed to go gallivanting around at night.'

She acted like she hadn't heard this and said, 'And I don't think madam has plans tonight,' giving me a sly look before returning her gaze to the coffee. 'So maybe madam could put Aliki to bed just for tonight? I will do extra duties next Sunday to make up for it.'

I was about to ask her where she intended to go; what was so important that she was willing to disrupt our routine. Perhaps she saw the disapproving look in my eyes, but there was no time for either of us to say anything because at that moment an avalanche of leaves was released over our heads. Nisha screeched, making a pantomime of it, waving her hands in the air and chasing Aliki, who was slipping away down a path that led into the woods. I could hear them after a while in the forest, like two children, laughing and playing, while I drank my coffee.

By the time we got home that evening, Nisha hadn't mentioned again taking the night off. She made dhal curry, and the house filled with the smell of onions and green chillies, cumin, turmeric, fenugreek and curry leaves. I looked over her shoulder as she sautéed the onions and combined the spices with the split red lentils, finally adding a splash of coconut milk. My mouth was watering. Nisha knew this was my favourite dish. I lit the fire in the living room. It had rained earlier that afternoon and from the living-room window I could see that Yiakoumi opposite had his canopy open, and the cobbled streets glimmered beneath the warm lights of his antique shop.

We do not have central heating, so we sat as close as we could to the flames with the bowls of dhal curry on our laps. Nisha bought me a glass of sweet *zivania* – the aromatic type with caramel and muscat, so warming on this chilly night – and tested Aliki on the nine times table.

'Seven times nine?' Nisha said.

'Sixty-three!'

'Good. Nine times nine?'

'Eighty-one! And there's no point in doing this.'

'Why not?'

'I know them.'

'But you haven't practised.'

'I don't need to. You just have to see the pattern. If you ask me what seven times nine is, I will know that the answer begins with a six. I know that the second number is always one lower than the previous one. So, eight times nine is seventy-two.'

'You're too cheeky for your own good, you know? I'm going to test you anyway.'

'Go ahead. If it helps you.' Aliki sighed and shrugged as if she had resigned herself to this pointless fate of learning something that she already knew. She had every bit the spunk of a nine-year-old girl.

Yes, I remember it all very well, the way that Aliki was munching and yawning and shouting out the answers, the way that Nisha kept her attention on my daughter, saying hardly a word to me. The TV flickered in the background. The news was on with the volume turned low: footage of refugees rescued by coastguards off one of the Greek islands. An image of a child being carried to the shore.

I would have forgotten all of this, but I have been over it again and again, like retracing footsteps on the sand when you have lost something precious.

Aliki lay on her back and kicked her legs up in the air.

'Sit up,' Nisha scolded, 'or you will be sick in your mouth. You've just eaten.' Aliki made a face but she listened: she perched on the sofa and watched TV, her eyes moving over the faces of people as they trudged out of the water.

Nisha refilled my glass for the third time, and I was starting to get sleepy. I looked at my daughter then; a monster of a child, she's always been too big for me, even her curly hair is too thick for me to get my hands around. Curls so thick, like the tentacles of an octopus; they seem to defy gravity, as if she lives in an underwater world.

In the light of the fire, I noticed that Nisha's face was pale, like one of those figs blanched in syrup that have lost their true colour. She caught my eye and smiled, a small, sweet smile. I shifted my gaze over to Aliki.

'Do you have your bag ready for school?' I asked.

Aliki's attention was on the screen.

'We are doing it now, madam.' Nisha got up hastily, gathering the bowls from the coffee table.

My daughter never really spoke to me anymore. She never called me Mum, never addressed me. At some point a seed of silence had been sowed between us and it had grown up and around and between us until it became almost impossible to say anything. Most of the time, she would talk to me through Nisha. Our few conversations were functional.

I watched Nisha as she licked a handkerchief and wiped

a stain off Aliki's jeans and then took the bowls and spoons to the kitchen. Maybe it was the alcohol, or the trip up to Troodos, but I was feeling more tired than usual, a heaviness in my mind and my limbs. I announced that I was going to bed early. I fell asleep straightaway and didn't even hear Nisha putting Aliki to bed.

3

Yiannis

THE DAY THAT NISHA VANISHED, before I even realised she'd gone, I saw in the forest a mouflon ovis. I thought it was odd. These ancient sheep, native to the land, are wild and rare. With a yen for solitude, they usually roam secluded parts of the mountains. I'd never seen one on flat terrain, never this far east. In fact, if I told anyone that I saw a mouflon on the coast, nobody would believe me; it would make national news. I should have known at the time that something was wrong. A long time ago, I understood that sometimes the earth speaks to you, finds a way to pass on a message if only you look and listen with the eyes and ears of your childhood self. This was something my grandfather taught me. But that day in the woods, by the time I saw the golden ovis, I'd forgotten.

It began with a crunch of leaves and earth. A late October

morning. I'd returned to collect the songbirds. I'd driven out to the coast, west of Larnaca, near the villages of Alethriko and Agios Theodoros where there are wild olive and carob groves and plantations of orange and lemon trees. There is also a forest of dense acacia and eucalyptus trees – an excellent spot for poaching. In the small hours of the morning, I'd put out the lime sticks – a hundred of them strategically placed in the trees where the birds come to feed on berries. I'd also hidden amongst the leaves devices that played recordings of calling birds, to lure my prey. Then I found a secluded spot and lit a fire.

I used olive branches as skewers and toasted haloumi and bread. I had a flask of strong coffee in my backpack and a book to pass the time. I didn't want to think about Nisha, of the things she had said the night before, the stern look on her face when she left my flat, the tightness of the muscles in her jaw.

These thoughts fluttered around me with the bats and I waved them away, one by one. I warmed myself and ate and listened to the birdsong in the dark.

So far, it was a normal hunt.

I fell asleep by the fire and dreamt that Nisha was made of sand. She dissolved before me like a castle on the shore.

The rising sun was my calling. I had a last shot of coffee to wake myself fully and threw the rest on the fire, then stamped out the remaining flames and forgot about the dream. The thick woods began to stir, to wake. I usually make more than 2,000 euros for each hanging, and this one was a good one – there were around two hundred blackcaps stuck on the lime sticks. They are worth more than their weight in gold. Tiny songbirds migrating from Europe to Africa to escape the winter. They fly in from the west, over the mountains, stopping here on our island before heading out to sea, towards Egypt. In the spring, they make the return journey, coming from the southern coast. They are so small that we can't shoot them. They're also endangered, a protected species.

I was always frightened at this point, looking over my shoulder, expecting that this time I would be caught and thrown in jail. I'd be totally screwed. This was always my weakness – the fear, the anxiety I felt before killing the birds. But the woods were quiet, no sound of footsteps. Just the birdsong and the breeze through the tree branches.

I removed one of the attached birds from the stick, gently prying its feathers from the glue. This one had tried hard to free itself, it seemed. The more they try to escape, the more stuck they get. I held it in my palms and felt its tiny heart racing. I bit into its neck to end its suffering, and dropped it, lifeless, into a large, black bin-liner. This is the most humane way to kill them – a quick, deep bite to the neck.

I'd filled up the first bag and begun to remove the feathers and berries from the lime sticks with my lips so I could reuse them, when I heard the crunch of leaves.

Shit. I froze for a moment and held my breath. I scanned the surroundings and there it was, in a clearing between the bushes. The mouflon was calmly staring at me. It stood in the long shadows of the trees and it wasn't until the light shifted that I saw the most extraordinary thing: instead of the usual red and brown, its short-haired coat was gold; its curved horns, bronze. Its eyes were the exact colour of Nisha's – the eyes of a lion.

I thought I must be dreaming, that I must still be asleep by the fire.

I took a step forward and the golden mouflon took a small step back, but its posture remained straight and strong, its eyes fixed on mine. Moving slowly, I removed my backpack from my shoulders and took out a slice of fruit. The mouflon shuffled its feet and lowered its head so that its eyes now looked up at me, half-wary, half-threatening. I placed the slice of peach in my palm and held out my hand. I stayed like that, as still as a tree. I wanted it to come closer.

. Seeing the beauty of its face, a memory came to me, sharp and clear. Last March, Nisha and I had gone to the Troodos mountains. She loved to go for long walks on Sunday mornings when she wasn't working. She'd often come with me into the forest to pick mushrooms, wild asparagus, blue mallow or to collect snails. On this day, I had wanted to see if we could spot a mouflon ovis. I hoped that we would see one in the depths of the woods or the verge of the mountains, at the threshold to the sky. We were so high up and she slipped her hand in mine.

'So, we're looking for a sheep?' she'd said.

'Technically, yes.'

'I've seen plenty of sheep.' There was a mocking smile in her eyes.

'I told you, it doesn't look like a sheep! It's a magnificent creature.'

'So. We're looking for a sheep that doesn't look like a sheep.' She was holding her hand over her eyes, scanning the area around us, pretending to look.

'Yes,' I said, matter-of-factly.

This made her laugh and her laughter escaped into the open sky. I felt in that moment that she had never been a stranger.

We'd been walking around for hours and were about to turn back, as the evening was closing in, when I suddenly spotted one standing at the edge of a steep cliff. I could tell it was female as it had smaller curved horns and no ruff of coarse hair beneath its neck. I pointed so that Nisha could see.

The mouflon saw us and faced us straight on.

Nisha stared at it in amazement. 'It's so pretty,' she said. 'It looks like a deer.'

'I told you.'

'Nothing like a sheep.'

'See!'

'Its fur is smooth and brown . . . and such a gentle look on its face. It's like it's going to speak to us. Doesn't it look like it wants to say something?'

I didn't reply and instead watched Nisha watch the animal, her face bright with curiosity.

There was a flash in her eyes, as if the colours of the forest shone through them, as if some secret energy, some nimble animal hiding amongst the trees, had suddenly come to life. She let go of my hand and took a few steps towards the mouflon. Strangely, it stepped away from the edge of the cliff and came slightly closer. I had never seen one approach a human before. Nisha was so gentle in the way she stretched out her hand, in the way she waited for the animal. But there was tension in her. This was all in her eyes: they burned with an emotion that I didn't recognise.

12

In that moment, I felt such a distance from her and the animal, like they shared something I couldn't understand.

However, in the next moment she turned to kiss me. One soft kiss.

Now, dawn in the forest, and the memory of that day brought a sharp pain to my heart. The mouflon ovis gazed at me, transfixed, tilting its head slightly, making a sound which was like a question. A question of a single word.

'I won't hurt you,' I said, and realised suddenly how loud my voice was in the woods, how it disturbed the peace. The Ovis shook its head and took another step back.

'Sorry,' I said to it, this time softly.

For the first time, it broke its gaze. It seemed to rest its eyes on the bucket of birds beside me.

'Sure,' I said. 'I don't blame you. I'm basically a murderer offering you a peach.' I laughed a bit, at the irony of it, as if the Ovis might share the joke.

I threw the slice of fruit on the ground, and this time I walked backwards, retreating into the shadows and the trees. I continued to watch the mouflon from there for a while, this incredible animal, strong and beautiful. It was very still, then it looked at something over to the left and turned its back to me and walked away, into the forest.

I removed the rest of the birds from the lime sticks as quickly as I could, so I could return home and find Nisha. I couldn't wait to tell her what I'd seen. I was hoping that perhaps this story about the mouflon would make her shine again.

13

4

Petra

I WOKE UP IN THE MIDDLE of the night because something broke. I heard a crashing noise, loud and clear, like a window smashing or a glass dashed on the floor with force. The sound had come from the garden, I was sure about that. The clock on my bedside cabinet showed 12 a.m. Could it be the wind? But the night was still and apart from the sound I had heard, there was a deep silence. Maybe it had been a cat?

I put on my slippers and opened the shutters, then the long glass doors to the garden. It was a clear night with a full moon. My house is a three-storey Venetian property in the old part of the city, east of Ledra and Onasagorou, leading to the Green Line that has divided the island since 1974. Sitting in the crystal blue waters of the eastern Mediterranean, our small island has long felt the influence of both Europe and the Middle East. We have been occupied by the Ottomans. We have been colonised by the British. And then we became a battleground between the Greeks and the Turks, our population split, until peacekeeping forces stepped in and, literally, drew the line. This partition continues to hold our island in a tentative peace, although missives about reunification are constantly in the news. Our city of Nicosa, on the Greek side, brushes the Green Line right where I live. When I was a little girl, I thought the end of our street reached the end of the world. There is no violence today with our Turkish Cypriot neighbors in the north, but it is an uneasy peace, to be sure.

We live only on the ground floor, each of our bedrooms looking out onto the garden. Two years ago, I rented out the storey above me to a man called Yiannis, who made a living by collecting mushrooms and wild greens from the forests. A bit reclusive, but he was a good tenant, always paid his rent on time. The top floor is empty, or full of ghosts, as my mother used to say, which would make my father scoff at her and respond always with the same words: *Ghosts are memories. Nothing more, nothing less.*

In the garden, there is boat. There were times in the past, on long nights when I couldn't sleep, that I would see Nisha sitting out in my father's tiny fishing boat, *The Sea Above the Sky* painted in pale blue on its hull. The paint is peeling, and the wood is crumbling. It's a boat that has made so many journeys. Nisha would sit in it and stare out into the darkness. The boat has one oar – the other has been missing for as long as I can remember – but someone placed an olive tree

15

branch in its place. Because my bed is next to the window, I would watch her for a while through the slits of the shutters, and wonder what was going through her mind, alone like that, in the middle of the night.

But on this night, she wasn't there. I looked around to try to determine the cause of the crashing noise. I was half expecting the crunch of glass beneath my feet. But there didn't seem to be anything broken or out of place.

The moon illuminated the pumpkins, the winding jasmine and vines, the cactus and fig tree to the far right, near the glass doors of Aliki's room, and, in the middle, on a slightly raised patch of earth, where the roots have cracked through the concrete, the orange tree – like a queen on her throne. I always felt, growing up, that this tree quietly commanded the garden.

Everything was so still. Still and quiet. Hardly a leaf moved. I walked around the garden. Near the steps that lead up to Yiannis's flat, I finally discovered the source of the noise: a ceramic money-box that I'd had since I was a child – it had smashed on the ground, its white shell broken and hundreds of old lira scattered about, making tiny pools of gold.

It was the kind of money-box that you have to break in order to get to the treasure inside. I remembered dropping in the coins, imagining a day when I would retrieve them. My aunt Kalomira had made it for me in the village of Lefkara, where she lived with her husband, who used to eat the balls of a goat or the brain and eyes of a lamb with lemon and salt. I had watched her spinning the clay on the wheel. Her husband offered me an eye. I refused. Later, she had

16

painted the pot white and added a funny sketch of a dog. It was ready for me and waiting on a shelf when I returned with my mother to see her many weeks later.

I had never broken it; the time was never right. So, I had left the coins safely inside, like wishes or secret dreams collected from childhood.

But who had broken it now? How had it fallen from the garden table?

I decided to go back to bed and ask Nisha to deal with it in the morning.

I pulled the covers over me and in the dark and quiet of my room, I remembered my mother by my side.

'What will you do with all that money?' she had asked.

'I will buy wings!'

'Like the wings of a bird.'

'No, more like the wings of a firefly. They will be transparent and when I wear them, I will fly around the garden at night and glow in the dark.'

She had laughed and kissed me on the cheek. 'You will be beautiful as always.'

The memory faded and I suddenly felt a deep pang of guilt for the absence of words and dreams and laughter with my own daughter. How had I lost her?

Or had she lost me?

5

Yiannis

WHEN I GOT BACK FROM hunting it was still early afternoon. I couldn't wait to tell Nisha about the mouflon ovis I'd seen in the woods. I wanted to describe its incredible beauty, how unusual its golden fur had been and how, oddly, it had had the eyes of a lion.

The more I said these things in my head, however, the crazier they sounded. I knew that Nisha would listen to me. She would look at me like I was bat-shit crazy, humour me with that slow nod of her head, but she would also suggest we return later that afternoon so that she could see it for herself.

I knocked on the glass doors of her bedroom and waited. I usually heard her flip-flops on the marble floor, but this time there was silence. I knocked again and waited a few minutes, then again and waited a further five. Maybe she had walked down to the grocery store, or she could have gone to the church. Although she wasn't Christian, she liked to light a candle and appreciate the peace and quiet. In church there were no demands of her, no tuts, no shaking heads. Nobody disturbed her. The locals just saw a good Christian woman praying amongst other good Christians. In there, she'd said, everyone was equal as long as you were one of them.

I decided to head upstairs and start cleaning the birds. I sat on a stool in the spare room and, one by one, I plucked out their feathers and threw the birds into a large basin. This was a task that took some time, and one that I never looked forward to. It was tedious work I did automatically, and left my hands covered in feathers and sticky blood. Once this task was complete, I would soak them in water or pickle them in vinegar, place them in various sized containers depending on the order, and take them out to various restaurants, hotels and venues around the island.

As I held one of the birds in my left hand, about to pluck its feathers with my right, I felt an unexpected vibration on my palm. I paused and looked down and noticed that the soft brown feathers on the bird's chest rose; its right wing twitched. It suddenly felt heavy on my palm, as if I was holding a paperweight, and the vibration seemed to travel through me – along my arteries, up my arm, until I felt a terrible sensation, a deep tremble in my chest.

I felt nauseous. I dropped the bird onto the table and shifted on the stool, taking long, deep breaths. The bird lay there, breathing, its chest rising and falling more visibly now.

I was four or five years old, walking with my dad in the wild fields of the mountains. He stopped to pick some hawthorn berries. On the ground something bright caught my eye: a yellow wagtail. Even at this age, I knew the names of some of the bird species, migratory and native, because my grandfather had taught me. I loved the birds. I watched them building their lives high up in the trees and sky. I was desperate to catch them, hold them in my hands, to look closely at their feathers and decipher their amazing colours.

Here was my opportunity! This yellow wagtail was motionless amongst the brambles. Even as I approached, it didn't move. I picked it up and nestled it in my palms – it was so dead that it was dry. I examined it: its small, silver-grey bill, brown tail and brown primary feathers; while its chin and breast, belly and under-feathers were the brightest yellow I'd ever seen. Its crown, shoulder and back were a darker yellow, greyish in tone. I examined its eyeline and eyestripe, its open blank eyes, its wing-bars and lores, its twiglike feet.

I imagined I was holding gold. In my hands I held pure gold.

I lived simply and saved money so that I could stop the poaching. All my neighbours thought that I made a living picking and selling wild asparagus and mushrooms, wild greens, artichokes and snails – depending on the season. I mean, of course, that kind of foraging was my day job and provided pocket money. But I would never have been able to build a future for myself relying on the measly income of selling vegetables and snails. Not after what had happened. It was a risk I couldn't take.

I hated lying to Nisha. I'd managed to keep the poaching a secret for so long: it wasn't difficult – when I came back with bulging bin bags, people would assume I'd collected other things from the forest. People didn't question much around here, and many of the houses were empty because so few wanted to live so close to the Green Line. It reminded them of the war, of division, of abandoned homes and lost lives. This isn't something one wants to be reminded of on a daily basis.

I had my reasons for choosing to rent a flat there. It was reasonably quiet, most of the residents were old, and I knew I could get away with more. And besides, I enjoyed sitting on the balcony in the evening, listening to the bouzouki from Theo's restaurant, and watching the old men eating, drinking and playing cards. I joined them sometimes, but mostly I kept my distance. In this part of old Nicosia there were brothel-type bars, and when the men finished eating and drinking at the restaurant, they usually made their way to them.

There was one such bar at the end of our street, called Maria's. Its windows were frosted, and through the old wooden door wafted the heavy scent of sweat mingled with cigarette smoke and old beer. The barmaid, in tight black clothing, served sliced apples and peanuts, olives and hummus. I have been there twice, on both occasions to meet Seraphim.

I watched the bird on the counter now, the way its beak opened and closed, the way its matted feathers twitched. I checked its neck and saw that the wound I had made wasn't that deep. It looked up at me, straight into my eyes, and seemed to be saying, 'You sick prick, I can see you.'

I put some water on my finger and bought it to its beak. At first it didn't drink but I kept my hand there for a while, and, after a few minutes, it dipped its bill into the droplet of water and tilted its head to swallow it. I decided to line a small container with a clean towel and I put the bird in there to rest. I sat there and watched it for a while. It was suspicious of me, kept giving me that look.

Some time later, I had filled a whole bin-liner with feathers. The little bird was lying still in the container, breathing steadily. The naked birds were piled up in the basin by my side.

I thought you were a different person, Nisha had said.

I put some water in the basin, using a hose, and left the birds in there for a while to soak. Then, I dipped my finger into a glass of water and bought it to the little bird's beak again. This time, it dropped its bill immediately into the water and tilted its head so that it could swallow. It seemed to be treating me less like a killer and this was reassuring. I did it a few more times until it didn't want any more.

I thought you were a different person.

After I had finished cleaning the birds, I made myself some supper and sat on the balcony, eagerly awaiting Nisha's knock

22

at the door. Most evenings, she would wait for Petra to go to bed before sneaking out into the garden. The staircase was on the far left, behind a large fig tree, so Petra wasn't able to see it from her window. Nisha didn't want Petra to know. She wasn't allowed to have a boyfriend. Nisha would slip out at around 11 p.m., unnoticed. She would stay with me for a few hours – we would talk for a while and make love and fall asleep. Then her alarm would go off at 4 a.m., and she would unfurl herself from my arms, go out into the garden and sit in the boat while the sun rose. I was never sure why she didn't just go straight to her room, but the time she spent alone in the old fishing boat seemed to be important, and I didn't question it. I would turn off the light and go back to sleep for a few hours.

When she came last night, things felt different. We sat by the open doors of the balcony, overlooking the street below, with the sound of the bouzouki and a sky full of stars. It was chilly and she had a throw wrapped around her. She was quieter than usual, as if there was something on her mind, but then she started telling me a story about her grandfather and how he'd ended up with a glass eye.

Nisha was in the middle of saying, '. . . and then he chased him with a baseball bat . . .' when I placed the ring in front of her on the table.

She looked down at it, then picked it up and put it, not on her finger, but on her open palm. She was gazing down at it so I couldn't see her eyes, just the soft darkness of her lids and lashes.

'Will you marry me, Nisha?' I asked.

She said nothing.

'I've had the ring for a while. I wanted to ask you this summer . . .' I paused there, as I couldn't finish the sentence: I couldn't bring myself to remind her of what had happened just two short months earlier. '. . . and then you were so heartbroken.'

She nodded.

'But I meant everything I said.'

She looked up at me. Straight lips. Hard eyes.

She didn't believe me.

'We can still do all of the things we were going to do. We can still go together to Sri Lanka, back to your home. You can be with Kumari. We can have a family.'

'I fell in love with you as soon as I saw you.' Her voice was barely a whisper.

I tried to remember the first time she'd seen me. What had I been doing? What had she seen in me in that moment?

'But I loved my husband too.' Then the muscles of her jaw clenched, her shoulders and body stiffened. She closed her fingers around the ring, tightening her fist, possessing it.

Without a further word, without a yes or a no, she walked towards the back door that led to the stone staircase.

'What was I doing when you first saw me?' I asked.

She stopped in her tracks, but did not turn around. 'Feeding the chickens.'

'Feeding the chickens?'

She didn't reply. Instead, she turned and looked at me over her shoulder, and then said, 'You see, I thought you were a different person.'

She didn't sit in the boat that night; she went straight to bed.

Around 11 p.m. I expected to hear Nisha's gentle tapping on the back door, but it didn't come. Sunday was one of the nights she usually called Kumari, so I was sure she would appear. She always spoke to her daughter in the middle of the night because of the time difference, and she liked to do it at my place due to the fact that I had a tablet and she wanted to be able to see Kumari while she spoke to her. Before she met me, she had talked to Kumari on the phone. To give her some privacy, I would sit out on the balcony and wait for her to finish.

However, she told me once that it was also her way of keeping the two worlds of her life apart, separate but in harmony at the same time.

'What did you mean by that?' I'd asked her one night, when she'd finished the call with Kumari. I came back inside and she crawled into bed with me.

'Well,' she'd replied, 'downstairs at Petra's I am nanny to Aliki. But when I come up here – and everyone is asleep and there are no demands of me – I remember who I really am. I can be a real mother to my own daughter.'

Now, I made myself a coffee and sat on the balcony and listened to the sound of the bouzouki. I took the little bird from the container and sat holding it in my palms. It took a bit of convincing to get it to stay there, but then it slept, breathing slowly, steadily, its tiny body expanding and releasing. When it woke up, I gave it water, drop by drop, until it didn't want any more.

An hour passed and still there was no sign of her. At midnight, I decided to go downstairs and knock on her bedroom door.

On the last step, something got tangled in my feet – one of the stray cats, the black one, the one with the different-coloured eyes. I lost my balance and grabbed on to a small garden table to stop myself from falling. The table tipped and from it fell an old ceramic money-box that belonged to Petra. It smashed on the ground, the coins spilling out, and when I saw the light of Petra's room turn on, I rushed back up the stairs, closing the door gently.

I couldn't sleep that night. I couldn't stop thinking about Nisha.

Where had she disappeared to?

Had I scared her away?

You see, I thought you were a different person.

I sat on the balcony with the bird for the rest of the night, until the sun began to rise behind the buildings to the east. Far away, I imagined the sun's rays lighting up the sea. And the little bird filled its lungs and began to sing.

The red lake at Mitsero reflects a sunset, captures it, holds
it, even when the sun has died.

Red lake, toxic lake, copper lake. Mothers and fathers
tell their children stories about it. Never go near the red
lake at Mitsero! Tales of deep passages underground,
where men crawled like animals and died in darkness.
Stay away from the red lake at Mitsero! By all means, run
along the dust paths and into the fields – as long as you
avoid the snakes and hornets – but whatever you do, keep
well away from the water.

On this day, in late October, there is a dead hare on
the rocky terrain by the lake. So fresh it is still intact.
The wind blows its fur the wrong way. Its footprints are
scoured into the earth beside it. There are no wounds
on its body; it seems to have run out of life, for one
reason or another. Soon the hare will return to the
earth, but for now it lies still, in a running position, as if

it had been hoping to make it further, like we all do.

What a beautiful lake it is. Copper bleeds into it from the past. The lake is a consequence of what has been left behind: when the mines were abandoned a crater was left. As winter approaches, just as it does now, the crater fills with water. After a rainstorm, rivers of yellow and orange trickle into the red water, changing its colour – this is how the sunset appears.

But why not a sunrise?

Because a sunrise is infused with the promise of a new day.

A sunset holds the expectation of something else – the hush and darkness of the night. The lake exists on the verge of darkness.

6

Petra

IT WAS 6.30 A.M. WHEN I woke up. Nisha would have just had a shower and gone out into the garden with long, damp hair, picking oranges and collecting fresh eggs. After bringing in the eggs, she would fry or boil them. When we had courgette flowers or wild greens, she would scramble the eggs over them and add lots of lemon and pepper. This was Aliki's favourite.

On this morning, Nisha was not outside. A silvery mist rested over the leaves, as if the garden had exhaled. The lira on the ground now glimmered in the sun.

In the kitchen, Aliki was sitting at the table, still in her pyjamas, swinging her legs and playing a game on her iPad. Her loose hair fell about her face and shoulders. By this time, it was usually in a neat ponytail and she should have been wearing her school uniform and finishing off her orange juice.

'Where is Nisha?' I said.

Aliki looked up from the screen and shrugged.

'Have you eaten?'

She tutted, no. I saw a stroke of uncertainty in her eyes. I thought she would speak but she slouched and sank further down into her seat.

I went into Nisha's room and found that she wasn't there. In fact, her bed looked like it hadn't been slept in.

Returning to Aliki, and with as much cheer as I could muster, I said, 'Why don't you go and get changed and I'll make breakfast? Then I'll take you to school.'

She got up, reluctantly, but did as I'd suggested. In the meantime, I called Nisha's mobile a few times, but it went straight to voicemail.

'Nisha,' I said. 'Where are you? Call me back.'

I began to boil the eggs and make toast, opening all the cupboards to find where Nisha kept the fig jam. I was becoming increasingly irritated – fear hadn't gripped me yet.

It was Aliki who had the deeper instincts that I lacked. After I had peeled the eggs and laid the table, Aliki still hadn't come back to the kitchen so I went to her room and found her in front of the mirror, crying. She'd put on her uniform, but she'd been unable to tie up her hair. The elastic band was stuck in a knot of curls.

I told her to sit on the bed and I perched beside her and gently untangled the band. Then, with a wide hair-brush, I tried to bring all that hair together into a high ponytail, like Nisha did. But the curls were wild and unruly

30

and tried to escape – as I brought one side up, the other side fell out of my grip and tumbled back down to her shoulder.

I could feel her shifting, uncomfortable and impatient.

'I'll tell you what!' I said. 'Forget the ponytail. Let's do something different.'

So, I plaited her hair and she pulled the thick black braid over her right shoulder and stood to look at herself in the mirror. Her patio doors were open and the room was full of sunlight and music from the birds. Even the mist came in, like a lost spirit.

Such a crisp autumn day, and it should have been a happy morning, like every other. But what I saw in Aliki's eyes as she stared at her reflection was a broadening expanse of worry.

I took Aliki to school, something Nisha usually did. I also had to leave work for an hour to collect her in the afternoon – my shop assistant, Keti, didn't work on Mondays. I then had to bring Aliki back to work with me for a while. We made our way through heavy traffic to Onasagorou Street, just by Eleftheria Square, to the main branch of my clinic, Sun City – I am an optician – which sat in a stately row of expensive boutiques, ice-cream parlours, patisseries, restaur-ants, galleries, cafes, and also the base of the British Council – a converted townhouse on Solomou Square. Aliki amused herself by trying out the least expensive pairs of glasses and doing impressions of people in front of the large mirror at the front. In a pair of metal-rimmed, round specs she pretended to be Gandhi; in some round transparent anti-blue light glasses she was a K-pop star; in a plain brown-framed pair she was Nisha, and she grabbed the feather duster and cleaned the shelves.

That night, Nisha still hadn't returned. I made some dinner, but Aliki wasn't hungry. She sat in front of the TV.

'Your food is on the table. I've covered it to keep it warm,' I said. 'I'm just popping out to speak to Mrs Hadjikyriacou next door. Find out if she's seen Nisha. I'll be outside if you need anything.'

Aliki nodded and continued to watch the news, which I'm sure she wasn't really paying any attention to. She seemed preoccupied, and she was sucking the knuckle of her index finger as she had done when she was much younger.

I'd never paid much attention to the other maids in our neighbourhood before. The maids here did everything – they were hired and paid (lower than the minimum wage) to clean the house, but ended up being child-carers, shop assistants, waitresses. Outside, two women, probably Filipinos, walked along the street with a young Cypriot child between them – a little girl with pigtails, holding each of their hands. She ran and skipped and they lifted her by the arms. In a house down the road a maid whacked the dust out of a rug on the railing of the porch. She waved at the two who were passing. Now, turning the corner, another maid was being pulled along by a huge sand-coloured hunting dog. Outside,

Yiakoumi's shop, yet another maid was bringing in the antiques – displayed on a table during the day – in order to shut up shop for the night. To the right, Theo's restaurant was starting to get busy, as it was close to dinner time. His two Vietnamese maids dashed about in their rice hats, holding drinks or trays of dips. Each time I saw one of these women, my heart dropped, hoping that Nisha might appear beside them.

Right next door, on a beach chair, sat Mrs Hadjikyriacou, who Aliki called the Paper-Lady. She sitting on her usual deckchair, in the front garden next door to ours. Her skin was so white and creased that she looked as though someone had scrunched her up into a ball and opened her up again. She sat there most of the day, and late into the evening, sometimes until midnight, watching the day go by, the seasons change, and she remembered everything – her mind like a journal, full of pages and pages of the past, or at least every bit of the past that has walked her way. It is a well-known fact that her hair turned white overnight, during the war, when the island was divided. That's when she started storing everything in her mind, so that nobody could take her soul from her. This is what she told me once, many years ago.

She sat there now, perched on her chair, watching TV, which had been brought outside; the wire was stretched to breaking point, plugged into a socket in the living room. She spat phlegm into a handkerchief, inspected it, then shouted at the TV. She was furious, it seemed, about a decision the president had made.

I hoped that she might have seen Nisha leave.

I watched as her maid came out with a tray of fruit and water, placing it on a small table by the old lady's side.

'I don't want any,' she said, flicking her wrist in dismissal, and the maid mumbled something in her own language before returning to whatever she had been doing inside. This maid was new and hadn't yet learned a word of Greek or English, so they communicated with their respective mother tongues, plus gestures and eye-rolls.

As usual the Paper-Lady was surrounded by cats, all of which Aliki had named. One of the cats was sitting to attention, staring at her, meowing.

'What is it, my dear?' she asked, with a sigh. 'What is it, my darling sesame dough? You want to drink? You want to eat? Come to me and I'll kiss you!' In response, the cat turned its back to her. Then, without even looking my way, she lowered the volume on the TV, and said, 'Petra, come over and have some fruit.'

I approached, with usual pleasantries about the weather, taking a slice of orange out of courtesy, and then I asked whether she had seen Nisha the previous night or, in fact, that morning.

Sitting back with her fingers laced together, she searched her mind, her head tilted slightly to the right, towards the light of Yiakoumi's shop. She fixed her gaze on the window display. 'According to seven of Yiakoumi's clocks, it was ten thirty when I saw her. According to one, it was midnight.'

I waited for her to say more but instead she scooped up

34

one of the cats and placed it on her lap. The black cat's eyes were gold, with an area of patchy blue that looked like the Earth from a great distance.

'Did she say where she was going?'

'She was in a hurry. She said something about meeting a man.'

'Who?'

'Do you think if I sniff my nails they will tell me the answer?' Her stock phrase.

She stared at me for a while, as if she was waiting for me to stop chewing. When I swallowed the last bit of orange she tapped the plate with her finger.

'Have some more.'

I could see that her attention would remain on the plate until I obliged, so I took another slice. She watched me as I bit into it, and as I wiped juice from my chin.

'Was there anything unusual . . . ?' I began.

'My daughter is coming next week from New Zealand. She's coming to see me from the other side of the world.'

'That's wonderful.' Through the crocheted curtain I could see her maid's silhouette; she looked like she was bending down to wipe the coffee table, the glow of an orange lamp behind her. She was shaking her head, talking to herself about the old lady, no doubt – unless there was something else that had peeved her so badly that she looked like she had taken a bite of a lemon straight from the tree.

Just at that moment, the bouzouki started playing in the restaurant and the cats, as if on cue, scurried off in that direction.

'Did she say anything else?' I said. 'Nisha, I mean.'

'No.'

'Which way did she go?'

She pointed to the right. 'Then she turned left at the end of the road.'

'But that way's a dead end,' I said. What would Nisha be doing going down there? It only led to the Green Line, to the military base and the buffer zone that separated the Turkish and Greek parts of the island. Nobody went that way.

Mrs Hadjikyriacou was looking up at me, examining me. From her corneas, triangular films of tissue threatened to take over her eyes.

'What's the problem?' she asked.

'I don't know where Nisha is. I'm sure it's nothing to worry about, she probably just—'

She interrupted me: 'Just what? You mean to tell me she hasn't returned?'

I nodded.

'I presume you've tried her phone?'

I nodded again and she looked up to the sky, her silvery eyes restless. She looked so worried that I suddenly had the urge to reassure her.

'Honestly, I'm sure it will be fine. There has to be a reasonable explanation.'

'No,' she said.

'Maybe she went to see a friend.'

'No,' she said again. 'Nisha would never take off like that, even for a day. You must know that. She is an extremely conscientious young woman.'

She picked up a slice of orange, bought it to her lips and, seeming to remember that she didn't want any, tore it up into sections, throwing the pieces on the ground for the cats when they returned.

Then she reached out and placed a sticky hand on my arm. 'Petra,' she said, staring at me hard, like she was trying to see me through a thick mist, 'there is something not right here.'

I returned home and checked on Aliki. I found her sitting on her bed in the dark. She was in her pyjamas and sipping a mug of warm milk, which she cradled in her palms. Her school bag was at the foot of the bed and her uniform was hanging ready, on the back of her chair by the desk. If I hadn't known better, I would have thought Nisha had been here.

'You've eaten?' I said, and Aliki glanced at me over the mug and nodded. 'You're OK?' Again, she nodded.

I went over and gave her a kiss on the forehead. That's when I noticed that the black cat with the different-coloured eyes was sleeping on the bed beside her, at first glance just a gleam in the moonlight, its shiny black fur oily in the darkness. I was about to say that she knew very well that cats weren't allowed in the house, but, anticipating my admonishment, she quickly said, 'Monkey has had a tough day. He needs some tender loving care.'

'You've named him Monkey?'

'Look at his long, bent tail. I think he swings from trees.'

I smiled. *My clever girl.* I backed out of her room and closed the door.

But I was on edge. I couldn't shake the feeling of Mrs Hadjikyriacou's hand on my arm, her insistence that something was amiss. I peered out of the window to see that she had gone inside, the street now dark and empty.

7

Yiannis

I N THE MIDDLE OF THE night, Seraphim and I drove
out to a beach in Protaras. Once a week, during the
autumn migration, he and I would go out to sea to
catch birds. These were our most lucrative hunts. We drove
to the east coast in Seraphim's van. Although it was cold in
the early hours, Seraphim had his window wide open and
drank in big gulps of air. He always did this as we approached
the water. I hardly spoke. I couldn't stop thinking about
Nisha. I tried to imagine where she might be, but my mind
met only darkness. I had tried ringing her many times but
her phone was switched off.

The villages around us were quiet, only one light was on
in a house on a hillside. Soon I could hear the waves.

You see, I thought you were a different person.

It was Seraphim who had got me into poaching. Seraphim

was in love with money – but I'd be lying if I didn't say the same about myself. Once upon a time, I had been an executive at Laiki Bank. I lived in a luxury apartment on the other side of the city – the sparkly, fashionable district. My grandfather was a farmer in his former years, and a park ranger thereafter. My ancestors lived the rural life, farmers and shepherds who worked the land. Father was determined that I would make it in the world. He encouraged me to study hard so that I would *climb from the soil to the stars!*

And, of course, I did. The banker's life was appealing, stable. I would be financially secure, rich even, and wouldn't have to rely on the weather and the seasons, like my forefathers had. At least this was what my father told me. I hadn't realised then that the financial world had its own storms and droughts.

Before the financial crisis of 2008, Laiki Bank was booming – it was set to become the European investment vehicle of Dubai's sovereign wealth fund, and it played a pivotal role in the island's financial services industry, welcoming fresh-faced Russian entrepreneurs who arrived with cash-filled suitcases then set up companies on the island, run by local lawyers and accountants. At one point, bank transfers between Russia and Cyprus were astronomical. Laiki had even handled the affairs of Slobodan Milosevic. His administration moved billions of dollars in cash through Laiki in the 1990s in spite of UN sanctions.

I loved to tell these stories at swanky dinner parties – people were always impressed. Teresa, my wife at the time, loved that sort of life. She would never have married me if

I'd followed the life of my grandfather. Our story was a simple one: she worked at Laiki's rival bank, we met, we fell in love.

But Laiki got into fatal trouble because of aggressive expansion into Greece. The balance sheet was overstretched and then the global financial crisis hit and everything went wrong. Laiki was placed under administration and I lost my job, my savings, my wife – in that order. But while the humiliating turn in the bank's fortunes reflected Cyprus's deeper troubles, the turn of events in my life shone a light on the black hole that existed at its centre.

The van rattled along a dirt path. Seraphim began, as usual, to hum an old children's song. He always hummed this rhyme as we approached the water, something that harked back to the days before the war. But the memory was too buried for me to retrieve it and I never asked him.

'You need to loosen up,' he said now. 'I've told you so many times, come down to Maria's with me – I'll get you sorted. Last night I was with the Filipino girl again. She's very sweet, you know. If it wasn't for my wife I think I might fall in love.'

I remained silent, staring out of the window, watching the approaching opaque darkness of the sea and sky.

'What's wrong with you?' Seraphim asked, flicking his eyes towards me. He was about two years older than me and, in spite of all his money, dressed like an odd-job man no matter the occasion. A small, dark man with large hands, his hair was mostly uncombed and was receding at the front. Usually unshaven, he reminded me of the rats that live in the sewers along the banks of the Pedieos River. He was married to a Russian woman called Oksana, whom he spoke about often and fondly; but most nights he visited the bars in old Nicosia, searching for the women who had to find another way to make ends meet – as he put it. Nice Romanian, Moldavian, Ukrainian girls – not too expensive – Sri Lankan, Vietnamese, Nepalese maids. Women who came here to make money, one way or another – as he put it. As if he was doing them a favour.

I turned a blind eye to the crap Seraphim spewed. He was dodgy to the core, but there was something charming about him, a certain warmth. And he was good at keeping secrets. He held steadily to the steering wheel as the van bounced over the rough terrain. Seraphim was the only person in the world who knew about my relationship with Nisha.

'Nisha's gone,' I said.

I could hear the sea now, below us to the right, breathing heavily. The clouds parted and the sky around the moon turned silver. I realised he'd been silent for too long.

'Nisha is gone,' I said again.

'That's not possible.'

'Why not?'

He was quiet again and he made a right turn now, onto the road that would lead down to the jetty of a small private cove. There was a tiny church made of limestone on this corner, with a huge white cross that was illuminated at night.

'Why would she leave?' he asked, finally.

42

'I don't know,' I said. 'She just disappeared.' I paused. 'I proposed to her on Saturday night and she disappeared on Sunday night. Well, any time on Sunday, I guess.'

'Sunday night,' he said. Not a question, but a statement. But before I could say anything else, he'd brought the van to a swift halt, turned off the engine and opened the driver's side door.

Vyacheslav was waiting for us as usual by one of the boats, holding his silver thermal flask, smoking a cigarette and reading the news on his phone, his hair so blond it was almost white. He grinned when he saw us, throwing the butt on the ground and greeting us as usual.

Seraphim and I pulled a huge, rolled-up mist net from the back of the van, one side each, rather like we were carrying a body. I kept looking over my shoulder, sweating. These sea-hunts were the most dangerous. If we were caught, we'd be fined 20,000 euros and land ourselves in jail. Each time we went out to sea, I thought: *Surely this time we will be caught.*

Vyacheslav began to unwind the mist net in order to attach either end to the two boats. He would sail with Seraphim, as usual, and I would go out alone. I think he preferred Seraphim's company.

'It's clear now,' Vyacheslav said, looking up at the sky, his eyes narrowing, his face creasing into a big smile. 'This'll be a good hunt.'

'Let's hope so,' Seraphim said. We all spoke to each other in English, in our respectively heavy accents.

Vyacheslav lit another cigarette and recited the main

headlines of the day, something he always did, while Seraphim made sure that the nets were attached securely. I placed a couple of calling devices in each boat.

Thousands of migrating birds sweep down as the sun begins to rise, coming to the island to stop for a rest on their arduous journey across the Mediterranean Sea. This island, this little sea rock, is along one of the major migration routes. The birds see the lights of the town and fly towards them. Some birds even use the coast as a leading line, helping them to find their way. The mist nets are so fine that the birds fly straight into them. Every attempt to escape causes further entanglement. It's not just blackcaps we catch, but all kinds – the nets are indiscriminate. Summer is relatively quiet, but during passage times, particularly autumn and spring, more birds move through – so many in fact, that we make a killing.

As we sailed out to sea, I was suddenly hit by the feeling that I was drifting further away from Nisha: that some invisible cord that kept us together was being stolen by an invisible but powerful current. She always seemed to know what I was feeling, or rather she carried my feelings, even the ones I didn't know I had. She would rest her chin on her fist, lying on my bed, or sitting at the dining table, and look into me with her lion eyes.

'What's making you so sad?' she would say, or 'Why are you angry today?' or 'Where have you disappeared to?' She knew my moods better than I knew them myself. The only other person who had ever paid me that kind of attention was my grandfather, when I was a boy. He was always so aware, as we walked through the woods: where I was stepping, whether I was too excited and would frighten the animals, whether I was tired, hungry. Once, after my dog had died, he let me talk about her all the way from Troodos to the East coast. We got off the bus, and although I was animated and told him joyful stories, he knew from the way I dragged my feet that my heart was heavy, and that when we went for our swim I would have sunk if I hadn't given him those memories to carry.

Last summer, I had shown Nisha a photo of myself when I was six, taken in front of the farmhouse in Troodos. There was a cow in the yard just behind me, and I was crouching down tying my laces and looking at the camera, smiling. It was my mother who had taken that photo; I remember her carrying my sister on her hip. She had come back from taking my father and grandfather their lunch in the fields, her face red, a scarf tied around her head. Nisha cried when she saw it. She was sitting naked on my bed by the open doors of the balcony, the air hot, sticky, full of night jasmine and the perfume of women who roamed the streets. It was nearly midnight and the music from Theo's drifted up to us. We had the fan rotating between us. Her yellow eyes had welled up and tears dropped down onto my wrist as I held the photo.

'Why are you crying?'

'You were just so beautiful and sweet,' she said, wiping her face with the back of her hands. Then she lay down in my arms and I could feel her tears on my chest. I held her tight, not knowing if I was comforting her or if in fact it was she who was comforting me. I didn't really understand what had made her cry. What had she seen in my face from all those years ago? What unfathomable dreams had she projected into the future?

As the boats went further out into the water, broadening the distance between us, the mist net stretched out, almost invisibly, just above the sea, between the two boats. The lights of the town became smaller as we drifted further, steering the boats so that the distance between them remained stable and we were running parallel to each other. It took some careful sailing not to tear the nets or let them droop, but I'd had a lot of practice and Vyacheslav had taught me well.

Once we had gone out far enough, Vyacheslav raised his hand in the air and we turned off the engines. The boats bobbed on the soft waves now, and we waited. The horizon was still black.

You were just so beautiful and sweet.

I must have fallen asleep because when I woke up I saw a thousand wings silhouetted against the sky, the sun cracking through the edge of the world. The birds that flew highest missed the net and made it to the shore; the others, the hundreds that skimmed the water or flew a few metres above it – their journeys ended there. They crashed into an invisible barrier, the fine threads of our massive net, and there they would flap, screech and cry. But there they would stay.

Before the sun rose completely, we steered our boats back to shore and the three of us pulled the net out of the water. Some birds were drowned, others were still trying to escape. We lay the net out on the sand and began to remove the birds, one by one. Amongst the blackcaps were robins and redwings, grey and purple herons, honey buzzards, red-footed falcons, goldcrests and some large wintering black gulls.

We threw the dead into the bin bags and the others – the ones that were still moving – we bit into their necks, severing the artery for a quick death, and adding their bodies to the rest. Other birds were still coming in to land on the shore, and tiny sparrows hopped beside us on the sand. A stray cat with bulging eyes came to sniff out what was happening, winding its way between us, head-butting our knees and elbows for attention. Seraphim threw it one of the birds and the cat took it in its jaw and sprinted off.

'You shouldn't do that,' Vyacheslav said, with creased brows. 'You might as well throw the vermin money.'

'It's only one!' Seraphim laughed. 'Keep your hair on, as they say in English. Cats are hunters, just like us.'

'They hunt to survive and they hunt for the sake of it, depending on their circumstances,' I said. I'd been quiet until that point, and the two men flicked their eyes towards me without much interest and continued with their task. The sky was lightening now and we had to be faster – we had to have all this sorted and cleared before people in the town began to wake up.

On the way home, I wanted to talk to Seraphim more about Nisha's disappearance, but he was distracted, giddy from our big take of the morning. He was jabbering incessantly about the plans for our next hunt: we would go to the

Akrotiri peninsula, a good place to trap – being part of the British military base there, it was largely undeveloped. We would take lime sticks and mist nets to the Akrotiri marsh reserve and to the pools behind Lady's Mile beach. We would need quite a lot of lime sticks, so he was going to prepare them in advance.

It was Seraphim who kept our small organisation running, and above him were men who gave him orders. We had the bags of birds with us in the back: Seraphim and I would take a few bags each, clean them, and then give Vyacheslav a cut of the profit. Vyacheslav was exempt from cleaning the birds because the boats belonged to him. We would each make about 3,000 euros from the morning's efforts.

As I got out of the van, I paused with the passenger door open. 'Sunday,' I said to him. 'Nisha disappeared on Sunday. Was there anything particular about that day? Do you remember anything?'

'No, why would I?' he said.

'Because earlier you said it wasn't possible. That Nisha wouldn't have run away. What did you mean by that?'

'I think you misheard me, my friend. You know what these women are like – they come and go like the rain.'

Not Nisha, I was going to say. But I didn't.

When I got home, I brought the bags of birds upstairs and placed them in the spare room. I proceeded to the kitchen to check on the little bird. It was sleeping. I stroked its feathers. I imagined that birds have no memory, that they

48

live only in the present, that the past washes away behind them and disappears like each wave on the ocean.

I thought of the bags of dead birds in the spare room. I had no energy to clean them, so I stored them in the industrial-sized fridge, and I decided to leave the job for the next day.

I had a long nap as I hadn't slept the night before. When I got up, it was already dark. I rang Nisha a few more times. Again, it went straight to voicemail. I made myself some dinner of couscous and snails and sat out on the balcony to eat, the throw that Nisha always used over my shoulders. The blanket smelled of her – wood polish and bleach, spices and milk. She felt so far away. Where had she gone? What had Seraphim meant? Did he know something? You never knew with him.

Seraphim is the son of an old family friend. When I was a kid, he would come with his parents and sister to visit a couple of times a year. Being two years older than me, he either ignored me or bossed me around. Then our families drifted apart, and I went off to university in Athens. When I returned, I moved to the heart of the city centre. Years later, after I lost my job at Laiki and started renting the flat above Petra's, I bumped into him again in the grocery store down the road. He recognised me immediately, embracing me, whacking my back with his big hands. He told me about his Jaguar (he collected antique cars), his property (a sprawling villa), and his beautiful Russian wife. It seemed that there should have been a parenthesis there too, but he left it out.

49

I was envious. There he was, his life pretty much sorted, while mine was falling apart.

'So, how are you, my friend?' he said. 'I heard you're flying high in the financial world?'

I had been about to nod and simply agree with him, but then he added, 'Or has this crisis been a blow?'

So, I told him, matter-of-factly, that yes, in fact, it had been a blow. I didn't mention, however, that I'd been looking for work with zero success and wasn't even sure how I was going to make next month's rent payment to Petra.

He nodded, thoughtfully. 'And I heard you got married . . . and so young!'

'Yes,' I said, 'she's wonderful. Very supportive.' I didn't tell him that I'd lost her too.

The first loss had led to the second, and those two had in fact led to a third – the loss of my naivety, which in reality I should have outgrown already. It was only when we knew each other better that I confessed to him that she had, in fact, left me.

'Do you live around here now?'

Yes, I had said, and told him the name of the street.

'Great. We're practically neighbours.' He had hesitated for a moment. 'I'll tell you what . . . I have a proposal for you. I think you'll like it. Will you meet me at eleven thirty tomorrow evening?' From his pocket he took out a crumpled-up receipt, flattened it out on the grocery story counter, and wrote down the name of a street, the name of a bar and his mobile number. He also wanted to take mine – 'Just to be sure,' he said.

I wanted to go and meet him. There was something about him, some energy, that said: *Follow me and I'll show you a life that's better.* He had an infectious smile and his eyes always shone with possibilities.

When I looked at the scribbled address, it turned out to be Maria's. I should have known from the time he wanted to meet – it ran until the early hours.

Maria's bar was an open ground for sex workers, pimps and drunk old men. Just off the main street with dark windows and a wooden door. On the dance floor, an older woman threw tiny pieces of paper into the air as if she was showering herself with confetti.

Seraphim was sitting at the bar talking to the barmaid, who was dressed in her habitual tight black. He spotted me straightaway and waved. He had clearly been looking out for me.

I joined him. Without asking what I wanted, he ordered a couple of beers. He was grazing on some nuts. He pushed the bowl towards me. 'Help yourself,' he said.

'No, thank you.'

'You must try them. Fresh from the trees. Lightly roasted. No added salt.'

I felt that I couldn't refuse. It was the same when we were kids. One time, when I was thirteen and he was fifteen, he convinced me to climb a tree. He told me about a beautiful bird he had seen up there, a rare species that he'd never encountered before. Of course, I was excited, and I went up quite easily, as I was agile and strong. But coming down was a problem. Trees are notoriously difficult to climb down. I was stuck up there for a good hour before my grandad came up the hill carrying two bales of hay on his shoulders, which he placed on the ground below me so that they would break my fall.

The nuts did look good and I'd been anxious about meeting him, curious about what this proposal might be, so I'd hardly eaten. Now I took a handful of them and threw them in my mouth.

The barmaid placed two bottles on the bar and Seraphim reached for his wallet to pay. I was his guest, he said, he would be treating me. I drank the beer quickly. On the stool beside us, a man with grey hair was playing with the hair of a young woman, her arms hung around his neck. She was dark skinned and looked barely eighteen. A few seats down a bald man was trying to kiss the neck of another woman – she looked familiar, but I couldn't think where I'd seen her. Seraphim ordered another couple of beers. This time the barmaid placed in front of us bowls of sliced apples, olives and crisps. This time he didn't pay. We were drinking the beers at top speed and the barmaid kept replacing the empty ones.

On a table behind us, two beautiful women sat in the laps of two very old men. 'Those are lovely Romanian girls,' Seraphim said. 'Not too expensive.'

The beer had started to go to my head. So far we'd spoken about nothing much. He had told me a bit more about his cars. A Porsche 911, in mint condition. 'There's magic in that car,' he said. 'You should come with me some time, we'll go up to the mountains. You'll see its power.' He told me about his Mercedes SL 300 Gullwing. 'One of the first sports cars of the post-war era. Silver. Doors open up like the wings of a bird. You can fly in that thing.' He preferred not to drive that one around too much, he said. He kept it in tip-top condition in his garage, took it out for a spin once a week, to keep it alive and breathing.

Even slightly pissed, I had been struck by how shabby his clothes were. His T-shirt was old and worn, as were his jeans; his hair barely brushed, it flicked out in various directions. With all that money I wondered why he wore clothes that looked twenty years old.

The beers kept coming, and I was drinking more slowly now.

Two Filipino women approached us: one younger, heavily made up; the other, slightly older woman, hardly wore a speck of makeup and her skin shone in the dim lights. Seraphim was well acquainted with them. There was a lot of small talk.

'When shall I take you two out in my car? Seraphim had said.

The older woman smiled politely but hadn't answered. The younger one brushed her hair away from her forehead and placed both of her hands between her knees. These small movements told me that the women were not comfortable. I downed another beer. The two women disappeared into the crowd.

Seraphim ordered couscous from one of the barmaids.

'Couscous?' I said, and he winked.

In a short while she returned carrying a ceramic pot on a silver tray. She placed the pot and two small plates and cutlery on the bar.

'Have a look at this, my friend,' said Seraphim. 'In season. Organic. You must love them.'

He opened the pot and dug into it with a fork – pulling out a tiny poached songbird. Steam wound in ribbons out of the pot, mixing with the cigarette smoke already in the air. He delicately placed a couple on my plate and a couple on his. Then he threw one into his mouth, crunching into its bones with relish.

'Go for it,' he said. Mouth full. 'You must like them. I've never met anyone who doesn't. Didn't you have them when you were a boy?' He spat on the counter.

I told him that I did. And that I knew that it was illegal to eat these birds.

'I'm not too hungry,' I said. 'I had a huge meal before I came out. Still bloated.'

'Looks like it might be harder for me to get you on my side than I thought.' Seraphim swallowed the last bit of bird and used the nail of his pinkie finger to remove meat from his tooth. I felt like gagging.

'I don't understand.'

'These songbirds – how shall I put it? They are on your plate courtesy of me. You can say that I'm keeping the tradition alive. But I catch them in their thousands. Another pair of hands would double my income. It's just a few traps a week during the hunting seasons.' He paused, considering me. 'After all, how did you think I lived so well?'

I didn't respond.

'I see your dapper clothes and your good looks are your cover-ups. But you're struggling, my friend – don't think I can't see that. I saw it in your eyes in the grocery store. It was right there, slashed across your face like a huge scar.'

Once again, I said nothing. But Seraphim had sussed me out. It was his mighty skill.

'You don't have to give me an answer now. Think about it, and I'll call you in a week. If you say yes, we'll start straight away. I need an apprentice. Someone I can trust. You've always been trustworthy, haven't you?' He grinned broadly for a moment and then pushed the plate towards me. 'If nothing else, at least try one. It'll take you right back to your childhood.'

I realised I had hardly touched my dinner. I got up and put it in a Tupperware box to store in the fridge. I gave the little bird some more water and it drank, drop by drop. I had put out a plate of seeds in the morning and it had eaten quite a bit. Then I nestled it in my palms and took it out, once again, to the balcony to wait for 11 p.m. I watched it as its jet-bead eyes opened and closed, its feathers fluffing up as it settled in my hands. I had an image in my mind of the other birds, the dead ones, thousands of them in the black bin-liners, feathers stuck together with their own blood and the blood of the other birds. Beady eyes open forever to the darkness.

I was even more uneasy that night. Below, on the street,

the light from Petra's living room shone on the cobblestone street. There were shadows on the stones, the movement of people within. Yes, one was Petra's – long and slim, hair up. The other was Aliki's – shorter and broader – coming to the window intermittently to stand silently, no doubt, beside her mother. Then, on one occasion, there was a third, softer, rounder – standing alone. This must have been Nisha. But I could hardly go and check. I rang her, and once again it went straight to voicemail. I could think of no good reason to knock on their door at this hour. But I kept Seraphim's words in mind – *She'll be back*. I mean, he was right – it wasn't as if she had anywhere to go. Unless she went back to Sri Lanka . . . No, I was sure that Nisha would knock on the back door at eleven, like she always did, and the memory of waiting for her would fade into the past and be forgotten.

Mrs Hadjikyriacou was outside again, talking nonsense to the cats. I couldn't hear was she was saying, though – the bouzouki wasn't playing that night; instead, a girl was singing in another language, and the foreign words flew in their hundreds over the streets and consumed them. I'd never seen her before, and she was beautiful: dark, with dark eyes. Her right hand was smaller and seemed damaged in some way, perhaps a birth defect. It remained scrunched up, close to her breast. Her left hand, however, danced as she sang, rose and fell with the mesmerising tone of her voice, her fingers tapping the air as if she was playing an invisible instrument. Her voice was extraordinary, clear as glass. On the tables around her, the men, many of whom had once been officers in the military, who probably had medals and flashbacks locked away somewhere, knocked back shots of ouzo, sucked snails with their gums, laughed – and ignored her. She was merely background noise.

I saw Yiakoumi come out of his shop. He sat down on a wicker chair to drink coffee and hear the music. The clocks behind him were lit up – it was 10.30 p.m.

I sat there holding the bird, listening to the music, waiting for the next half hour. But Nisha didn't come.

At 3 a.m. I was awakened by the sound of my iPad ringing. I jumped up to answer it, thinking it was Nisha, but the name that was flashing brightly on the screen was Kumari. I stood and watched it for a while not knowing what to do. What would I say to her?

In a moment it stopped. But not even ten seconds later, it began to ring again and once more I could do nothing but stand there, imagining the little girl on the other end, waiting eagerly to speak to her mother.

8

Petra

THE NEXT MORNING, AS SOON as the cockerel started to crow, I made myself some tea and toast and went to Nisha's room. I looked around, without knowing what I was searching for. Her makeup was on the dressing table, neatly lined up. The brushes sparkled with rouge. Then I noticed a journal and, resting on top of it, a gold engagement ring. I had never seen her wearing this before – it was simple, with a decent sized diamond in a raised clasp. I placed the ring on the dresser and opened the journal. On the first page was a rough sketch of the garden – there was the boat and the orange tree. The rest of the pages were full of writing in Sinhalese.

In the drawer of her bedside cabinet, I found a gold locket. It was heart shaped and inside were two, roughly cut out photographs – one of her, and one of a young man. She never wore this locket but sometimes, in the evenings, when she sat down to rest and watch TV, she held it tightly in her palm or coiled the gold chain around her finger, like a Christian would their rosary.

In another drawer, I found a lock of hair.

'That's my Sri Lankan sister's hair.' I turned and Aliki stood in the doorway. 'Her name is Kumari. She is two years older than me – she's eleven.' She stared at me. 'Did you know that?'

'Not really,' I said. It occurred to me that I had never bothered to ask about her daughter, about what she looked like, what she was like, how she was doing without her mother by her side. When did Nisha even speak to Kumari?

The lock of hair was in a clear plastic bag, the type you might keep coins in to take to the bank.

'But my hair is curly and hers is straight.'

I nodded.

'That is a locket that Nisha's husband gave her before he died. He is inside that heart. She would never, ever leave without him.'

So, these were Nisha's most precious possessions.

None of Nisha's clothes or shoes were missing. She owned three handbags, but only two were there, lined up at the bottom of her wardrobe. Her reading glasses were resting on her pillow. Her bed was neatly made, the covers folded at the corners meticulously.

Turning around to ask Aliki a question, I realised that she had slipped out of the room. Probably gone to make herself some breakfast.

There was a small antique desk by the glass doors and when I opened the top drawer, I found her passport. At this point I sat down on the chair, I was so confused. A part of me had hoped that I wouldn't find these items, particularly the passport. I wanted to believe that Nisha had taken off somewhere – and that would mean she was safe. But, if she had, why would she leave her passport? The locket? I opened the journal again and ran my fingers over the foreign words, the beautiful lines that ran along the paper like the vines in the garden. I wished I could read it, hoping it would give me some clue to Nisha's whereabouts.

She had simply vanished.

I took the locket and held it tightly in a closed fist, like Nisha did when she watched TV. It reminded me of Aliki's tiny heart, during the last ultrasound I had had when I was pregnant, before going into labour.

Stephanos hadn't been there. He had been an army officer and worked at the British base, which was why we had decided to stay here – in my parents' house – after we got married. Stephanos was a British Cypriot, born in Islington, raised in Edmonton. His parents moved to London as refugees after the war. He'd enlisted in the army in England, but one summer he came to Cyprus to stay with relatives and we met and fell in love. After that he requested to be transferred here. The British still have a base in Cyprus, a remnant of their occupation of the island until its independence in 1960.

It was convenient for him to get to work, as he could walk

there in ten minutes, or drive in two. By that time, Mum had already passed away and Dad had moved to a small flat in the mountains, so we moved into this beautiful Venetian property in the old city – the house I had grown up in.

It belonged to my dad's aunt, and for a few years, between the ages of five and seven, she lived above us, where Yiannis now lives. I remembered her as a tiny, pretty, old lady, with silver hair, which she always wore in a net. She used to sit in the garden and embroider tablecloths, curtains, wedding dresses and veils. She told me stories about the beginning of time and the end of time, her hands always busy, sewing. She told me once that she was buying time, that she would weave until she was ready to leave this world and reunite with the man she loved – my father's uncle, who had died fighting for the British in the Second World War.

Stephanos was diagnosed with cancer when I was five weeks pregnant with Aliki. It travelled from his prostate, to his bones, to his liver. He went from a man leaving the house in his military gear every morning, a man who ran laps around the old city in the evenings, a man who made me laugh till I burst, into a . . . something. Something shrivelled, not human. Something not alive and not dead. A creature; a tiny, dying bird.

Aliki continued to grow. She grew and she grew like a fruit on a tree, like a plump fig, growing and expanding my insides till I was ready to burst. She writhed and wriggled and pushed, and that's when the idea of an octopus came to me.

By the time of the mid-pregnancy ultrasound, Stephanos

61

was bed-bound. I promised to bring him the scan to see. He hoped, he'd said, that Aliki would be as beautiful as me. He had chosen her name. When he spoke like that, looking right into my eyes, I knew that he was still there. But then I would take in the rest of him; how alien he looked – bones crumbling, spine twisted, neck bent forward like a vulture's – and I had a feeling that I wanted to melt away. I wanted to disappear into him, into his eyes, so that I could rest inside him and hold on to his soul. I began to see his eyes like tiny doors, leading to the man that I had always known. I would wait for him to wake up each morning, sitting by his side in the hospital. I would look at this shrivelled form on the bed, wired up to machines, and wait for those doors to open. When his eyes closed forever, I'd lose him completely.

The day of the scan, the nurse spread gel over the bump and ran the cold wand over my skin. But I couldn't bring myself to look at the screen. I just thought of the first scan at twelve weeks. Stephanos had come with me to the appointment – we knew his diagnosis by then, but he hadn't deteriorated yet. We had both stared rapt at the screen, not even sure what we were looking at. The foetus, the size of a raspberry, had barely looked human. The heartbeat was faint and muffled, so far away. But now if I looked at the screen there would be a real child, and I wasn't ready to imagine her. Not without Stephanos. Still, I heard her heartbeat. It was steady and strong and full of life; it knocked on the boundaries of this world demanding to be heard. I heard it. Oh, I heard it! I had no choice. Aliki was announcing herself, forging a path for her arrival.

At the same time, my heart vanished. It turned to mist and disappeared.

I hired Nisha as soon as Stephanos died. She was even there for the birth. Most of the other women in the city had domestic workers, so I saw no harm in having one too. I did my research and realised that it wouldn't be too expensive, no more than I could afford. I would offer her accommodation and food, so the monthly fee was minimal. The fact was, I couldn't manage on my own and I knew I would need to return to work sooner rather than later. It was my own business, after all. This is how I reasoned, anyway.

Aliki was an 8lb baby with a full head of hair. She looked exactly like Stephanos. I'm petite with mousy-brown, straight hair and olive skin. I saw nothing of me in her. Even my breasts were too small for her and I never produced enough milk. She pulled at my skin and sucked my nipples raw, trying in desperation to get more than I could give her. I have to admit, I was jealous of how Nisha was able to love her, hold her in her arms, so close to her skin.

Aliki would cry and cry.

'Madam,' Nisha would say, 'your baby is crying. Go to her, she needs you.'

I couldn't go. I couldn't move. 'Please, Nisha, can you go, just this once? I will go next time.'

'OK, madam, if that is what you want.'

She would pick up the wailing child and walk around, but Aliki would not stop. Then, one day, for some reason, Nisha decided to lie on the floor on her back, lift up her top, and place the baby on her naked chest. Aliki suddenly stopped crying. She whimpered for a while, then slept. Sitting back in the armchair and watching them like that – Aliki's white, curled-up body against Nisha's darker skin – reminded me of the night cradling the moon.

Aliki fell in love with Nisha: she desired her odours and the warm touch of her skin. I imagined that in the beating of Aliki's heart, Nisha could feel that of her own child. I didn't want to think about this. I dashed the thought aside, to a safe place, where the guilt couldn't reach me.

Nisha never gave up trying to bring me closer to my child. She tried to get me to hold Aliki, to be still with her. But I couldn't. In Aliki's face, in her eyes, in the soft curve of her chin, the pink freshness of her skin, even in the mole on her cheek, I saw Stephanos. I had nightmares. I would sit up and see huge white spiders the size of shoes crawling to the baby's room. I'd follow them, stamp on them, trying to keep them from reaching my baby. Then I would wake up, standing over the cot, Nisha by my side with her hand on my back, rubbing it.

'Shush now, shush, madam. Everything will be OK.'

She would take my hand and place it on Aliki's chest so that I could feel her chest expanding as she breathed,

'You see,' Nisha whispered beside me, 'your daughter is just fine. When she wakes up, you can take her outside and enjoy some sunlight. It will be warm tomorrow.'

Then she would calmly lead me back to bed, holding my hand, tucking me in, whispering, 'Sleep now.'

No, Nisha would never leave Aliki without saying goodbye. This I knew for certain.

I placed the locket back in the drawer and, taking the passport with me, headed outside to see if Mrs Hadjikyriacou was there. She was sitting on the deckchair by the front door and her maid was kneeling in front of her, rubbing *zivania* into her legs, her translucent skin creasing like tiny waves under the maid's fingers. It was warmer but windy that morning. When she saw me, she shooed her maid away and propped her legs up on a stool.

'It's a bit early for you,' she said, without even looking in my direction. She was gazing up at the sky and straining her neck to do so. It was early; Yiakoumi hadn't even opened his shop yet, and all his timepieces, apart from one, read seven o'clock.

She straightened her neck now and turned to look at me. The wind blew stronger and the alcohol evaporated from her legs and drifted towards me. She smelt like she'd spent the whole night in a bar. I bought my hand up to my nose and she noticed the passport I was holding.

'My darrrrling,' she said in English, then in Greek: 'Where are you going?'

'Nisha hasn't returned.'

'I know,' she replied, nodding.

'This is her passport.'

65

'Ah.'

'If she'd intended to leave, then wouldn't she have taken this with her? She's even left the locket her husband gave her before he died, and her daughter's lock of hair.'

I waited, expecting to hear another *ah*, but Mrs Hadjikyriacou remained silent. She seemed to be thinking.

She looked up and down the street then turned to face me, her eyes filled with anxiety, with intensity. 'She was wearing a long-sleeved black dress,' she said, 'with white trainers. She had a green scarf wrapped around her neck, which partly covered her mouth. She wore that scarf like it was the middle of winter, though I know it must have been a warm Sunday night because my woman didn't bring me a blanket.'

'Why was she dressed like that?'

'Do you think if I sniff my nails they will tell me the answer?'

I rolled my eyes without her seeing.

One of the cats jumped onto the stool and walked along her leg as if it was a tree branch, then settled in her lap. She stroked it while it purred. 'Petra,' Mrs Hadjikyriacou said, 'if she's not back by tomorrow, you must go to the police.'

I looked down at my watch. There was no time to think about this right now, as I needed to get Aliki ready for school.

Once again, I left work early to collect Aliki from school in the afternoon. I had no option but to bring her to work with me again. This time, she sat behind the counter doing her homework with Keti's help. She was learning the periodic table.

'It's amazing to see all the elements of the whole universe on one page!' I heard her saying with excitement, as I led a client into my office for an eye exam.

That evening, after work, I made some pasta with haloumi and mint for dinner. Aliki and I ate in silence. Aliki's eyes flicked towards Nisha's empty chair now. The photograph of Stephanos in his uniform sat behind her on a console table. Sometimes I would catch Aliki stop in front of it while she was playing, pausing to stare at it. Could she see how much they looked alike? Their pale skin, wide-set eyes and round faces – even the small moles on their right cheeks.

I tried to engage Aliki, ask her questions. How was school, and do you have homework tonight? She replied with a nod, a shrug or a shake of the head, but she never spoke. Not a word. Sometimes I thought she wanted to speak, but then whatever words were hovering would be swallowed, gulped down with the pasta.

When we had finished, I helped Aliki with her homework at the kitchen table, then settled her into bed. We both pretended she was going right to sleep, but no doubt she would stay up reading for a while.

When I heard no more sounds from her room, I tiptoed to the front door, quietly closing it behind me before crossing the street to Theo's restaurant. He was in the kitchen shouting at the chefs. I stood and waited for him to stop and finally he turned to me with a smile. 'Petra, my dear, table for tonight? A late supper?'

'No, Theo, I've come to speak to your maids.' He raised

his eyebrows. 'It's about an important matter regarding Nisha. She's gone missing and I want to see if they know anything.'

'Take a seat,' he said. 'I'll bring you a coffee on the house. They are busy in the back but they can take a break soon.'

I sat down beneath the vine-covered trellis, sipping my coffee. It was just after 9 p.m. and there were a few diners at the table and a couple of punters at the bar. After about fifteen minutes, the women emerged from the kitchen, both in black trousers and white shirts, their usual rice hats tied at the chin with a red ribbon. It occurred to me then how awful it was that Theo was making the women wear these hats; I couldn't imagine that it was their own choice. This wasn't a Vietnamese restaurant, after all, it was Greek. The hats were exotic, a fetish, of course. The men ogled from their seats. How had I never noticed this before?

Theo gestured in my direction, and they approached my table, clearly tired but smiling.

'Madam,' said the one on the left. 'Sir said you wanted to talk about something important.'

'We are just having a break. We've been working from six this morning,' said the other, in a tone that was both joyful and irritated.

The shorter one nudged her and gave her a look to be quiet. 'Sorry, madam,' she said, holding out her hand. 'I am Chau and this is my sister, Bian.'

I shook both of their hands. 'I live across the street,' I said. 'I am Petra.'

They both laughed. 'We know, madam,' said Chau. 'We see you every day and we are friends with Nisha.'

'I was hoping you might know where she is. I haven't seen her since Sunday evening.'

'No, madam,' said Chau, shaking her head. 'She comes to say hello every morning after taking Aliki to school, but we have not seen her for a few days. We were thinking maybe she went away.'

'We work here in the morning for the breakfast customers,' added Bian, 'then we go to sir's house to clean, then we come back here in the afternoon until very late. We see Nisha once in the morning and sometimes in the afternoon. Now, for few days, nothing.'

The word 'nothing' stabbed me like a knife. It reminded me of the emptiness that Nisha had left behind.

Bian eyed Theo watching us from behind the bar. Several customers had left their tables, and dirty dishes had started to pile up at the bussing stations.

Chau looked over, concerned. 'We must go,' she said. 'Sir will be angry. We have much more to clean before closing time.'

'Hold on,' I said. 'Please, if you hear anything, will you come and knock on my door straightaway?'

They both stared at it me for a moment too long and then nodded.

'Of course, madam,' said Bian. 'We will come to tell you first.'

When I got home, the house was quiet. I peeked into Aliki's room and she was asleep, a book lying across her chest.

Feeling restless, I went to the garden to collect the pieces of broken money-box and coins from the ground. I put all the lira in a glass bowl and sprayed them with water until they gleamed. The black cat sat by my feet and watched.

Then I went out to the front porch to sit for a while. I watched the neighbourhood go about the business of shutting down. Mrs Hadjikyriacou was indoors tonight. Yiakoumi's maid was taking the antiques inside in order to shut the shop. To the right, Theo's restaurant was getting quiet, just a few customers remained, finishing drinks and paying their bills. Bian and Chau dashed about, wiping down tables and preparing them with fresh tablecloths for the next day.

I had started to see the rhythm of these women with new eyes – how the whole neighbourhood pulsed with their activity. They had been invisible to me before Nisha had gone missing: all I had seen before was a little Cypriot girl walking excitedly down a street with two adults; the shining antiques outside Yiakoumi's shop every day; the clean and well-kept front garden down the road; the happy customers at Theo's. I had not really seen the women.

When I went to bed, I heard my daughter's voice; it struck me, since I had craved the sound of it all through dinner. I had the window slightly open, the sky a deep blue, when her voice came to me with the wind. Such a soft voice, but textured, rising with excitement, falling with lilting sadness. I peered out of the shutters and was surprised to see her sitting in the boat. When had she woken up? This time she

70

was holding the oar and the olive branch but not rowing. Then she laughed, holding her sides, as if someone had said something funny. I called her inside and lay back on my bed and closed my eyes.

I must have fallen asleep because when I woke up it was completely dark and I heard knocking coming from the garden. I got out of bed and opened the glass doors. Yiannis was standing by Nisha's room, tapping on the glass.

Startled, he turned to me. 'Petra,' he said.

'What are you doing?'

'I heard a noise.'

'But you were the one making the noise,' I said. 'Was there another noise?'

He didn't respond to this.

'Do you know where Nisha is?'

'No,' he said, bluntly. And then it seemed that he regretted this and said, 'I knocked for her on Sunday, too. I wanted to ask her something. Do you know where she is?'

'Unfortunately, I don't.'

Then there was anguish on his face, anguish in his eyes. The moonlight illuminated the streaks of silver in his hair and I thought to myself what a beautiful and lonely man he was.

A gallows frame looks over the red lake at Mitsero, a colossal rusty carcass that creaks in the wind. It is quiet by the lake, on this bright day in October. The hare is exposed to the sun, its body bloated as gases stretch its insides and skin, as bacteria eat soft tissue. The hare is still intact, in the running position, but its powerful hind legs have lost their purpose. It is lying on a slab of yellow stone about five metres from where the crater wall drops to the water.

A praying mantis flies down – green as another land in another time – all five eyes alert for any movement or changes of light. It scuttles a short distance across the yellow stone where the bloated hare is lying, back legs pushing its green frame forward, the front two – sharply spined – reach out and capture and hold a roaming fly.

The hare's head is slanted slightly upwards, away from its front paws. It would seem that it is looking at the mantis eating the fly, but its left eye, the colour of amber, is flat against the earth, and its right eye looks directly into the sun, golden. The hare's black-tipped ears give the impression that they are blowing backwards in the wind. As if it were running.

No vegetation grows around the lake, the soil is arid. But, further out, the soil is rich in copper and pyrite and gold, and there are barley and wheat fields and sunflowers leading to the village. There are fruit trees in the fields beyond the village, and from there come the distant sounds of life – of leaves rustling, wings flapping, animals moving amongst the cherry and pecan trees as they begin to shed their golden leaves.

The hare's carcass reeks now, and the smell is carried by a soft breeze over the red water of the lake, through the hollow gallows frame into the fields, where it meets rosemary and thyme, eucalyptus and pine.

9

Petra

I CALLED UP NISHA'S AGENCY. I asked them if they'd
heard from her.

'No,' the woman said, after checking the system. 'We
log everything and there's nothing here.'

I told her that Nisha had gone missing three days ago,
that I couldn't get through to her on her mobile, either.

'Well,' the woman said, 'keep us posted because she still
has an outstanding debt.' She had a voice like a foghorn. It
was awful and too loud, and it said nothing helpful.

'How much?' I said, but the woman wouldn't tell me, it
was confidential information. However, I knew that the agencies charged the workers a considerable amount of money
to sign up and secure a placement abroad.

Then I rang Nicosia hospital to see if Nisha had been
admitted, but they had no record of her.

When I got off the phone, I looked around and saw that the dinner plates from the night before were still in the sink unwashed, and the ones from breakfast were piled up on top of them. Dust had gathered on the furniture and the marble flagstones.

It was only 9 a.m., but I felt like I'd already had a full day.

I'd woken up early, left a message for Keti to tell her I'd be taking the whole day off, made breakfast for Aliki – finding a jar of her favourite fig jam in the cupboard felt like a small victory – and rushed Aliki off to school.

Now, I went to Nisha's room and gathered what I needed: her passport, her contract, the locket and the lock of hair. I was going to the police station.

I drove to Lykavittos station at Spyros Kyprianou, an old white building with blue shutters. I'd passed the building many times but had never been inside. I told the officer at reception that I wanted to report a missing person. The woman took down my name and asked me to take a seat, saying someone would be with me in a minute.

A minute turned to five, ten, twenty, half an hour. Phones rang in rooms along unseen corridors; occasionally an officer would pass by and wish me good morning. Footsteps on flagstones reminded me for a moment of all those hours I had spent in hospital waiting-rooms, praying for Stephanos: the intermittent whispers, the soft footfalls; disinfectant and coffee; smiles from distracted doctors. I would nod politely, but I found that I couldn't smile, my hand resting on my stomach as the baby grew day by day, week by week, month by month.

'Mrs Loizides?'

Looking down at me, as if from a great height, was a man in his sixties, taller than the average Cypriot, stomach spilling over his trousers, sleeves rolled up.

'Yes,' I said. 'That's me.'

He held out his hand, either to shake mine, or to help me to stand – for a moment I wasn't sure, and hesitated.

'Vasilis Kyprianou,' he said.

'Nice to meet you,' I said, and shook his hand, and with a smile he led me down one of the corridors and into a small room with a cluttered desk, a filing cabinet and a fan that was blowing some paperwork to the floor. He rushed to scoop up the papers with large, clumsy hands, straightening them into a pile and plonking it back on the desk – whereupon, once again, when the fan arced back around, the paperwork flew back down to the floor. This time he left it and picked up a small cup of coffee and took a sip. He grimaced.

'Cold,' he said, noticing that I was looking at him. 'Always.'

With the shades drawn, the office was dim, streaks of sun reaching through the dusty slats. He sat down, the light cutting across his face and highlighting his white stubble. He signalled for me to take one of the vacant chairs opposite him.

'Loizides,' he said. 'Why does that name sound familiar?' He thought for a moment. 'Ah, it was an old colleague of mine. Yes. Nicos Loizides. We trained together. Do you know him?'

'No. I don't believe I do.'

He smiled and leaned forward on his elbows. His face

77

reminded me of a red helium balloon that had begun to sag, those balloons that slowly deflate after a birthday until they are wrinkled and bobbing on the ground.

'So, how can I help you today?'

I took Nisha's things out of my handbag and laid them out on the desk. 'My maid has gone missing,' I said. 'Her name is Nisha Jayakody. She is thirty-eight years old and she's been missing since Sunday night.'

'Today is Wednesday,' he said, as if I didn't know.

'Yes.' I opened the passport and placed it in front of him. I explained everything in detail: the trip to Troodos, Nisha asking me if she could take the night off, returning home, what we had eaten, what time we had eaten, how I had gone to bed leaving Nisha to take care of Aliki, and, how I had woken up in the morning to find that Nisha had gone. Finally, I explained that a reliable neighbour had seen Nisha heading out at ten thirty that same night.

'She hasn't taken her passport,' I said, pushing it still closer to him, because he had not yet even looked at it. 'If she had intended to leave, she would have taken this with her.'

'Ha,' he said simply, bringing the back of his hand to his mouth, wiping it as if he had just finished eating, and leaning back in the chair.

'Where is she from?' he asked.

'Sri Lanka. She has been working for me for nine years. She has helped to bring up my daughter. Nisha would never leave without saying goodbye to her.'

There was a moment of silence. Then Officer Kyprianou sighed deeply, and looked me straight in the eyes, as if willing me to understand his thoughts, like I was missing some joke. Then he said, 'It's only been a few days. Why don't you leave it and see how it goes?'

'But she's never done this before,' I said. 'I know something is wrong. Look' – I tapped the locket and the lock of hair on the desk in front of him – 'these are her most prized possessions. She wouldn't even wear the locket for fear of losing it. It was a gift from her late husband. This is a lock of her daughter's hair. She hasn't seen her daughter for nine years, since she came here. She would never leave these items behind.'

He picked up the coffee again and took another dissatisfied sip, nodding his head as if to himself.

I wished I had a pin to burst his big, hollow head.

'I was wondering if you could take down Nisha's details, investigate—' but he interrupted me before I had even finished speaking.

'I can't concern myself with these foreign women. I have more important matters to attend to. If she doesn't return, my guess would be that she's ran away to the north. That's what they do. She's gone to the Turkish side to find better employment. These women are animals, they follow their instincts. Or the money, more likely. That's what I have to say on the matter. You would do best to go home and start cleaning out her room. If she's not back by the end of the week, call up the agency to find another maid.'

With that, he stood up to signal that our meeting was over, holding out his hand to me.

I rose from my chair and looked at his hand, but didn't

shake it. There was so much I wanted to say, but it was clear this man wasn't capable of hearing me. I gathered Nisha's things from the desk and tucked them back into my bag, purposely stepped on the paperwork that was scattered on the floor, and walked out of his shabby little office.

When I got home, I saw that Yiakoumi's maid was in the antique shop, polishing things. I went across the street to have a chat with her, to see if she knew anything.

Yiakoumi was in the back with his feet up on a messy desk. He nodded at me when I entered. 'Get Nilmini to help you,' he said. 'I'm waiting for an important call.'

'Nilmini,' I said. She was sitting on a stool amongst items of copper. She looked up. How young and self-contained she was. A beautiful Sri Lankan woman in her early twenties, with such long hair it looked as though it had never been cut.

'That's a lovely name,' I said.

'It means "ambitious woman".' She continued to polish an old urn.

I noticed behind her a pile of tattered books – *Alice's Adventures in in Wonderland*, *Huckleberry Finn*, *Peter Pan*. One of them was open on the floor in front of her, pages held back with two pebbles from the beach. She saw me looking.

'I love reading, madam. In Sri Lanka I wanted to study literature. Sir bought me these books from the market. He said I can read as long as I do my work.'

I nodded and glanced up at Yiakoumi, who was yawning and reading something on his phone.

'I am wondering, Nilmini, if you have seen Nisha or heard from her.'

She paused and looked up at the ceiling where a brass chandelier hung above her.

'The last time I saw Nisha, madam, was Sunday night.'

'What was she doing?'

'Usually, madam, she comes to say hello. This time she was walking very quickly.'

At that point Yiakoumi's mobile rang and he got up to speak in the storage room at the back.

'What time was that?' I asked.

'I arrived here maybe an hour earlier, so I think it was after ten. Sir wanted me to work Sunday night because customers come in the morning. I cleaned his house in the morning, had a break and then came here at nine o' clock.'

'Did Nisha say anything to you?'

'No, madam, she said nothing. Normally she waves, sometimes she comes in and makes a joke and we laugh, often she brings me fruit. No, she didn't stop to see me and I tell you, she looked worried.'

'Are you sure?'

'Yes, madam. I have been working here opposite Nisha for a year. I know her face. I know my friend's face when she's happy, sad, angry, tired. This time I tell you she was worried.'

'Do you remember anything else at all?'

'Well, madam, maybe this not an important thing, but the cat was following her.'

'The cat?'

'Yes. I looked down the road as she walked off. I was outside. The cat followed her all the way and turned the corner when she turned. So the cat might know where Nisha is.'

I stared at her. Was she being serious?

'It was this cat, madam.' She pointed out of the window, where the black cat with the different-coloured eyes was sitting on the table, washing itself amongst the pots and vases. The one my daughter now called Monkey.

That afternoon, I picked up Aliki from school. I didn't take the car because I wanted to walk with her. She was wearing her favourite K-pop idol girl T-shirt with some light blue jeans, and she'd released her hair from its ponytail so it hung in thick waves over her shoulders.

'Aliki,' I said, 'I went to the police today.'

She quickly glanced up at me, cheeks rosy.

'I went to report Nisha missing, but they wouldn't help me. They said she's probably run away to the north. But I don't believe them,' I said.

Suddenly, her eyes filled with tears.

'I'm not saying this to upset you. I want you to know what's happening. I'm looking for Nisha but I'm confused. Did she say anything to you? Do you know anything that might help me to understand what is going on?'

Aliki looked down at her feet as she walked.

'Aliki?' I said. But this just made her withdraw further –

she walked over to a shop front and stared at the shoes on display. She'd cut herself off from me completely.

At home, I made potato salad. The vegetables in the fridge had started to rot – Nisha had always done the shopping – so I chopped them all up and threw them in the salad: red peppers, tomatoes, spring onions and parsley. Aliki poked at the food with her fork, humming something under her breath.

Later, I stood by the large window at the front of the house, looking out onto the street, hoping with each second that passed that I would see Nisha turning the corner. I couldn't tamp down that hope. Maybe any moment she would appear in the lights of Yiakoumi's shop and Theo's restaurant, coming to our door and turning the key in the lock, putting down her handbag and explaining where she had been.

I must have stood like that for half an hour, maybe more. Like a cat, Aliki came in and out of the living room, standing beside me for a while and leaving again. She was anxious. I could hear it in the way she moved, in the urgency of her footsteps.

The olive tree opposite was illuminated by the shop lights. Yiakoumi came out and sat beneath it with a coffee. A woman was singing at Theo's restaurant – I couldn't see her because the men sitting beneath the grapevine at the tables around her obscured the view, but her voice was pitch-perfect, so full of pathos, so full of beauty and sadness, that something welled up inside me and I began to cry.

Who was this woman who sang in a foreign tongue? Where had she come from? What had she wished for before coming here? These questions brought me back to Nisha in a way that I had never thought about her before. I had failed to recognise that she, too, was a woman with pain and hopes. I had known this only as a distant thought – I had never absorbed it into my heart. For she, too, had lost her husband. She, too, had come from an island ravaged by war over the years, one besieged by colonialists. Its beauty and its people had suffered, too. And these things live on: they carry themselves silently into the future. Who was Nisha? What had life taught her? Why had she travelled such a great distance? To save her daughter . . . from what?

I had never asked these questions.

I knew that she treasured the locket. I knew how she loved Aliki. I knew the taste of her food, the spices and curries and creams. I knew how she dusted and hoovered, how she ironed the clothes, how she wrote careful shopping lists, taking her time with each letter, each word, as if she were writing a poem. I knew how she packed the groceries in perfect order so that she could unpack them more easily. I knew she had a copy of the Buddhist scriptures by her bed and a fat little statue of the Buddha beside it. I knew that when she washed fruit, she'd watch the water fall and get lost for a while.

I didn't know Nisha.

Now that I could hear this woman's song – a melody that told a story I couldn't understand – I hoped with all of my heart that it wasn't too late.

84

I felt Aliki standing beside me; I thought she was going to put her hand in mine. But when I turned, she was nowhere to be seen.

Aliki was sitting out in the garden in the boat again. She was rowing and humming to herself. I went outside, turned an empty plant pot over and sat on it, a little distance away from her. The trees around the garden created a shelter from the wind. Above, the moon shone brightly in the dark sky but, around it, thick clouds were gathering – an indication of a brewing storm. The black cat was in the garden now, sprawled across the patio, purring. I watched it, contemplatively. If only it could speak.

'Would you like to come in?'.

I turned and saw that Aliki was looking in my direction. 'You want me to sit in the boat?' I asked.

She nodded.

So, I climbed in opposite her and she gave me the olive branch to hold. The cat jumped in with us and snuggled up against her thigh. I glanced over at the glass doors of Nisha's room.

'She loves me,' Aliki said, and I wasn't sure if she was talking about Nisha or the cat.

'I know,' I replied, and whichever it was, this seemed to satisfy her as she started to row with the oar she was holding.

'You have to row on the other side, because if you don't we'll end up just going around in circles. This is why it's

85

important to be balanced. Because then you'll go around in circles if you're not.'

Her words made me chuckle there was so much truth in them. I moved to sit beside her, and began to row with the olive branch, to the rhythm that Aliki had set.

'Where are we going?' I said.

'To the sea above the sky. This is where I go with Nisha. It's lovely up there. Sometimes a bit scary, but not always.'

'I see,' I said, matching her movements still.

I was hoping that she would tell me more, but she had fallen silent. Her last words had floated away, high into the sky, and were mere dots up above, like helium balloons at carnivals when I was a girl: after all the sweets and colour and noise, I would release them at the end of the day and watch them float away.

Finally, Aliki spoke. 'Mum, please find her,' she said. 'I really want you to find her.'

At that moment, the sky opened, and rain began to pour down on us.

The hare is drenched. Its fur looks oily in the sunlight
that shines intermittently through the clouds. The rain
falls into the red lake. The rain falls onto the yellow rocks,
forming streams of gold. The rain clangs against the steel
of the gallows frame and the metallic structure creaks.
Water begins to fill its hollow shell.

In the fields beyond, it falls through the leaves of the
pecan and fruit trees. It falls down upon the wheat and
barley fields. No one is out today; even in the village,
doors and windows and shutters are closed, and water
runs from the eaves of buildings.

Rain is always a surprise. The villagers are relieved
because the earth needs to drink. Not so long ago were
the scorching summer days when the water barrels were
empty, the land dry as a bone. Now, the trees are cool in
the drenching. When the rain stops, the locals will come
out to collect the pecans before the crows do.

There is a chapel in this village which is silent and empty, but slightly further away, in Agrokipia the church bells can be heard this morning and every morning. Built by the Hellenic mining company, the church served as a protector of the miners, who risked their lives underground. Far away, across the dividing line, the birds can hear the very distant sound of morning prayer from the mosque.

Somewhere in the middle, amongst the rainfall, the two sounds meet and touch and join in union and fall down upon the hare, washing away the dirt and the hatching maggots, washing away the dried blood, the skin that has cracked open into wounds.

10

Yiannis

FOR TWO DAYS IT RAINED. It was so bad that water streamed into small rivers along the cobbled streets. At night, the customers at Theo's reluctantly went inside because nobody could sit beneath the vines in the pouring rain. We can survive the cold – with the warmth of outdoor heaters and clay ovens in the taverns – but the rain, though rare, sends everyone indoors. Even Mrs Hadjikyriacou locked herself away. Even the cats disappeared.

For those two days I stayed in. It took me almost that long to clean all the birds from the hunt with Seraphim, to pull out their feathers and soak them. I had to do it in batches. In the spare room I had three large fridges, industrial size. I checked the orders and separated the birds into containers of various sizes and labelled them, before storing them in the fridges. There were one or two establishments – a hotel and a restaurant in Larnaca – who had requested the birds be pickled, so those I soaked in vinegar.

During these dark days, I tried not to think about Nisha. But it didn't work – of course it didn't. The rain pelted down on the window from the gutters, drowning out all other sound, so that I felt my solitude keenly.

Nisha's absence was even louder than the rain.

Down in the garden, the boat filled with water and looked like it was going to sink, like it was doomed.

Nisha loved the rain. She would lie on my bed, near the long glass doors, and watch it coming down. She liked to watch water falling. It reminded her of something, she'd said, though what that thing was, I didn't know. A secret memory.

When it rained, she wanted me to make her Turkish coffee in a small cup, with some sesame biscuits in a saucer.

'It's nice to be served sometimes,' she said, laughing. How she savoured that coffee, dipping the biscuit in until it became moist and dark.

'Back home we drink tea and chew betel,' she would say. Always. A mantra. As if she couldn't quite allow herself to enjoy the pleasures of one world without being pulled into the other. Her home was always waiting for her. This was the feeling I had and it made me want to touch her, to feel the soft dark skin on her thighs and stomach, to wrap my limbs around her and hold her there. But instead,

I would simply sit beside her, sensing that at these times she needed company more than comfort.

'It's weird to think,' she said once, 'how the British occupied both of our countries. What they took and what they left behind . . .' and the sentence remained incomplete as Nisha's sentences often did, so that I had to imagine what might have come after. I guess we both finished her sentences with our own thoughts.

She told me about Nuwara Eliya, up in the hills of central Sri Lanka, far from her hometown of Galle in the south. 'That's where most of the English people settled,' she said, 'up there – because they liked the cold weather. It's about fifteen degrees! And they built *typical* English houses.' There was a note of disgust in her voice on the word *typical*, a scrunching of her eyes.

I felt close to her at these times – there was this thing we shared, the British occupation, something we could both understand: tales passed down, culture and land stolen, that insatiable fight for freedom and identity. I imagined these houses built with red brick and slanting roofs and neat front gardens, misplaced amongst the rainforest and blue magpies and jackfruit trees. But then, I had never set foot in the place where Nisha had grown up, never seen the paddy fields that she'd speak of so often.

'*Tiryak* is one of the six realms of rebirth in Buddhism,' she said once, when the rain had just stopped, and she was watching snakes and snails coming out on the street below, the birds re-emerging from the trees. 'This is when one is reborn as an animal. It makes me wonder . . . imagine being reborn as a snail!' She had taken a sip of thick black coffee and been thoughtful for a while. 'When I was a child in Galle, there was a frogmouth owl that visited me at night. It was a female, so lightly spotted and white, about twenty centimetres tall, with a large head and a flattened, hooked bill. In the daytime it must have slept in the forest. Its wings were so soft that it flew silently. One night, on my sister's eleventh birthday, it came to our bedroom window. After that, it came every night for a week, so I started to leave the window open, and then it would fly in and sit on my sister's bed. But she wasn't there. She had already died.'

'You had a sister?' I asked. She had never mentioned a sister before.

'She died when she was ten. She was born with a broken heart. This is what my mother said – that some babies are born with a broken heart because they felt so much sadness in a past life, and they are not ready to live again. She had an operation when she was three, had a scar running down her chest like a beautiful tree branch. Sometimes she got me to draw flowers around it, with my mum's lip pencil. She wanted the scar to look pretty, like the places in the tropical forest. That's what she said. One day, she just didn't wake up.'

I reached out and took Nisha's hand in mine; it was warm, and she squeezed my fingers.

'The owl would come in and sit down on my sister's favourite book – *The Mahadenamutta and His Pupils*. She loved

92

those stories. She would ask me to read them to her every night. One day, I shooed the owl off the book and started to read. The owl sat beside me and watched me turning the pages. I think it was listening! It came again and again for a whole year, and I read that book every time. On my sister's next birthday, it disappeared.'

She squeezed my fingers again and remained silent. She looked out of the window, and I did too.

'I love the way the snail trails glimmer in the light,' she had said.

'I love you, Nisha,' I had replied.

There wasn't even a pause.

'I didn't come here to love *anyone*,' she said, pulling her hand out of mine. 'I came here to send money to my daughter.' She was so deliberate with her words, as if she had rehearsed them. The way she had stressed *anyone*, with a fierceness in her eyes, made me reluctant to say anything else to her. I nodded and she put her hand on my knee, then dunked a biscuit in the coffee.

Remembering this now, I was all the more convinced that I had scared Nisha away with my proposal, that it had finally been the thing that had been too much for her. She had probably packed her belongings and gone home without telling me. But I had proposed on Saturday and she had left on Sunday. How would she have had time to reserve a flight so quickly? Something didn't quite add up. Perhaps she had already decided to leave before my proposal? And, once I had proposed, that had made it even harder to tell me, so she had just left. I decided that this was the most probable explanation. But I still couldn't be sure.

I noticed that the little bird was struggling to open its right wing. I filled up a smaller container with about an inch of water and placed it in there to bathe. I didn't think its wing was dislocated and I hoped it was bruised rather than broken. The bird moved around in the container, splashing its beak into the water, turning once or twice to glance in my direction. Each time it did this my heart fell to my stomach. When the bird finished its bath it hopped out, without opening its right wing at all, and ate some of the berries that I had put on a plate beside the container.

Eventually, it stopped raining and the sun came out. I decided to head to the river to find some snails: there'd be an abundance of them now after the rain, and I just couldn't sit still.

It seemed that the river had overflowed, carrying along with it all manner of detritus. There were plastic containers and plastic bags, barbed wire, car wheels and hubcaps, a pair of sunglasses, a yellow foam mattress clinging to the side of a tree, even a dead cow. A stench travelled along with it, most likely from the north part of the island, which was often polluted by spills from a badly maintained sewage system. The smells travelled across the water with a southern blowing wind, like today.

Suddenly, I heard a voice – a woman's cry – so quick and sharp I wasn't sure I actually had heard it. I couldn't distinguish voice from wind from rush of river.

'Hello?' I called across the water. But no reply came, even when I called again.

In the mountains, the water is clear and fresh, nothing like the water down here. Before it gets contaminated by human waste, you can drink from it and swim in it; there are waterfalls that pour down amongst the trees. It's the kind of water one might imagine in paradise, if such a place existed.

I went up with Nisha last winter, up to the hills above the valley to sit by the river. She wanted me to show her where my grandparents and parents had lived, where I had grown up – the old farmhouse with the arches was now owned by tourists, who came only in the summer. The rest of the time the building was dark and empty. Nisha wore an abundance of clothing: a scarf, a woolly hat, thick gloves, two pairs of socks, thermal tights beneath her jeans, a thermal top beneath her jumper, and her big puffy coat with the fake fur running around its hood. All this, and her teeth were still chattering! 'See,' she had said, 'isn't it nice to see the place where you grew up, because now I think I know you better.' She planted a big, cold kiss on my cheek.

You see, I thought you were a different person.

If I followed the river through time, would I find Nisha at the top dressed in all her cold weather abundance? Would I find my father and grandfather there with flocks of sheep, both with high boots so they could walk easily though the fields, sheepdogs by their side? The sheep roamed free in the pastures – back then, the borders between farms were fluid, they weren't divided by fences but instead by trails of wild herbs, like rosemary and thyme.

There had been two sheds attached to the farmhouse, one for churning the milk to make haloumi and *anari*, and the other for spinning wool into yarn. My mother and grandmother used the yarn to knit blankets. The men – including me, though I was just a boy – would load the mules with cheese, yoghurt, milk and rolled-up warm woollen throws and head out to the farmers' market. My grandfather, strong as an ox and with a head of thick white hair, loved his animals, caring for them as if they were his children; although it's true that he killed around four or five lambs a year – one especially for Easter after the long fast. The meat was clean and pure. We also had some chickens for fresh eggs, and a dozen turkeys.

I told Nisha all this when we went to the hills, and she had a similar look on her face as she did that day when she had seen the photograph. She held my hand tightly, as if the wind might blow me away.

What I didn't tell her was that sometimes my grandfather and I would go hunting for songbirds. I didn't want to tell her this. My grandfather had shown me how to make the lime sticks. We would make them together in the farmhouse and put them out in the sun to dry, then we would go to the woods and catch about ten birds. He had a singing bird mechanism which had been made in Paris by a French watchmaker who had perfected the sound. There was a bird on this automaton, meticulously crafted, adorned with real feathers. A wind-up key animated the bird and produced the sound. This device, which fit comfortably into the palm of my grandfather's hand, was made of brass and steel components and had a leather bellow. When he wound the key, the movement pumped the bellow which sent air through a tiny whistle, producing the most extraordinary song. If the key was fully wound, the bird would sing for about half an hour.

He would always ask me to wind the key, while we stood in the forest of the mountains, just above the valley. Then he would balance the device in the branch of a tree, covering the metal with leaves so that the birds would not see it glinting in the sun. He made sure not to put up too many sticks. He didn't want to kill any birds unnecessarily. He just wanted to catch enough so that the family could eat some meat in the winter months. Once the glue sticks were set, we would find ourselves a spot in another part of the woods and wait. To pass the time, he often told me stories – Greek myths and legends of Panhellenism and of fantastical beings – all things that, according to my grandfather, had spurred the Greek Cypriots to fight for independence but, at the same time, had convinced some of them of their invincibility. They had a sense of entitlement and desire to join with Greece that was fierce and unforgiving. 'The voice of myth is powerful,' he would say. These were his favourite words.

But sometimes we just waited quietly, listening to the sound of the machine, which was loud and clear, even at a distance.

'Sounds like a real bird, Grandad,' I said, on one such occasion.

'It has a voice of brass and steel,' he said. 'Never confuse the two things.'

At the time, I had no idea what he meant, but I nodded dutifully, like I always did.

He went on: 'You see, we have to eat, and we have to survive, and yet we must protect our dignity and our identity. There are things we do to achieve those things. But we can respect the land and the animals that are on it. Always be kind to the land, the people and the animals that are on it. Remember that. It's the most important rule in the world.'

This was just after the war, when the island had been divided. My father had fought, and he came back without his right hand and with a new voice. When he came trudging up the mountain, a week after we'd heard on the radio that the war had ended, his eyes were different – they had spots of blood in them, and he barely spoke. He only opened his mouth to complain, or yell about one thing or another. I remembered how his voice would suddenly break the silence. Our Turkish friends had disappeared from their houses in the hills and now we were supposed to refer to them as our enemies. The only thing my father said in his old voice – which I remembered as so earnest, so thoughtful – was that he'd killed a friend down there. Though he never told us who it was.

After the war, I learnt a lesson I would never forget: how a person can disappear inside themselves, and that, sometimes, like my father, they are never able to find their way back.

There it was again – the sound of a woman's voice. As if the wind had opened its mouth and let out a cry. I suddenly remembered where I was: the river to my right, the field to the left. Was that just the wind? A crow maybe? Was my mind playing tricks on me? I looked around.

'Is anyone there?' I called again, but there was no reply. I walked up and down the river, I trudged through the rain-soaked land, I walked far and wide, covered as much distance as I could, until I was convinced that I was alone.

I hadn't collected any snails, and the memories of Nisha and my childhood had drained me. I decided to head back home. But I couldn't spend another night wondering about Nisha, thinking I had seen her shadow, questioning whether she had gone or not.

So, before heading up the stairs to my flat, I knocked on Petra's front door.

11

Petra

ALIKI LOOKED OUT OF THE car window at the rain
pelting down on the pavement as we waited at the
traffic light, on the way to school. She seemed
thoughtful and faraway. She'd done her own hair – two plaits
hung over each shoulder – and she was wearing a bright blue
raincoat over a grey tracksuit and her P.E. trainers. I knew
she didn't want to get any of her Converse wet and dirty.
She had about six pairs of various colours and designs, some
with flower patterns, others with stars or planets or polka
dots. Sometimes she purposely wore odd pairs; how she
matched them was of some importance. She kept them in a
neat row against the wall just outside her bedroom door, and
I'd watch her from time to time as she tried out different
combinations, sometimes shaking her head and trying
another until she felt that her look was just right. She was

very particular about her footwear; she wouldn't even let the cats sleep on them: pointing a finger, and in her most adult voice, she instructed the cats to sit *beside* the shoes, not *on* them. If they didn't cooperate, which they often didn't, she showed them the door. As a rule, I didn't allow cats in the house – they are vermin in these areas – but still they would stroll in when doors were left open in the summer months.

I stood at the gate, as Nisha would have done, and watched as Aliki walked to the entrance of the school. She was slow in her movements, avoiding the puddles as if they were landmines. Normally she would jump in them in order to make Nisha scold and laugh. Nisha would tell me about it later: 'That daughter of yours! She drenched her shoes and trousers. She jumps in those puddles like she is Indiana Jones!'

As Onasagorou is pedestrian only, I parked in one of the back streets and made my way on foot through the rain. By the time I arrived at Sun City, Keti was turning over the open sign on the shop door. She stepped aside to let me in and ran to get me a towel and a coffee. Always eager to please and to learn, she was an aspiring eye surgeon, training at the university of Nicosia, who worked part-time as my assistant. She was brilliant at her job, attentive, meticulous. Sun City attracted an elite clientele; indeed, the city's most important politicians, actors, hotel owners – and even an Indian prince – came to us so that they could see the world more clearly and with style, so I only hired the best staff. Keti had 20/20 vision, but shrewdly wore a pair of Chanel tortoiseshells without prescription: she knew how to represent our interests. We sold the latest designs from Tom Ford, Cartier, Versace, Dior, Bulgari and Chopard. I even had embroidered eyewear by Gazusa, and in an alarmed cabinet behind the counter, I kept the most expensive pair – gold framed with pink lenses and encrusted with 2.85 carats of pink diamonds. I loved the craftsmanship of the individual glasses, each a work of art.

'Where is Nisha?' Keti said, handing me a warm mug of coffee.

'Nisha?'

'It's Thursday,' she said. 'And you are late – we were meant to go through the stock and you have a client in' – she looked at her watch – 'twenty-three minutes.'

'Thursday?' was all I could say at this point. Thursday was the day I bought Nisha in to clean the shop. She would be relieved of her household duties for the day and join me at Sun City to mop and clean the floor, wipe down the shelves and polish the glasses. She would then clean my clinic, followed by the kitchen at the back. She put her heart into it: she knew how important it was to make the shop sparkle.

'Are you OK?' Keti had lifted her glasses, as if this would make her see better, and she was examining my face closely.

'Yes, I'm fine.'

'So where is Nisha?' she asked again.

'Nisha,' I repeated.

Once again, she waited, glasses hovering above her eyes.

'I have no idea.'

She creased her brow.

'I have no idea. I don't know where she is. She's gone.'

'Gone?' She now lowered the glasses onto her nose and bombarded me with questions: Where did she go? Did she say she was leaving? Do you think she went back to Sri Lanka? Any chance she had enough of you? ('Joking – don't look at me like that!')

I answered her questions as best I could. I was exhausted. I realised in that moment that the last few days had caught up with me.

Soon, our first customer came in to collect her prescription sunglasses: Porsche Design with an 18 carat gold frame. She was a new client, with an accent I didn't recognise. Tall, severe blonde bob, sharp fringe, dressed all in black. She'd first visited the shop a couple of weeks earlier when I'd given her an eye test. She put the glasses on now, and stared at herself in the mirror for a while, then she popped the case into her handbag, paid the rest of the money – she had left a deposit of 250 euros – and went out into the rain wearing her new sunglasses.

Keti would normally have had a great deal to say about a customer like this. She would have mused about who she was, where she might have come from. She would have come up with ludicrous and yet at the same time almost plausible stories about why she needed to wear such an expensive pair of sunglasses in the middle of a storm. But today she was quiet, and she looked over at me from the back of the store, where she was checking the stock, and I could see that she was concerned.

The morning proceeded with a few more appointments, some cancellations due to the weather, and just one or two browsers, but it was a mercifully quiet day. Keti went out at lunch and came back with warm haloumi and tomato sandwiches for us both; she closed the shop and brewed coffee. We sat in the kitchen to eat, while the rain continued to fall outside.

'So, let's examine this,' she said, placing one hand on the table, opening it, palm facing up, as if she was holding an eyeball that she was about to dissect.

I nodded.

'She decided to waste her one day off to spend it with you and Aliki in the mountains?'

I nodded again, ignoring Keti's little embellishments, which I had been expecting anyway.

'And while you were there, she asked if she could take the evening off – seeing as she had spent the day practically looking after Aliki – in order to visit—?'

I nodded.

'To visit whom?' Keti prompted.

'I don't know,' I said, and added reluctantly, 'I interrupted her before she could finish her sentence.'

'So, you told her, quite clearly, that she couldn't go.'

'I didn't say no, as such. But it was clear that I disapproved.'

'And you have no idea whom she might have wanted to visit?'

'None whatsoever.'

'So, you went back home, she made dinner, you all sat together to eat, right?'

'Right.'

'Then what?'

'Then I went to bed. I was tired, I wanted an early night. I left Nisha to put Aliki to bed and ready her things for school in the morning.'

'And then in the morning . . .'

'In the morning she was gone. She left her passport and a number of other things that are very special to her. I also found a gold ring, like an engagement ring, on her dresser, that I'd never seen before.'

Keti nodded now, presumably at a loss.

'It's Thursday today,' she said. 'You've been to the police?'

'Yesterday.'

I told her about the whole sorry encounter at the station: what the officer had said, and how I had finally walked out of his office, stepping on his paperwork. But as I relayed the story, I felt a dull ache in my stomach, like something was amiss, something I didn't understand. And it was then that I realised the officer's voice had sounded somehow familiar, as if I had been hearing an echo of something that was coming from inside me.

I couldn't say this to Keti, but I felt a bloom of guilt at this acknowledgement. Blushing self-consciously, I focused on her.

'You've got to search for her yourself,' she said, slapping her hand meaningfully on the table between us.

'How? I don't even know where to begin.'

'You'll figure it out. You can't leave it like this! You can't let a woman who has lived with you and helped you for so many years just vanish, as if she was meaningless.'

I nodded. She was right.

'And your instinct tells you something is wrong?'

'Yes. Absolutely.'

'And this is out of character?'

'Yes.'

'Well, then. You have no other choice.' And that was the last thing she said, before looking at her watch and informing me that lunch was over and our next client would be arriving in about three minutes.

That evening it continued to rain. The boat was brimming over with water. Water fell through the trees in the garden; it saturated the soil and made the patio glisten like a lake. Aliki stalked around the house, holding onto the black cat as if it was her salvation. Sometimes the cat obliged, purring and rubbing its nose on her ear; other times, it pushed her face away with its paw, scrambled out of her arms with a hiss, and dashed for the window.

I couldn't eat that night, but I made a light meal for Aliki. I couldn't stop thinking about my conversation with Keti and the things Nilmini had said. I walked in and out of Nisha's room, hoping to spark a memory, a revelation. Was there something I had missed? Had she mentioned anything that I'd forgotten? It was like attempting to recall a half-forgotten dream.

I kept hearing Keti's words: *You've got to go and search for her yourself.* Heavy words; words that hit me hard with the weight of responsibility. And last night Aliki had asked me to find her.

Yes, this was something I had to do, although I hadn't the slightest idea how.

I decided that I would speak to more of Nisha's friends. It seemed like a place to start. I wondered if they knew anything – and if they did, whether they would tell me.

I knew Nisha was friends with the maids at the gated mansion at the end of the street, the one with two hunting dogs so, on Friday afternoon, I shut my practice early and headed home. The rain had finally stopped, but very few customers had come in – I had been alone in the shop, as Keti studied at university on Fridays.

I decided to make dinner early, then walk over to the gated mansion down the street. But before I'd even started cooking, while Aliki was in the garden attempting to empty the boat of water, the doorbell rang.

It was Yiannis from upstairs. The light from Yiakoumi's shop glowed around him and he stood there staring at me for a moment too long before he spoke.

'Petra,' he said, 'sorry to disturb you. I am wondering . . .' There was a pause, and a shuffle of his feet, as if he was about to change his mind and walk away. '. . . is Nisha in?' He was almost a silhouette, so I couldn't see the expression on his face, but there was something guarded, uncertain, in the tone of his voice.

'No,' I said. 'I'm sorry, Yiannis, but she's not.'

He ran his hand through his hair, streaks of silver illumi-nated in the light that poured from the display window behind him. His movements were so hesitant that I could almost hear all those clocks ticking.

'Do you know where she is?'

'Why?' I said, perhaps too quickly, and he bought his hand to his face and rubbed his stubble. Then he looked over my shoulder, into the open-plan living room, his eyes scanning.

'Well . . . because I haven't seen her,' he said. 'I haven't seen her all week, and I've been worried.'

There was a desperation in him now that I didn't understand. He was lost and vulnerable, like those stray dogs that wander the neighbourhood looking for someone to love. Why was he so concerned about Nisha? There was something niggling at me, something I think I had known for a long time but refused to believe, and it was this thought that made me invite him in.

He was dressed nicely, as if he was heading to a bar for a drink – a perfectly ironed black shirt, opened slightly at the collar, a pair of dark blue jeans – but mud covered his shoes. Mud that hadn't yet dried and crusted.

He stood awkwardly in the middle of the room: it was the first time he'd been inside, and he glanced left and right at the furniture, the photographs on the console table, the dining table. He looked over to the kitchen, where Nisha had spent so much of her time, scrubbing and cooking. It was strange, though – he looked around like he knew the place.

Now, in the light, I could see clearly the desperation that I had sensed in the darkness; it was mainly in the deep crease of his brow and the restlessness of his eyes. We stood there for a moment, neither of us speaking. He was a good-looking man: very dark eyes with thick lashes, and a soft beard that was neatly trimmed, partly black, partly grey. It was strange to have him standing in my living room. We hardly ever spoke, apart from short pleasantries in the garden about the chicken pen or the weather or how the tomatoes and shoe-figs were doing.

I wanted to understand his connection to Nisha. I had seen them talking many times in the garden; I had seen the looks they gave each other, of course I had – a touch of the hand, low whispers in the evening . . . but, if there had been something going on between them, I may have needed to dismiss Nisha, even though I couldn't imagine my life without her. Nobody allowed their maids to have sexual or romantic relationships – it was almost unheard of, apart from those maids who ended up marrying their employers.

I couldn't help glancing down at the mud on his shoes, wondering where he'd been. I suddenly realised I should have told him to take them off at the door – *It's not as though Nisha's here to keep the floors clean.* And that thought alone made me suddenly feel so alone, the house so empty without her.

I offered him a drink and he thanked me and asked for alcohol. 'Anything,' he said. 'Something strong.'

I went to the kitchen and poured us both some *zivania*.

When I came back, Yiannis had taken off his shoes and was standing by the console table in his socks, looking at the photographs. He must've seen me looking at his feet.

'I'm sorry that I came in with such muddy shoes,' he said. 'I was out collecting snails. I've had so much on my mind that I'm finding it hard to think.' Before I could respond, he said. 'Is that your husband?' signalling with his eyes Stephanos in his military gear.

'It is.'

He nodded. 'Your daughter looks like him.'

I noticed now that his shoes were lined up neatly by the door.

I put the drinks down on the coffee table and lit the fire. He joined me, perching, uncomfortably, on the edge of the L-shaped sofa. He took a long gulp of *zivania* and for a second it made his jaw clench and his eyes shine. This wasn't a man who was used to drinking spirits.

I wasn't sure if he was waiting for me to speak, but I didn't know what to say anyway. I could have started talking about Nisha, telling him what had been going on this week, but apart from being my tenant, this man was more or less a stranger.

He took another big gulp from his glass and this time scrunched up his eyes. Then he ran his finger over the rim of the glass, again lost in thought.

Eventually I said, 'So, you're worried about Nisha? Do you know her well?' This made him put the glass on the table and rub his eyes with his hands, as if I had just woken him up. He nodded and picked up the glass again.

He was nervous, I could see that, and he opened his mouth a few times to say something, but at first no voice came out. 'When was the last time you saw her?' he eventually asked.

'Last Sunday evening,' I said, cautiously. 'I woke up in the morning on Monday, and she was gone.'

This seemed to worry him even more and he stood up and paced up and down in front of the fire, his feet padding softly on the rug, so that his faint moving shadow drifted over the furniture. I thought how absurd it was that this man was in my living room all of a sudden, in his socks.

'I don't know where she is,' I said.

'Do you think she went home?'

'No.'

'How can you be so sure?'

I thought for a few moments, while he stared at me with wide eyes, waiting for an answer. Perhaps it was the fact that he seemed to share my confusion and concern, that I went into Nisha's bedroom and came back with her belongings, those I had taken to the police station. I didn't bring the gold ring. I placed them all on the coffee table without saying a word.

He sat down again and looked at the items. He opened the passport and stared at her picture for a long time. Then he picked up the locket, as if he'd seen it before, and wrapped his hand around it. As for the lock of hair in the plastic bag – he pressed it between his palms, so tight, that I could see blue veins bulging in the backs of his hands.

'So she hasn't gone home.' He said this more to himself than to me. His voice had changed: it rang out clear, filling the quiet room, hovering over us for a while, much like the sound of a gong that reverberates before vanishing into silence.

'Have you been to the police?'

'Yes, I went on Wednesday.'

'What did they say?'

I paused, considering whether to tell him the whole unpleasant story. 'They were no help. They have no interest in searching for her. They said she's probably run away to the north to find other work.'

'Nisha would never do that,' he said. And suddenly I understood clearly – it was the way her name rolled off his tongue, as if he'd said it a thousand times before – that he knew her. He loved her.

There were questions – so many – I could have asked him. But I decided to keep us on our shared concern and knowledge that anyone who knew Nisha even a little bit would know that she would never take off in that way.

'The only time she went away,' I said, 'was a few months ago. She went for the entire weekend to stay with a cousin of hers in Limassol. This woman was about to leave Cyprus and Nisha wanted to take her some things to give to Kumari. She gave me the woman's name, her employer's name, their telephone number – in case her battery went dead or something . . . she didn't just take off. It was all organised.'

Yiannis was silent for a while.

'When was this?'

'In August,' I said. 'Yes, I'm pretty sure that's when it was. I remember the heat that day. She packed an overnight bag and wore an orange linen dress that I had given her. I dropped her off at the coach station in the early morning. She was teary in the car. When I asked her what was wrong, she said she was going to miss Aliki. I remember saying, "Don't be silly! You're only going for a weekend!" But since

Aliki was born, Nisha has never spent a weekend away from us.'

Realisation hit me. Nisha had lived here for nearly ten years and in that entire time, had only spent two days away from us. She had taken care of my daughter and loved her, she had scrubbed my floors and toilets, she had made us hot dinners and kept the garden looking beautiful. She even polished the frame of Stephano's photo every day, and it broke my heart when I recalled the look on her face as she did this. She had lost a husband, too. She gave us everything. In this generosity, she had been the heart of this house. And yet, I had no idea about her life. I knew she held the heart locket some nights, and I knew there was a new gold ring on her dressing table that I had never seen before. How had her husband died? She had never told me, and I had never asked. How had she felt? What was it like to feel something for another man, after losing him? Had Yiannis given her the ring? Had she loved both these men in the way that I had loved Stephanos? Did she love this man sitting before me? Or did he have something to do with her disappearance? I could barely hold one thought before I jumped to another.

I heard a soft bump and saw the toe of a red Converse poking out from the doorway. Aliki was eavesdropping, but the intensity of Yiannis's words surrounded me and pressed down on me. I didn't want to break the spell to scold her.

'Did she say anything?' Yiannis asked now. 'Before she disappeared. Did she say or mention anything that could help us to understand where she might have gone?'

'We went up to the mountains on Sunday for a day out. While we were there, she asked if she could take the night off. It seemed as if she wanted to meet someone.'

'Who?'

'I have no idea. She didn't say. And I didn't approve of her going.' I didn't tell him about the whole conversation I'd had with Mrs Hadjikyriacou – that she had seen Nisha leaving that night around ten thirty. Something told me not to.

'So, on Sunday afternoon she was with you in the mountains.' He seemed to be turning this around in his mind. 'And there was someone she wanted to meet that night. You say you didn't approve of her going, but you haven't said if she went or not.'

'Nisha came home with us and I went to bed at nine o'clock. Nisha was here, putting Aliki to bed. Look,' I said, standing up, suddenly exhausted, 'I can see that you're concerned but there's nothing more I can tell you.' I saw that Aliki's shoe had vanished from the entrance to the hallway. 'And plus, it's late, and I haven't made dinner yet. Aliki hasn't eaten and I've been working all day.'

He stood up too, looking dismayed. 'Yes, of course – I'm sorry, Petra. I didn't mean to bother you.' He hesitated for a moment, as if he wasn't sure whether to go out of the front door or the back – either way, there was a stairway that would lead him to his flat. Then he seemed to remember his shoes and went to the front door, bending over to put them on. The mud had dried now and was breaking off in flakes on the rug.

'Thank you for your time, Petra. And if you hear anything . . .'

'I will tell you straightaway.'

He left. After closing the door, I went to the window and saw that he was standing again in the light of Yiakoumi's shop, staring up at his flat, reminding me again of one of those wandering dogs, the ones that people leave on the streets when, for whatever reason, they are no longer good for hunting.

At night, a bat circles the lake, almost invisible against the black water. For a brief moment, the clouds part and the moon catches its large wings, its fragmented flight. The new moon quickly disappears behind the clouds, as if it had never been there.

The earth around the crater smells fresh from the rain, and the fur of the hare has begun to dry. Earlier, when the sun was high and the air was warmer, the blow flies returned to lay their eggs once more in the open wounds of cracked skin, while the flesh flies deposited larvae around the eyes and in the mouth.

On this night the earth and the sky join without a seam. There are white flowers in the fields, hundreds and thousands of them. Had there been a fuller moon, had there not still been thick clouds in the sky, they would glow like stars, and heaven and earth would be mere reflections of each other.

A man arrives, by foot. He lights up the path with the light of his phone. He has walked for miles along the bank of the river. The artificial light has a metallic quality. He has nothing else on him, no bag, no wallet, just the phone that he holds like a torch in his hand. The light drifts over the hare – he winces – then he directs the light over the lake and it catches the flight of the bat. He walks a few yards until he reaches the gallows frame, his heavy army boots leaving prints in the forgiving soil.

12

Yiannis

I COULDN'T GO UPSTAIRS. I WAS restless.

'Darrling,' a voice said in English to my left. I turned and saw Mrs Hadjikyriacou on her deckchair, a thick throw over her shoulders. Then she reverted back to her native tongue, a concerned look on her face: 'My love, you look heartbroken.'

I said nothing at all.

'How about some baklava?' On a small table beside her, she had an assortment of miniature cakes, as if she was expecting visitors.

'No, thank you, Mrs Hadjikyriacou. I think I'm going to go for a walk. It's a nice evening, if a bit chilly.'

'I wouldn't know. I'm numb to the cold. I have felt nothing, not heat, nor cold, since the war. It's Ruba – she insists on putting this stupid blanket on me. She says I'll catch my death. I tell her I've already caught him, many times before. And I'm stronger than him.'

I nodded. I was sure she was right.

'And I've said to you before, call me Julia. Mrs Hadjikyriacou makes me sound old.' This almost made me laugh, because she looked as though she'd fought her way out of the grave.

She reached over and selected two small portions of baklava, then gingerly folded them in a tissue and pressed them into my hand. She insisted that I looked malnourished and hungry – but then again, every person without a huge gut looked hungry to Mrs Hadjikyriacou.

Thanking her, I took her carefully wrapped parcel and walked past Theo's, where outdoor heaters had been lit and smoke rose from the ovens. Some of the men waved at me and I raised my hand and tried to smile. I continued on down the road, nearing the Green Line, where cats darted from one end of the street to the other, jumping over the dividing fence into the buffer zone. Everything seemed so surreal, like the world was ticking away without me. The only thing that seemed true was the moon.

A cat was trying to get my attention, chirping, weaving through my legs as I walked. The black cat that often hung around with Aliki and Nisha.

I thought about Nisha's passport – the fact that she hadn't taken it with her clearly meant that she had not gone back to Sri Lanka, as I had suspected. This made me feel relief and anxiety at the same time. If she hadn't gone home, then where was she? Why had she not informed anybody? I thought about the locket her late husband had given her and the lock of Kumari's hair. She would absolutely never leave without those two items. Even when she had gone away for those two days, she had taken them with her, neatly tucked into her wallet.

The cat yowled at me now and, when I paused, sprawled itself expectantly on the ground in front of me, paws up, stomach exposed.

I leaned down and stroked it, felt the vibration of its deep, contented purrs. I sat down on the ground, cross-legged, and continued to pet the cat. It seemed to have decided that this was what we both needed to do right then. The street was dark, deserted, with no lights on in any of the houses: most of them probably abandoned this far down the street, near the buffer zone. A new moon hung in the sky, still tinged with red.

I thought about Nisha's orange linen dress and the weekend she had left to stay with her cousin Chaturi in Limassol. The story wasn't as simple as Petra thought.

It began one Sunday in August. Petra had left Nicosia to spend the day with Aliki at Makronisos beach in the east. They'd left early in the morning, as it was a two-hour drive, packing deckchairs, towels and sun hats into the boot of the car. Petra had informed Nisha that they would be gone all afternoon, and would likely have supper in Ayia Napa with a friend. So Nisha and I had the whole day and evening to laze about together. It had been too hot to go anywhere except the sea, and Nisha hated the sea, so we had decided to stay in the cool darkness of the bedroom, with the balcony doors wide open. I will never forget that day. There was hardly a breeze: not even a leaf stirred on the trees. The sound of the cicadas and the smell of jasmine filled the room. Whenever the wind blew, it was hot and bought no relief.

Before noon, Nisha spent some time talking to Kumari on my tablet. She sat at the desk while I lay on the bed, listening to them speaking in Sinhalese, their voices sometimes joyful, sometimes serious, a few words in English. Though I couldn't understand their conversation, I knew Nisha well enough to pick up on the fact that she was distracted. I went to the kitchen and made us both some frappe, with lots of ice cubes and extra milk and sugar for Nisha, just as she liked. I handed it to her as she finished the call; she took one small sip and left it on the side of the desk, then she sat staring out of the open doors, hardly saying a word. We made lunch together, eating hoppers – Sri Lankan pancakes. She stirred the mixture and said a few things like, 'Pass the rice flour' or 'Splash some coconut milk into it now.' I added a ladle of batter to the wok and swirled it around, then she cracked an egg into the bowl-shaped pancake and began to make the garnish of onions, chillies and lemon juice while I fried the rest. 'Don't you think that one's ready?' she said, when I'd left the pancake in the wok too long, because I too had become distracted, wondering what was wrong with her. I knew she didn't like to be asked, so I waited.

Later that night, a full moon hung in the sky. Theo's was bustling with people, the bouzouki was playing and Nisha was lying on her side looking up at the sky. She wanted all the lights off: she felt cooler that way, she'd said. The moonlight was cool. She stared at it, her eyes glazed, as if she was staring at the space between her and the moon.

After what felt like a long time, she sat up, folded her legs, and faced me. I did the same. She looked at me straight in the eyes.

'I'm pregnant.'

'Pregnant?'

She nodded.

'You're pregnant.'

She nodded again. 'We were so careful,' she said. I could make out no obvious expression on her face, it was as blank as a stone. But then she leaned into me and rested her head on my chest and we lay down together.

'What are you thinking?' she asked.

'I think it's great.'

'Do you?'

'Yes.'

She turned on her back, took my hand and placed it on her stomach, then she rested her hand on top of mine. I'd never felt as close to anyone as I did in that moment. Our bodies connected – mine, Nisha's and this little foetus that was growing inside her. Our baby. Mine and hers. A wave of happiness came over me, like someone had opened a window that overlooked the landscape of my childhood and reminded me of what it felt like to be filled with love and wonder. What would this child look like? Perhaps these were premature thoughts, but I imagined that he or she would be everything like Nisha. These images fell into my mind as fresh and cool as rain in the heat of that room.

123

'What are you thinking?' she said again.

'I think it's wonderful. I love you.'

'That's because you're feeling and not thinking.'

'That's not true,' I said. 'My feelings and thoughts are perfectly in sync!' Then I added, 'For once!' And I laughed at how often we'd both said the words *feelings* and *thoughts*.

But Nisha didn't laugh. She gently lifted her hand from mine, lifted my hand from her stomach and continued to gaze out of the window. Finally, she said: 'I will lose my job. Nobody wants a pregnant maid.'

'We'll find a way. I'll help you find something else to do. Or I'll take care of you. Whatever you want, we'll make it work.'

'You don't understand,' she said. 'What about Kumari? I have to send money. If I lose my job, how will she live? I have debts to pay off. I have debts with the agency, Yiannis – I'm still paying them for bringing me here. And what about my mother? She is relying on me, too. It's because of the work I do here that they have money to eat and live and go about their everyday lives. What would happen if I lost this job? It's not just you and me and this baby.'

She said all this in one breath and her voice broke, though tears didn't come: she seemed to swallow them.

'I understand,' I said. I bought her closer to me, held her. 'What if I helped you financially? What if I gave you money to pay off your debt and also to send back home?'

'With what?' she said. 'Wild asparagus and snails?' Her voice held an edge of derision.

And she was right, because if that was the whole truth

124

then I'd be nothing short of a lunatic. I wanted to tell her about the songbirds. But if I told her, it would break her heart.

'The thing is,' she said, 'if I didn't have this debt, I probably would have been able to go home by now, and we wouldn't be here ... we wouldn't be in this situation anyway.'

She was matter-of-fact, decisive; her words a brutal blow to a fragile dream. But then she took my hand again, and this time pressed it down onto her stomach so that I could feel the weight of her love in that small push.

The following evening, I decided to tell her about the songbirds. It was the only chance I had to get her to believe that I had the means to help her financially. I wanted this baby, our baby, more than anything. It was late when she appeared at my door – we were back to our usual 11 p.m. rendezvous, since Petra and Aliki had returned from the beach. After Nisha had made them dinner and put Aliki to bed, she came up to my flat. I took her by the hand and led her to the spare room. I unlocked the door and for a few moments she stood there, confused, looking around, resting her eyes on one of the industrial fridges.

'What is all this?' she said.

'I have another way of making money,' I said. 'I want you to know that I've saved enough and I can support you, Kumari, and your mother.'

'But you told me this door was always closed because it was such a mess in here.'

In fact, it was relentlessly tidy and I could see her taking all this in, looking around at the lime sticks, the wicker shoulder-pouch I took with me on hunts, the black calling devices lined up on the small desk, the containers stacked against the wall.

'It's like Indiana Jones with fridges. What have you been doing?' she said

'After I lost my job at Laiki, I became involved in hunting. I was desperate. I could never have survived selling mushrooms and—'

'Hunting what?' she interrupted me.

'Songbirds,' I said, quietly.

'Songbirds?'

She went straight to one of the fridges, opened it and looked inside. Luckily, they were all empty on that day. Then she shut it and opened the second fridge, and the third. Leaving this last door open, she turned to face me.

'Where are they?' she asked.

'I don't have any right now. I just made a delivery.'

She nodded, and there was a look of disappointment on her face. But this feeling belonged only to her; she wasn't willing to share it with me in words.

'I don't want to do it,' I said, trying to make her understand. 'Once you get into it, it's hard to stop. It's a bit like drug dealing – there's a huge underground organisation, and they won't let you go, it's too risky for them.' I didn't tell her that the previous week a man I knew had handed in his notice, and that night his boat shed had mysteriously burnt to the ground.

'Who are *they*?' Nisha asked.

'The men at the top.'

'So, once you make a decent amount of money, you want out and you're stuck?'

'Yes.'

She closed the fridge door and bought her hand to her stomach, her eyes to the ground.

'What I'm saying to you is that I'm going to find a way out of this. I will. But I have more than enough money to be able to support us until I find a different job. The recession has passed now. I have experience in finance. I know the way I made my money isn't ideal, but we can be a family.'

'Not ideal.' She repeated faintly. She turned and walked out of the spare room, then headed for the back door. Her hand on the door knob, she turned back to me and said, 'I'll think about it,' then disappeared down the stairs.

After that, she didn't come to see me for several days. But about a week later, she turned up at my door – I remember it was a Friday morning and I was surprised to see her in the light of day. She looked so beautiful, in a vibrant orange dress that bought out the gold in her eyes. Her hair was tied up in a ponytail. Her lips glimmered with gloss. On her feet she still wore her practical, scuffed, high-impact walking sandals.

I wanted to reach out and hold her. 'Come in,' I said.

'No. I've just come to tell you that I'm going to Limassol for the weekend, to stay with my cousin Chaturi. Do you remember when she came to visit me?'

'Of course,' I replied.

'Well, she's leaving to go back to Sri Lanka next week and I'm going to give her a few things to take to Galle.'

I nodded.

'I need some time away from here so that I can think.'

I nodded again.

'Don't call me or try to contact me. It's just for a few days.'

'Don't worry,' I said, 'I understand.'

Her lips broke into a small smile, but her eyes carried a lingering sadness. Then she walked down the stairs and I watched her as she went into her bedroom through the patio doors.

After the weekend passed, Nisha returned. Late on Monday night, I heard a knock at the door. She was standing there in a bright white nightdress, a pink cardigan draped over her shoulders. Her hair was loose, her face flushed like she'd been running.

'I couldn't wait to see you,' she said.

She put her arms around me immediately and tucked her face into the crook of my neck; I felt the damp warmth of her body against mine, her breath against my skin. I was flooded with relief, joyful at her return, grateful to have her in my arms again.

'I wanted to come last night, but Aliki was running a fever. I couldn't leave her,' she said.

We lay down on the bed. There was a soft summer breeze. She lay on her back, I on my side; I kissed her shoulder and stroked her hair, just as she liked. I almost couldn't believe that she was there.

'How is Chaturi?' I asked.

'Do you like my nightdress? She gave it to me as a gift. She made it herself. It's beeralu lace.'

'It's beautiful,' I said. And it was so beautiful. I ran my hand over the fine patterns of flowers. It was like a pure white garden.

'She drew it on graph paper first, then attached it to the *kotta boley* with pins. She then took each thread around the pin. Can you imagine what a task it is?'

'I can.'

'Her employers were away this weekend, so we had the house to ourselves. I helped her with the chores, then we sat the rest of the time in the garden. We talked while she weaved. She was desperate to finish it before I left. She said she had a feeling she would not see me for a very long time.'

Over the years, Nisha had seen Chaturi every couple of months, usually when Chaturi came with her employers to Nicosia for a Sunday visit. They had family there and they would drop her off at Petra's for the day, then collect her in the evening before heading back to Limassol. It was always a special occasion for Nisha. The two women would spend time making *aluwa*, a nutty sweetmeat with cashews, or my favourite, *aasmi*, made with coconut milk and the juice of cinnamon leaves. Chaturi would leave with a couple of Tupperware boxes filled with sweets. Nisha would always set aside a few slices in foil and bring them up for me later in the evening, telling me all about their conversations, Chaturi's jokes, the news from home.

'I hope she is wrong about that,' she said. 'That it will be a long time before she sees me again.' She ran her fingers over the flowers of her nightgown.

'I'm sure it won't be too long' I said, reassuring her.

She paused a moment, and then said: 'I made an appoint-ment at the clinic in Limassol to end the pregnancy, but I couldn't do it.' Her eyes were wide now, fearful. 'This baby is going to start growing and I'm going to be left without a job and without a home. Do you know what happens to women like me who break the rules?'

Her words were tumbling from her mouth now, and I could barely keep up.

'My friend, Mary, from the Philippines, well, her employer saw her jumping over the fence at night to see her boyfriend and fired her on the spot. It was almost impossible for her to find work after that, because this employer was very well known in the community, and respected. She had to move into a hostel with fifteen other women on the other side of the island. The conditions were so bad that she ended up selling her body to stay in an old man's villa by the sea with three other women.'

I reached for her, but she pushed me away. She distanced herself from me, so she could look me in the eyes.

'And little Diwata down the road, well, her ex-employer beat her. She had bruises on her arms and legs and was only allowed to eat such a small amount of food each day that she ended up shrinking down to nearly nothing. She looked like she was twelve! Well, she was lucky because she found another employer. He has bought her a car, he never bruises her body, and he buys her new clothes and gives her his credit card to buy whatever she likes. Why do you think that is?'

She stared at me without blinking. I said nothing.

'Petra will fire me. She will. Who knows where I will end up? And if I want to find another job, I will have to give up the baby. But what if I can't do it? Just like I couldn't terminate the pregnancy.' Tears fell from her eyes now and she briskly wiped them with the back of her hand. 'I stepped through the door. I actually went to the clinic.'

There was nothing I could say. I wanted to tell her it would be OK, that for her the outcome would be different, I would help her. But what did I know of her world? Of what she owed. I couldn't bring myself to make promises I couldn't understand.

After a silence, she finally spoke. 'Whatever happens,' she said, 'you have to promise me that you will stop what you are doing to the songbirds. It's not a good thing.'

'I promise,' I said. 'I can promise that.'

Suddenly the cat's ears flattened and it hissed. From behind I heard footsteps approaching. I turned and saw Spyros with his poodle. Spyros, the postman. A well-built guy, covered in tattoos from the neck down. His poodle, tiny, well-groomed, in a khaki military bomber jacket designed especially for dogs. In the summer it had a sun umbrella attached to its leash. The discrepancy between them always made Nisha laugh when she saw the pair from my balcony on Sundays. She would lean forward carefully, so that prying neighbours would not see her, and whistle the theme tune of Indiana Jones, and he would whistle it back. It meant: *I know you're there and your secret is safe with me.* Spyros the postman knew most things, everyone in the neighbourhood knew that Spyros the postman knew most things, but his lips were always sealed. Nisha loved this game they played – it made her feel more accepted, more human, she said. She had told me that *Indiana Jones and the Temple of Doom* had been filmed in Kandy in the eighties, and as a child she had loved to imagine all the adventures taking place just 200 km or so from her home.

The cat now hissed, circling Spyros's dog, who growled in return, making a show of pulling at his lead. The dog bared its tiny teeth and the cat hissed again. It was an amusing stand-off, and if I hadn't been so upset, I would have laughed.

'Sit, Agamemnon!' Spyros said. The dog obeyed – sort of – continuing to growl from deep in its chest.

'What are you doing here, mate?' he asked, looking down at me.

'Thinking.'

'On the ground? In the middle of the street?'

'Yes.'

He sat down beside me. 'Something's wrong.'

'Nisha is missing. I don't know where she's gone.'

'How long?'

'Nearly a week now. Last Sunday night or Monday morning.'

Spyros furrowed his brow, seemed caught up in thought. 'I saw her on Sunday,' he said, 'around ten thirty in the evening. I took Agamemnon out later than usual because my mum had come to visit. I took my usual route, I was heading down *this* street and she walked past me pretty fast. She was in a rush. I asked her where she was off to and she said she was going down the road to Maria's bar to meet Seraphim.'

'Seraphim?' A jolt like a rush of ice went down my spine. 'Why?'

'I have no idea,' he said. 'That's all I know. But I saw her and I'm certain it was Sunday night.'

The cat followed me home like a tiny shadow, then disappeared into the darkness of the back garden. I was surprised to find the little bird sitting on the rug in the hallway near the door when I arrived. It was hopping about now. I put out some fresh water and bread and went out to sit on the balcony. I opened a cold beer and drank it quickly. Why was Nisha meeting Seraphim? And why had he not told me he had seen her? And what in God's name would she be doing in a place like that? I knew the bar. It was the place I had met Seraphim back when he first recruited me.

I couldn't sleep for thinking about it all, and was awake when, once again, at 3 a.m., my iPad started to ring. I got up and saw Kumari's name flashing on the screen. It stopped and started again. Once again I could do nothing: I was frozen to the spot. But the name begged me to answer, it pounded at the darkness with desperation.

I answered.

Kumari blinked at me, shocked to see my face. 'Where is Amma?' she said in English, stretching her neck in an attempt to see behind me. The girl was wearing her school uniform and had a rucksack with purple straps on her shoulders.

'I'm Yiannis,' I said. 'Do you remember me?'

She nodded. 'Of course I remember you, Mr Yiannis. We have spoken so many times! You are Amma's friend.'

'That's right. Is your grandmother there? Can I speak to her?'

'She just go to shop.'

'Your mum is at work. She left the tablet here with me. She told me to tell you that she loves you, to be good at school and that she'll speak to you very soon.'

Kumari nodded. 'Okay, Mr Yiannis,' she said. 'Thank you. You be good at work too.' Then she smiled. There was a cheekiness to her, like her mother. It made my heart ache.

Then she was gone, and the screen was blank once more.

13

Petra

O N SATURDAY MORNING, I DECIDED to visit the gated mansion at the end of the street. I told Aliki that Mrs Hadjikyriacou would be keeping an eye on her, but she was free to play in the garden. She nodded, without seeming too bothered, picking up a favourite book and heading out the door to the boat. She got in and started reading. I brought her out a plate of orange slices and kissed her head, then thanked Mrs Hadjikyriacou and told her I wouldn't be gone long. She knew my errand and was happy to help.

My first stop was Yiakoumi's shop. I had brought Nisha's journal with me and now clutched it to my chest as I stepped into the shop. There were no customers yet this early on a Saturday, but, as I had expected, Nilmini was there cleaning, bending over wiping dust from the glass cases under the counter. Yiakoumi was nowhere to be seen.

'Good morning,' I said.

'Good morning, madam,' she said. She paused in her dusting, standing up and eyeing the journal in my hands.

'Nilmini, will you do me a favour? Or, in fact, a favour for Nisha?'

'Of course, madam,' she said.

'This is a journal that Nisha kept,' I said, placing it on the counter. 'Would you be able to read it and tell me if there is anything in it that might help me to find her?'

She took the journal from my hands and opened it, flicking through, glancing at the pages. 'I will do it, madam,' she said. 'I will read this for you.'

I was in a hurry so I thanked her and left, and she watched me from the large window and waved as I continued down the street.

I walked past the church and caught wafts of lavender from its garden. The sun was still low in the sky in this early part of the day, and it promised to be a sunny and crisp autumn afternoon. A maid swept the path in front of the church, clearing it of leaves and cockroaches. She looked up and nodded as I passed.

There was a sculptor's workshop further down the street: a terraced property with no front wall or door or window, just a large mouth of an entrance that was always open – there was not even a shutter which came down at night to secure the premises. The cavernous space was strewn with broken planks, rusty nails, boxes of tools and twisted tree branches scattered about like severed limbs. From time to time the owner, a middle-aged man called Muyia, appeared in there, working, but more often than not it looked like a ramshackle, abandoned garage. However, Muyia was there this morning and I could see that he was focused on a piece of wood, chipping away, shaping something that seemed to mean very much to him: his concentration was so intense, his brow was furrowed and his lips were pressed together tightly.

Hearing my footsteps, he looked up and then raised his hand in greeting. 'Petra! How was your trip to the mountains?' he called.

'Mountains?' I said, coming up to the entrance.

'Yes, Nisha said she was going with you to the mountains. Come in, come in! Let me show you something.'

I stepped over bits of twisted wire and scrap wood. The space was deep and should have been dark but he had two bright lamps over his work station. This was the first time I'd been inside, and I realised that it wasn't as much of a mess as I'd thought. In fact, there was a gigantic shelf that held beautiful, carved wooden sculptures. They were mostly faces of people, but also animals: a snake, an elephant, three dragonflies hovering on invisible strings. There were finely carved flowers and various birds and fish, even a globe of the Earth – all crafted intricately with minute, precious details. They were unpainted, so they retained their soft honey colour and you could see the wood's grain. I felt as though I'd stepped into some kind of magical forest.

'Do you like them?' he said.

'They are extraordinary.'

He smiled at the compliment, and said, 'Have a look at this.'

I turned to see the piece he had just been working on. It was a Madonna and child, enormous, almost life-sized. There was a quiet beauty to the woman, to the curve of her cheek bones and the soft sweep of her eyes and nose, her heart-shaped face. A strand of hair fell down over one eye, and a small owl perched on her shoulder. But what truly struck me was how life-like she was – not just in her fine appearance, but in her essence, her energy; her strength and practicality. It was in the soft but certain gaze of her eyes as she looked down at the child in her arms, the firm and tender touch of her fingers on the child's thigh.

'She is holding *her* child,' he said, deeply emphasising the word *her*.

He looked at it now, staring at his creation, as though he had forgotten that I was there. Squinting his eyes, he ran his thumb over the wing of the owl. 'Hmm,' he said, 'I need to fix that bit. Do you see how the angle there is too sharp, in the wing? It gives the character of the bird the wrong quality, wouldn't you say?'

'I wouldn't know what quality the owl is supposed to have.'

At that point he looked at me for a moment, then creased his brow and nodded slightly, as if he had understood or remembered something. Then he said, 'You know, we've never really spoken before. Imagine, all these years as neighbours and this is the first time we've said more than a few words to each other.'

138

I looked again at the statue and saw something I hadn't noticed before: there was a deep sadness in the woman. It emanated not just from her eyes, but from everywhere, her posture, her enduring silent touch, even her stillness; it was even in the grain of the wood. And there was something else about her – she looked remarkably like Nisha.

'Would you like a coffee?' he said. 'I can bring another stool for you to sit down.'

'No,' I replied. 'I'm afraid I'm out on an errand and I don't have much time.'

Suddenly, I felt a desperate urge to leave. My mind was rattling with questions, but I wasn't ready to ask them. Did she pose for this statue, was she his muse? How many other men in the neighbourhood did she know? I had started to become worried about what else I might discover about this stranger who had lived in my house, brought up my daughter, orchestrated our lives, made our house a home after Stephanos died. Who was this woman who I had previously seen only as a shadow of myself? A dark and beautiful shadow, who rattled around in old sandals and with fire in her eyes.

It struck me now that it was I who had been her shadow.

I quickly took leave of Muyia, stuttering my apologies and promising to come back for a coffee another time. I did want to speak to him more, but I had to sort out my questions. And anyway, I'd already been delayed and didn't want to leave Aliki with Mrs Hadjikyriacou all afternoon.

I hustled along the street, to the gated mansion, a colossal neoclassical building with balconies flowering at every window. I pressed the buzzer and looked into the intercom. After a moment there was a crackly voice: 'Madam, come in!' followed by a loud click. The gate creaked open.

I'd visited Mr and Mrs Kosta's mansion once before when they'd thrown a New Year's party. All the neighbours – well, the ones they deemed worthy – had been invited, and I had made the cut. I supposed it was because I mixed with the rich and famous in my work; perhaps they thought I would have some good stories. This oversized house was their retirement home: they'd repatriated from the UK, where Mr Kostas had owned a chain of insurance firms in London.

I walked along a path, through the meticulously kept orchard: on one side were shoe-fig trees, cacti and apple and pear trees; on the other, lemon, cherry and apricot trees, grape-vines and tomato plants. Winter was approaching so the trees were losing their leaves, but I knew in just a few months tiny buds would appear on the branches and in a few weeks after that this whole place would smell like a perfumerie.

Halfway down the path I hesitated, expecting someone to come out to greet me.

'Madam, come in!' a voice called, and I followed the path around the house to the back garden, where there was an open lawn and a large metallic cage that held two sand-coloured hunting dogs. They were lean and muscular, and should have looked fierce, but their eyes were docile and calm. Inside the cage, one of the maids was bent over, cleaning the dog's backside.

'Madam,' she said, standing up, holding her gloved hands

behind her back, 'Binsa . . . she opened for you. She is inside. Please go inside.' She pointed at the door beneath the terrace. 'I have to clean the dog, he has a bad stomach today.' While she spoke, the dog remained with its hind up in the air, its front paws stretched in front, obediently waiting for her to continue.

I thanked her and walked up a couple of steps to the patio, where a glass door was open and smells of cooking wafted out.

'Madam, this way!'

Binsa was in the kitchen, deep-frying. 'I'm sorry, madam, I couldn't come to the door. I am making *keftedes* for sir and madam. You know, you can't leave these things in the oil. It is no good for them. And how is Nisha, madam? She hasn't come to the gate to talk for a long time. We miss her. I called her phone but nothing. You know that madam doesn't let us go out, so I couldn't come to see her. I hope she is OK, madam?' She flicked her eyes towards me now, but swiftly returned her attention to the oil and the fire.

'Where are sir and madam?' I said.

'They're out shopping today, madam. If you come back in one hour, they will be here.'

'Actually, Binsa, it was you I wanted to speak to.'

She looked up from her work again for a moment, furrowed her brow, then quickly said, 'OK, madam. I will take out this lot, three minutes, and talk to you before I do others. Can you wait a few minutes?'

'Of course, Binsa,' I said. 'Take your time.'

On the counter by her side there was a large platter full

141

of raw meatballs dusted with flour, ready for the oil. Nisha had spoken to me many times about Binsa and Soneeya from Nepal. Both in their twenties, about ten years younger than Nisha, their journey to Cyprus was the first time either of them had been away from their families. Before making the decision to migrate, Binsa had been a young radio host at her local radio station, and Soneeya had been a nursery nurse, I think. Their English wasn't as good as Nisha's, because Nisha had learnt it back in Sri Lanka when she was a little girl. But Binsa and Soneeya had been here for two years and were already speaking quite well. Apparently, Mrs Kosta gave them classes in the evenings. Nisha had told me how they were not allowed out of the grounds because the Kostas were worried that they would be led astray.

Soon Soneeya came in, taking off her blue rubber gloves, chucking them in the bin and washing her hands thoroughly with plenty of soap. Before long, I was sitting in the living room with a cup of tea in my hand, the two women looking at me intently.

'I'm worried about Nisha,' I said.

At this, Soneeya nudged Binsa hard in the thigh with her fist and scrunched up her lips, saying something in Nepali. Then Soneeya got up and left the room, returning with something shiny in her hand. She offered it to me. It was a bracelet, a silver bangle with a single evil-eye charm. I held my breath and picked it up, turning it around in my hand. And there it was. The inscription of Aliki's name, engraved on the inner side of the bracelet. We had given this bracelet to Nisha for her birthday a few years earlier. She wore it every day. The clasp was broken now.

I looked up at Soneeya and Binsa. 'How do you have this?' I asked, my breath quickening, panic blooming in my chest.

'I told Binsa many times this week to ask madam to give us your phone number so we could call you, madam. We tried Nisha's mobile and there was no answer. I didn't ask madam because Binsa is her best maid. I am number two here. Binsa needed to ask her.'

'Soneeya found it, madam,' Binsa quickly broke in. 'She was walking the dogs, to the end of the street by Maria's. There is an old house there. No one lives there. Soneeya sometimes lets the dogs go do their business in that yard,' she said, shooting Soneeya a reproving look. 'And she saw something shiny by the front door. It was Nisha's bracelet. We became worried.'

'Very worried,' agreed Soneeya.

'And then Nisha didn't answer her phone,' Binsa said, 'and we thought that maybe Nisha went to see her cousin, maybe she went away again. It is none of our business. This is what I said to Soneeya.'

I put the tea-cup on the coffee table. 'The thing is,' I said, cautiously, 'I have no idea where Nisha is. She has simply disappeared. She left her passport and other important items. I can't get through to her on her phone, either. Her friend Yiannis has not seen her, but several neighbours say they saw her going out on Sunday evening.'

I waited as the women looked at each other and chatted,

143

quickly, passionately, in Nepali. Soneeya's voice rose now and then with alarm, whereas Binsa sounded calmer.

'Madam,' Binsa said suddenly, 'have you been to the police station?'

I explained to them that I had, but the police would not help; leaving out, of course, what Officer Kyprianou had said about foreign workers.

'I came to you,' I said, 'because I was hoping you might know something about where she went.'

They both shook their head.

'Did she ever mention leaving me? Maybe going over to the north to find other work?'

'Never!' said Soneeya, quickly. 'Madam, Nisha would never even think of doing this. That is not Nisha.'

I nodded. I knew of course that she was right.

'Do you know anything about Yiannis?'

The girls started speaking in Nepali again, whispering, as if there was a chance I might understand them. They were clearly in disagreement, but after some time, Soneeya turned to me.

'Madam, Binsa is unsure about speaking to you but I think you care about Nisha. I would like to say this to you because Yiannis maybe knows something that you don't know.'

I sat up straighter at this point and I think Binsa noticed, as she looked concerned. She mumbled a few words under her breath and Soneeya shushed her.

'This man, Yiannis, he loves Nisha so much. He *loves* her, madam. I don't know how to say this to you. He *loves* her from here to the moon.' She made a huge gesture with her hands at this point, opening them wide.

'I see,' I said. 'Does she love him, too?' It seemed like a reasonable question to ask.

'Yes, madam,' said Soneeya. 'If anybody knows a thing about where Nisha is, he will know. She tells him all her secrets, everything.'

I nodded, a knot forming in my stomach, like a stone. It was clear from how anxious Yiannis had been last night that he did not know a thing.

'Madam,' said Binsa now, interrupting my thoughts, 'do not tell Nisha we told you this information. She will be unhappy with us. She loves her job too, madam, she never wants to lose this job with you. She worries that you will not like her being with Yiannis.'

'I promise,' I said. 'I won't say a thing.'

At that point the sound of a buzzer rang through the room.

'Ah!' Binsa exclaimed, jumping up and heading to the large front window. From her apron pocket she retrieved a gate remote and clicked it a few times.

'Sir and madam are here!' Soneeya said, beginning to gather up our tea-cups.

I heard the creak of metal gates and the soft sound of an engine, followed by the thump of car doors. Quickly, I riffled through my purse, found an old receipt and wrote my phone number on it. 'Soneeya' – I pressed the paper into her hand – 'please call me if you think of anything else. Anything at all.'

Soneeya nodded and tucked the receipt into her pocket, spiriting the tea tray off into the kitchen.

Binsa opened the front door and Mr and Mrs Kosta came in. They were both wearing soft cashmere jumpers, with jeans and tennis shoes. Mrs Kostas lifted her gold-framed Armani glasses (I recognised them; I'd sold them to her), pushing them up into her hair.

'Petra!' she said, 'how nice to see you. What brings you here?' Before I could reply she turned to Soneeya. 'Soneeya, the shopping's in the car. Go.'

Soneeya nodded and said, 'Yes, madam, I'll go now.' She rushed out to help Binsa, who was already bringing in bags from the car and placing them in the hallway.

Mr Kostas, with a mop of thick brown hair, greeted me and excused himself to make a phone call. Binsa now returned to the kitchen, working quickly to finish the meatballs she had left during our chat, clearly trying to make up for lost time. Mrs Kostas placed her keys in a large bowl in the middle of a round marble table and hung her bag on a coat stand by the door, then turned to speak to me.

'Petra, have you been well? I haven't seen you for so long. Did my girls take care of you? I do hope so. They are improving. I've been teaching them, but I tell you, I'm thinking of separating them, sending one to work elsewhere. They distract each other too much when they're together and, realistically, do I really need two maids?' She paused in front of me now and lowered her glasses onto her nose again. It was clear that she'd had some work done on her forehead and her lips.

'Well, I don't know,' I said. 'I guess it depends how much needs to be done.'

'I'm *inundated* with work from the charity events I organise. And this is *such* a big house.' She laughed and sighed and shook her head, as if there was always way too much work to even mention, and then she offered me a seat in the living room with a wrinkled hand that was tipped with long, red, coffin-shaped nails.

'Oh, thank you,' I said, 'but I really must be going.'

'But I've only just come through the door!'

'Actually, I came to speak to Binsa and Soneeya.'

'Oh?' She eyed me suspiciously.

'The thing is that Nisha, my maid, my . . . girl, has . . . well, how shall I put this? She has been gone for several days and I wanted to see if Soneeya and Binsa have heard from her or if they know anything.'

'I see,' she said, glancing over to the kitchen, where her maids were working. 'I doubt they know anything, as they really don't have many friends and acquaintances. I make sure of that.'

Soneeya came out of the kitchen holding a tray with a tea-pot and two cups with saucers.

'Are you sure you won't have a drink? I could get Soneeya to bring an extra cup, there's always plenty in the pot. Soneeya! What did I tell you? We drink our tea with milk in this house! Go and bring some. Pour a little into the small jug. Goodness, I've told her so many times. These girls have the attention spans of fleas.' She sighed, then continued. 'Petra, dear, don't look so worried! Don't overly concern yourself. If Nisha has gone, she's gone. They do that some-times, you know? These women can drift around the world

147

without a second thought. Oh, how I wish I had that luxury!'
Her face creased into a grimace, but her forehead remained
smooth as stone.

'Well . . .' I began.

'Well,' she said, in a pronounced whisper, 'no more distrac-
tions for Soneeya and Binsa, hmm?' With that, she stepped
towards the front door, signalling that our chat was over, and
waved at me as I weaved back through the orchard to the
gate, which was now creaking open. 'Come again for a coffee!'
she called. 'Call me soon!'

In the late afternoon light, the sunset and the lake are one.
Beautiful streaks of pink and red wash through the sky,
which is luminous and silky. The hare is no longer
distinct. Its skin has ruptured further and is almost
completely decayed. Fly eggs have hatched into maggots
in its eye and in the expanding wound around its neck,
while the larvae in the mouth have grown, feeding on
flesh. The same kind of larvae have also filled the rotten
hole in the abdomen; feeding and feeding, converting the
tissue of the hare into their own. The hare is slowly
disappearing. But its hind legs still look strong and its ears
still look as though they are blowing in the breeze; its fur
is still the warm colour of the earth.

The rusty metal of the gallows frame looks ochre,
bathed in the pink light. On clear and quiet afternoons
such as this, the locals believe they can hear the ghosts of
the men underground working, endlessly working until

they die. Their effort is lost now but it was also lost then – not to their families, no doubt, but to the rest of the world. On they worked, like ants, while copper blazed in the light of the upper world.

If you listen carefully, apparently, you can still hear them calling to one another beneath the soil.

14

Yiannis

WHY WOULD NISHA HAVE GONE to the bar to meet Seraphim? I had been stuck on this since Friday night. All day Saturday, packing up the birds and preparing for deliveries, ticking off the orders against the containers, making sure all the inventory was properly distributed, I thought about it. I wanted to call him and confront him, but he had gone away for a couple of nights so I decided to wait. I'd be meeting him for a hunt in a few days and I would rather speak to him face to face, see his expression as well as hear his voice.

On Sunday, I set out on deliveries. They would take me all day, and most were usual customers, so I could drive the route practically without thinking. While part of my mind steered my truck down the narrow streets, navigating intersections and traffic, another part of my mind travelled the past.

I thought about the night Nisha came to my apartment, after her visit to Chaturi. It had been the middle of August and extremely hot. When she told me she could not terminate the pregnancy, I had gone out the next day to buy her a ring. I visited the jewellers on Ledra Street and bought a simple gold ring with a blossom-cut diamond. I was not *simply* going to propose, but suggest that we leave Cyprus together, and move to Sri Lanka. In my mind, this would solve two problems: the first, that Nisha would finally be with Kumari; the second, that I could stop the poaching without having to face the consequences. I reasoned that it wouldn't be too difficult for me to find a job in Sri Lanka, particularly with my background in finance and my experience working with foreign markets. I am fluent in both English and Greek.

While this may sound well thought out, it was impulsive. It is my nature, and it's what made me good at banking. But the truth is, I was following my heart and not my head and therefore failed to recognise the challenges to my plan. Like how Nisha would feel being completely reliant on me financially. Like whether we would have enough money to settle Nisha's debts to her hiring agency in Cyprus, or did I think we could just run out of town and leave them unsettled? Like whether Nisha would want to leave Petra and Aliki – as much as she wanted to return to her own daughter, would it be so easy for her to leave behind the Cypriot girl she had raised? All of these thoughts, these contingencies, I tucked away somewhere, refusing to derail my dream of a free life with the woman I loved.

The weekend after her return from Chaturi, I went to the supermarket to buy the ingredients for Nisha's favourite vegetable rice and curry. I had some *kakulu* rice at home, plus basics such as coconut and turmeric, and some chillies that Nisha had grown and dried in the garden. I bought pineapple, sweet potatoes, aubergines. It was a simple meal, but one that I knew reminded Nisha of home.

That Sunday, she sat on a kitchen chair while I made lunch. Aliki and Petra had gone to the beach again and wouldn't be back until very late, so Nisha had the whole day and night off. I didn't want her to lift a finger: she was constantly working, hardly ever taking a break for herself. She had her bare feet up on the chair, arms around her legs, chin resting on her knees. She was wearing a pale blue summer dress, a pass-me-down from Petra. One of the straps had fallen off her shoulder, which was smooth and golden-brown. The chalky blue contrasted with her skin so much that it almost glowed. She was beautiful. Nisha was always beautiful, in every single way.

I was dicing the pineapple when she said, 'I'd recognise you if you were a lion.'

'What?' She often came out with bizarre things, but this was odd even for her.

'If in another life you were a lion, I think I would recognise you and still love you.'

'What if I were a snake?'

'Still, I'd know it was you.'

'A jellyfish?'

'Yes.'

'Cockroach?'

'Absolutely.'

'Is this assuming we are both lions or both cockroaches?'

'Yes,' she said.

'OK, what if you were a deer and I was a lion? Would you still love me?'

She thought about this as I threw the pineapple in the wok and began to cut the aubergine.

'I think we will meet again in all our future lives.'

I added the spices to the vegetables and began to boil the rice.

'Do you mind if I lie down?' she said.

'Of course. I'll call you when it's ready.'

She went over to the bedroom and I could hear that she had turned on the fan. I thought about what she had said: *I'd recognise you if you were a lion*, and suddenly a different meaning came to mind. Because, in fact, in this life, I *was* a predator. First with stocks and shares, and now with the songbirds. Had she been somehow referring to this? I could not be sure. But a deep feeling of guilt overtook me. I had promised Nisha that I would stop hunting and I was planning on keeping that promise. But was it enough? Would that change who I was, a hunter, a predator? Or was the poaching only part of that truth?

I had the odd feeling that she was in love with the man I should have been.

I poured myself a large glass of wine and gulped it down to wash away all the questions.

When dinner was ready, I went into the bedroom to tell

154

Nisha. She was lying on her back on the bed with her eyes closed.

'Are you asleep?' I whispered.

She shook her head. I sat beside her on the bed.

'In one story,' she said, 'a married couple ask the Buddha how they can remain together in this life and be together in future lives as well. The Buddha said, "If both husband and wife wish to see one another not only in this present life but also in future lives, they should have the same virtuous behaviour, the same generosity, the same wisdom." I know you're not my husband but if we want to stay together we have to try and be on the same . . .' She hesitated, wincing.

'What's wrong?' I said

'It hurts.'

'Where?'

She took my hand and placed it low on her stomach, close to her pelvis, in exactly the same location she had placed my hand two weeks before. I leaned down and kissed her just below her belly-button. When I sat up, I noticed that blood was leaking from beneath her body onto the white sheets.

Either she saw the expression on my face, or she felt the dampness on her skin, for Nisha jumped from the bed and looked down at the covers. I noticed in that moment that the back of her dress was soaked and blood was trickling down her leg.

Trying to keep my hands from shaking, I called my doctor's emergency number to request a home visit. Nisha had made her way to the bathroom and was sitting on the toilet with the door open.

Her face was red and bloated with pain, drenched knickers around her ankles, streaks of red on her thighs. She was mumbling, saying something to me that I couldn't understand.

I sat down beside her and took her hand; she held it tight, as if she were about to fall from a cliff. Her words became more audible: she was repeating something in Sinhalese, maybe a prayer.

I couldn't move or speak, I just held her hand to stop her from falling into the black abyss that had opened up before us.

Dr Pantelis arrived silently: I saw only the headlights of his car distorted through corrugated glass of the bathroom window. I tried to release my hand from Nisha's so that I could open the door for him, but she wouldn't let go.

'Can you get up?' I asked.

She nodded and stood, slowly and with great effort. She held on to me as we made our way to the front door. By this time Dr Pantelis had come up the stairs. He took charge immediately, swiftly and professionally. Only then did Nisha allow her hand to loosen from mine. He asked me to fetch a chair. I did so. My next task was to get a glass of water. I did that too. Meanwhile, he had opened his bag on the floor and checked her blood pressure and oxygen levels, her heart rate and pupils. He then gave her a small canister of oxygen to hold over her mouth.

Once she started breathing into it, I could see her shoulders relaxing. She glanced at me over the mask and I knew what her eyes were saying.

The doctor and I lifted her onto the bed and I tucked the covers around her. Then, at his request, I led him into the bathroom as he wanted to see what had come out of her body.

He looked into the toilet bowl.

'I'm afraid she has lost the baby,' he said, bluntly, but with a softness to his voice that made me want to break down and cry.

I swallowed hard. 'What can I do?'

'Make sure you keep giving her oxygen through the night. Stay with her. If you find she bleeds again and it doesn't stop, you may need to take her to the hospital. But for the time being she is fine to stay here.'

I stayed by her side all night. I peeled her out of her wet clothes, helped her into one of my T-shirts and sat by her side. We did all this without speaking. She wanted me to hold her hand so she could sleep.

'How are you doing?' I would say, whenever I saw her eyes flicker open.

'Yes, I'm doing OK.'

Beyond the glass doors of my bedroom, I could hear murmurs from the people passing in the street, the barking of a dog, the wheels of a car, footsteps, clattering plates at Theo's. It all seemed miles away. I was in between worlds: behind me was a road that reached a dead end and would never now open up; a child that would not come into existence. Yet, I could see him or her, a half-formed shadow with Nisha's bright eyes. Maybe I'd been too hasty. I'd made too many plans. I had been too sure of myself. This unliving child was so real to me. It filled the cocoon in which I sat and Nisha slept, like the light from the sun and the song of the birds that came through the window that morning.

Of course, I thought, *birdsong glows like sunlight.* A strange thought, which was snatched away from me as sleep tried to catch me. I stood, by the window, making sure to stay awake.

When Nisha woke up around five o'clock, I was seated upright on the bed beside her.

'Good morning,' she said, with such sadness that it broke my heart.

'Good morning. Did you sleep OK?'

'Yes,' she said.

'How are you feeling?'

'The pain has gone. I'm tired.'

I nodded, kissed her on the cheek and went to fetch a glass of water, which I held to her lips. She had a few sips and handed it to me.

'I'm empty,' she said. A clear and quiet truth.

The air in my apartment was heavy and humid. I had sweated through my clothes. There were a few items of clothing that Nisha had left over at mine – some underwear, and a red beach dress with yellow flowers that she often wore in the garden. I helped her to get dressed. It was as if she was half-asleep, her arms and body malleable, like soft clay – she allowed me to move her without resistance. It was the first time I had seen such vulnerability in her. Nisha was always strong, fearless, practical. Now, she had handed her power over to me.

She said only a few things. Namely that she would tell

Petra that she was unwell with a stomach bug and that hope-fully after a little more rest she would be able to return to her duties. With every word she spoke, every small decision she made, I could see her strength returning, her back straightening, the colour gradually returning to her face.

We walked through the garden to her room. The red dress kept reminding me of her blood-soaked blue dress. I tucked her up in bed in order for her to get some rest before Petra and Aliki woke up.

'Stay with me for a few minutes?' she said, quietly, and I heard the deep sadness in her voice again.

'Of course.'

I sat beside her on the bed and stroked her hair.

'You know,' she said after a long silence, 'every person comes into this life with a certain amount of breaths. You live until those breaths run out. It doesn't matter where you are or what you're doing, if you have no breaths left, your energy will pass. This baby just didn't have enough breath to come into this world.'

I took in her words but said nothing. There was a stillness in the room; the fan was off and the heat was immense.

'When you die,' she said finally, 'your energy passes into another form. Imagine having two candles. You pass the flame from one candle to the other.'

I knew she was talking about our unborn child, the child that would never be born as our daughter or our son. But I didn't respond. I found it hard to speak, to know what to say. I simply listened and stroked her hair. Soon she was asleep.

I looked around the room. On the nightstand was a religious statue and her reading glasses. On the old wood dressing table, her makeup and jewellery. In the far corner of the room was an ironing board next to a laundry basket filled with clean and fresh towels and bed linen that had already been ironed. Behind this, a feather duster and a couple of multicoloured aprons hung on a hook on the wall.

Of course, I'd seen her tending the garden, but I had never, ever imagined her life beyond her bedroom door, her life as a maid in this house.

I gave Nisha a soft kiss on her forehead as she slept and left her room through the glass doors. Back in my flat, in the bathroom, the toilet was still full of Nisha's blood and what looked like clots and grey tissue. I heaved. There was nothing else I could do but flush the toilet and leave the room.

The meal we had not eaten was still in the kitchen, the glasses empty on the counter. The ring was in my pocket. I took it out and stared at the light bouncing off the diamond. Then I put it away in the cabinet. I knew I couldn't propose now: I would have to wait until Nisha was better, wait for the right time.

The sun was setting as I made my final delivery. I was ready to return to my apartment, the spare room now empty and, well, spare. But not for long. Seraphim and I would be hunting again in just under a week. And I had a lot to ask him.

15

Petra

ON MONDAY MORNING AT THE shop, I showed Keti the bracelet. She examined it closely, turning it over in her hands, her brow furrowing at the broken clasp.

'It doesn't look like she took it off herself, on purpose,' she said.

'No.'

'Will you take it to the police?' she asked.

'What's the point?'

Keti nodded in understanding.

'Why don't we make posters,' she suggested. 'Maybe someone saw her . . . I could draft a flyer on the computer,'

'Could you?' I nodded. 'I think it's a good idea.'

'Do you have any photographs of Nisha on your phone?' she asked.

I scrolled through and found one. It was a close-up I had

161

taken of Nisha and Aliki on Aliki's birthday almost a year ago. They were in the garden beneath the tree, Nisha's arm around Aliki's shoulder. They were both smiling.

Keti sat down at the computer in the back office and drafted a flyer:

MISSING PERSON
IF ANYONE HAS SEEN THIS WOMAN
PLEASE CALL 9-------
THERE WILL BE A GENEROUS REWARD

She cropped the photograph I had given her to remove Aliki from the photo, and zoomed in on Nisha's face. Her eyes were arresting: anyone who saw this would recognise her immediately if they'd ever seen her. Nisha's eyes aren't something you forget.

Keti printed many copies of the flyer and we split them between us. Even though Keti lived near the university, we thought it wouldn't be a bad idea to show them beyond my neighbourhood.

Before we locked up that night, I thanked Keti heartily.

'Of course,' she said. 'Nisha was a friend. You don't have to thank me.'

Soon Nisha's face stared out of flyers on every street in the area.

I was managing to keep my business running smoothly– no small thanks to Keti, who had even begun coming in early

162

to dust and sweep the shop, trying to make up for the cleaning that Nisha would have done. I couldn't bring myself to hire a new cleaner, not yet. It would feel like an admission that Nisha was really gone.

Life at home, however, was falling apart. My mornings were put back by having to make Aliki breakfast and take her to school, and I had to let Keti open the shop on her own. I would run out after lunch to pick up Aliki, and Mrs Hadjikyriacou would watch her in the afternoons, while I returned to work. I would come back again in the evenings often later than I had planned, due to trying to finish enough work at the shop, squeeze in as many appointments as I could. I was exhausted. I felt like I was failing on all fronts.

At home, Aliki was restless. She would wander around the house, putting on and taking off her Converse trainers. She would match different colours then regret the choice. She'd walk around with one pink shoe, one chequered. Then one green shoe, the other striped. The cat called Monkey followed her around, sniffing her feet, rubbing its face against her hands as she tied the laces. She avoided the garden and I could hardly blame her: the garden was covered in snails. On the boat, particularly, there must have been about thirty, of various sizes, with their glossy shells and nimble eyes at the tips of their tentacles, slithering over the bow and stern, climbing languidly up its hull. After rain, Nisha would have peeled the snails off the boat, one by one, gently so as not to hurt them. But in her absence, nature had taken over.

On Tuesday night I had to stay at work very late. When

163

I got home, it was past nine o'clock and Mrs Hadjikyriacou was asleep in the armchair by the fire. On her lap, with her hands resting on it, was the framed photograph of Stephanos in his military gear. When she heard me, she opened her eyes. The fire was dwindling.

'Ah, Petra,' she said. 'You're back.' And then she seemed to remember that she was holding the photograph, and she looked down at it and ran her white fingers over the glass.

'He was so handsome, wasn't he?' she said.

I nodded.

'And such a kind heart. He would always bring me BBQ when he made it. And do you remember that time he came to pick me up from the airport? It was a Sunday and his only day off, but he came.'

'I do remember.'

'I'm sorry, my love,' she said. 'I'm sure you don't want these things darkening your heart right now. I always feel lonelier at night, don't you?'

I nodded again.

'You're lucky you have Aliki. She's a little genius, that girl. She tells some good stories too. She told me a story from *The Mahadenamutta and his Pupils*. Fascinating and hilarious!' She handed me the photograph and slowly got up.

I thanked her for helping me out, for watching Aliki and for staying so late.

'It's my pleasure, my love,' she said, and went home, where I suspect Ruba was waiting up for her.

I found Aliki sleeping on Nisha's bed with Monkey. In her arms she held the little Buddha that Nisha kept on her

164

bedside cabinet. I didn't wake her; I put a throw over her and kissed her on the cheek. She didn't stir. The cat gave me a dirty look for disturbing it and went straight back to sleep.

I considered Nisha's room. It was so austere, with only the barest of essentials. She had hung a few pictures on the wall, but after living here for nearly ten years, it still felt temporary. My eyes fell on Nisha's dressing table, and it occurred to me that I hadn't searched the drawers there; I had just searched the desk, the most obvious place.

Aliki was sleeping comfortably and, quietly, so as not to wake her, I pulled out the dresser drawers one by one. In one, I found Nisha's underwear – cotton, white and cream-coloured knickers – all neatly folded. How strange it was to find her undergarments, to be rummaging through another woman's most intimate things.

In the third drawer, underneath a pile of neatly folded T-shirts, I found a photo album. Its cover was soft blue leather, the colour of the sea. The first photographs were from Nisha's wedding day. She was so much younger, her face fresh; she looked like a different Nisha to the one I knew. She was a young woman with dreams for the future. Her husband had been young too, clean-shaven, quite small in build, and he seemed to sparkle. I imagined that he would have been the kind of man to tell jokes at parties. She was wearing a white dress, embroidered with red flowers. She held a small bunch of red roses. There were dates beneath each photo that I could barely make out in the half-darkness.

The album was a window into Nisha's life back in Sri Lanka. A visual story. Her husband standing on his own on the side of a street carpeted with red flowers, on the road a red bus with a lit-up sign on its front reading 22 Kandy, above it the canopy of trees adorned with red blossoms. Another of a waterfall, rushing down a cliff, falling somewhere behind a bustling market; amongst this crowd Nisha and another woman both waved at the camera. I could almost hear the sounds that these people could hear.

Towards the end of the album, her husband was suddenly missing, and I knew these photos must have been taken after his death.

The final pages of the album were pictures of Kumari, from when she was a baby until she was about two years old, the age she was when Nisha left and came to us. My eyes rested on the last photograph in the album, where Nisha was holding Kumari in her arms. It reminded me of Nisha holding Aliki in her arms at that same age, but my daughter had been a plump toddler, though both girls had similar thick, shiny, dark hair. Nisha held them the same way.

I thought of the wooden statue that Muyia had made. The mother and child. It was Nisha. Yes, I was sure. The woman holding the child was Nisha and the child was Kumari. I lay down beside Aliki and the now-purring cat and fell asleep.

The next morning, while Aliki was eating her breakfast, I went to see Nilmini.

'I know you said you'd read Nisha's journal,' I said to her as she swept the floor, 'but I also found this photo album last night and I wanted to give it you as well, in case it helps you to identify anyone from the journals.'

Leaning the broom against the wall, Nilmini took the album from my hands and held it to her chest, just as she had done with the journal.

'I suppose I just thought you might like to see it.'

'Thank you, madam,' she said. 'I have begun reading the journal. What I can tell you is that in this journal are twelve letters written for her daughter Kumari, during her first year here in Nicosia.'

'So there is nothing more recent?'

'No, madam. They are dated.'

'I see.'

I must have looked disappointed and at a loss, for she said: 'Madam, even if we do not find anything obvious, there may be other information which might give us a better under-standing.'

'That's true,' I said, smiling. And, just for a moment, she grabbed my fingers and squeezed them with hands that were softer and warmer than I had expected. I looked up and saw she had tears in her eyes.

'It is beautiful, the journal. Nisha should be a writer. In the letters, she tells all about her life back home and about her life here. I can hear my friend's voice as I read. I miss her very much.'

'I know Nilmini,' I said, 'So do I.'

'I'm sorry, madam.'

167

'What for?'

'Because I have not found what you are looking for.'

In the evening I invited Mrs Hadjikyriacou to stay and join us for supper. She demurred at first, saying that Ruba wouldn't know what to do without her there for the evening meal, but Aliki pleaded and finally she agreed. I made dhal curry but it was nothing like Nisha's – it lacked flavour and I added way too much coconut milk so it was like mush. But Aliki ate it regardless. After dinner, we sat by the fire drinking tea.

Mrs Hadjikyriacou's cloudy, silvery eyes regarded me with certainty and warmth. Then she turned her attention to Aliki. 'Come here, child,' she said. 'I can tell you a story. What is your favourite? And why in God's name are you wearing odd shoes?'

Aliki giggled. 'I like odd things,' she said. 'I'd like to hear a story.'

It was lovely to hear Aliki's voice, I drank it in. With Nisha gone, my daughter had no one else to speak to at home. Except the cats. Her voice was lost to me, we both knew that.

'Fair enough,' Mrs Hadjikyriacou said. 'Sit here beside me. I'll tell you about Foinikas, or Palm Tree village, the place where I was born. I lived there all my life, I got married there and had five children there. It's such an old place. People lived there since the times of the crusaders. Do you know about the crusaders?'

Aliki nodded. 'We learnt about it at school. Is that when you were born?'

'No!' She laughed. 'How the hell old do you think I am, you little monkey? Eight hundred years old?'

Aliki laughed and laughed and then she quietened at the sight of the old woman's knitted brow.

'Well, let me begin,' she said. 'Are you ready?'

Aliki sat straight and nodded.

'The knight commander's residence was built on the highest point of the village. The village was abandoned in 1974 after the war that divided the island. Today it is often flooded by water from the dam, but back in the day – well, what can I tell you, it was a place of beauty.'

Seeing my daughter held rapt by Mrs Hadjikyriacou's tale, I felt a pang of jealousy. I had never been able to command Aliki's attention, but then what did I offer her? Nisha had told her the stories, Nisha had played the games, teasing her imagination and teaching her how to see the world. I remembered the day we had gone up to the mountains and Nisha and Aliki had sat together on the bus, while I sat opposite them across the aisle, next to an old man who had been carrying a jasmine plant on his lap. He must have been growing it indoors by a sunny window for the flowers smelt as if it were summer and I remembered how strange it was to be enveloped by the scent during that chilly October day. The old man had snored, his head bopping gently to the movement of the bus as we headed up the mountain, and Nisha and Aliki had played I Spy.

'I spy with my little eye, something beginning with N!'
Aliki said.

'Hm, that's a hard one,' Nisha said. She pretended to look
all around the bus, then leaned over Aliki and made a big
deal of looking out of the window.

Aliki giggled.

'Hmmm, let me see. Nature?'

'Nope.'

'Erm . . . nuts!'

'Where do you see nuts?'

'There are almond trees on the hills.'

'Well, if there are, I can't see them.'

'How about' – Nisha was looking around again, this time
at the other passengers – 'novel!'

'Nope.'

'Aliki, this is too difficult.'

'Keep going!' she said.

'Nylon? And before you ask, the woman who is reading
the novel – to your right – is wearing nylon tights.'

'That's very good,' Aliki said. 'But no.'

'Necklace.'

'No.'

'Neck!'

'No.'

'Nun?'

I remembered Aliki looking around her at this point, then
she started to laugh again. 'Nisha, where do you see a nun?'

'We passed a church and a nun was outside in the garden.'

'You see everything,' Aliki said.

'You should be more observant,' Nisha said.

'OK, do you give up?'

'Let me try one last time . . .' There was a long pause. 'Nostril!'

'The answer,' said Aliki, 'is Nisha.'

'Me?'

Aliki had nodded.

'That's cheating! I can't see me!'

'Why?' she said. 'I see you!'

'I would never have guessed that. I could have gone on all week and I would never have guessed that.'

'Isn't it funny,' Aliki said, in her most adult voice, 'that you saw everything but yourself?'

On Friday night, around 10 p.m., I received a phone call from Soneeya. She was frantic. 'Madam, please come meet me at the gate, I have some information. Will you come right away?'

I told her yes, of course. I looked in on Aliki, who was sleeping peacefully in her room. Mrs Hadjikyriacou was still out, sitting in her garden as usual, and I asked if she wouldn't mind coming in and staying with Aliki for a while.

'Of course, my love,' she said, placing her hand on mine. 'My daughter is no longer coming to see me – something to do with work – they had to cancel the trip. So I have all the time in the world. Go and do what you need to do and don't worry about me.'

I thanked her by placing a kiss on her cheek, like I would have done with my own mother or grandmother, and left

171

her sitting in the living room by the fireplace flicking through a fashion magazine.

When I arrived at the mansion, Binsa and Soneeya were both waiting for me, standing behind the bars of the huge gate, beneath the glare of the security light. The two hunting dogs were out of their cages. One had its nose pressed between the bars of the gate, sniffing the air; the other lay flat, its huge head resting on its front paws. Their sand-coloured coats were shiny, their muscles defined in the spotlight.

'Madam,' Soneeya said. 'There has been another woman vanish.'

'What do you mean, Soneeya?'

'Soneeya is saying there is another woman who is missing. This week, we called on a few friends to see if anyone has heard from Nisha. Our friend told us that her friend's sister, who works in a house with a family on the other side of Nicosia, well, she vanished one day. She went out at night and never came back.'

I tried to sort this out in my head.

'How long ago?'

'About three week ago, madam,' said Binsa.

'And they've heard nothing from her?'

'Nothing, madam. Not one thing,' replied Soneeya.

This made my mouth dry. I was still hoping that, at any moment, Nisha would return, but here they were telling me a story of another maid going missing without explanation.

'We don't know anything about the circumstances,' I said. 'There could be very good reasons why your friend's sister is missing from her place of work.'

172

Soneeya shook her head but said nothing.

Binsa reached into her apron pocket and took out a small scrap of paper. 'We have a number, a person for you to call. You can go see him.'

Through the bars, I took the piece of paper from Binsa's hand and read the details that had been hastily scribbled across it: *Mr Tony The Blue Tiger, Limassol 09 ----------------*

'Who is this Mr Tony? What is the Blue Tiger?'

'The Blue Tiger, madam, is a place I have never been. It is a lovely place, they say, where all the workers meet on Sunday and make food and dance and eat. It is Mr Tony's restaurant the rest of the week. But Sunday he looks after all the workers. He finds them jobs. He helps them when they're in trouble. Sometimes girls stay at his home until they find an employer who is kind. They say Mr Tony is a good man and he knows so many things. If there is a problem, every maid goes to Mr Tony.'

'I don't see how he will be able to help me,' I said. 'The Blue Tiger is in another town. What information could he possibly have about Nisha?'

However, I remembered that Nisha had recently been to Limassol. Maybe he would know her, or her cousin Chaturi?

'He knows about the other woman who vanished. We do not have any more answer, but Mr Tony, he may have more answer.' Soneeya's eyes penetrated mine with urgency, as though she were about to take flight and go and find Nisha herself – if only she had had the freedom to do so.

The dogs picked up on her restlessness, for they were both pacing about behind her. With their coats golden in the

173

lamplight, their heads bowed, muscles rippling, tails down, for a moment they looked to me like lions. Lions in captivity. Lions who had been stolen from their land.

As I turned towards home, it occurred to me to go to the late-night bar by the Green Line, Maria's, which was located at the end of the street in the direction that Mrs Hadjikyriacou had seen Nisha heading the night she had disappeared. I wondered if someone there might know something about Nisha. I knew I was on borrowed time with Aliki home in bed, but maybe I would just stop in. Even just leave a flyer with them.

Two women were standing outside beneath a lamp-post smoking. In spite of the chilly night, they wore strappy tops and mini-skirts and were deep in conversation. I entered a place full of smoke. It reeked of beer. On a nearly empty dance floor there was a belly dancer in sequins and bright pink, rolling her stomach and tinkling bells. Men lined the bar. Waitresses in tight black clothes came and went with silver trays of dips and drinks. Candles had been lit on some of the tables, but nothing could make this bar look elegant: it was seedy and dark and it smelt of lust and greed and desperation.

I felt very out of place in my jogging bottoms, trainers and woolly cardigan whose sleeves were too long, but I was inside now, and knew it would be worth asking some questions. A few men turned with leering eyes to look at me but, to my relief, turned away again. I went to the bar and ordered a sparkling mineral water: I wanted to keep my wits about me in this place. The man beside me had a girl who barely looked eighteen sitting on his lap. As she licked his ear, he played with the strap of her pink dress and kissed her upper arm. I looked away. On my other side, a woman sat alone, smoking an e-cigarette that smelt like cherries. Her black hair reached the small of her back.

Once I paid for my drink, I asked the waitress if I could speak privately to the manager.

'Why?'

'I'm looking for work.'

She looked me up and down as if to say *Really?* and pointed to a wooden door at the back of the bar.

'He's in his office,' she said. 'Knock three times and wait.'

I did as she said. I waited for more than five minutes before the door opened and a small man who looked a lot like a hamster opened the door. He had a huge grin, dead-white teeth and a pot belly that spilled over his trousers. But he carried himself like a king.

'What can I do for you, young lady?' he said.

'Well, I'm not exactly a young lady anymore,' I said.

'You'd be surprised.' He smiled widely.

I had no idea what he meant.

He invited me into his office and I sat on a low stool by a high antique desk. He sat in a pivoting office chair – soft leather with broad arms – and looked down at me.

'You knocked three times. You're looking for work.'

'No.'

He raised his eyebrows and, for the first time, irritation erupted on his face. He glanced at the clock on the wall. In spite of the music outside, this office was strangely quiet.

'I know that many foreign domestic workers *work* here,' I said, 'and because of that I wondered if you have ever seen this woman.' From my handbag I pulled out one of the flyers Keti and I had made and pointed at Nisha's picture.

From the top pocket of his shirt the man retrieved a cheap pair of gold-rimmed glasses and put them on, taking the flyer from me and studying it. He seemed deep in thought for a very long time. Finally, he looked at me and said, 'No.'

'You've never seen her?'

'No.'

'She's never been in here?'

'Well, if she has, I never saw her. But I don't sit by the front door and memorise faces.' He glanced again at the clock and stood up.

'There are so many foreign workers here, they might have seen Nisha, they might know something,' I continued, desperately.

'Nisha, huh?' he said and smiled. 'Do you know that in Sanskrit, Nisha means "night"?'

I told him that I didn't know that.

'All the women I have ever met called Nisha are beautiful and mysterious. If I had met her, I definitely would have remembered. Leave the flyer with me and I'll put it up. Don't worry.'

I decided to hand out flyers to some of the women. Many of them were foreign domestic workers; there was a chance that they may have known Nisha, or at least someone may have seen her that night. The women here were usually tucked away, wrapped up safely in our domestic routines. It struck me how one person's emancipation sometimes relies on the servitude of another. These thoughts tormented me. I feared that I would never be able to tell Nisha what I had understood.

I stood there in the candlelight, clutching on to Nisha's flyers.

On the table near me, three young women sat talking. They laughed. They drank hot tea in tiny glasses.

'Hello,' I said, awkwardly, feeling that I was intruding.

All eyes looked up. 'Good evening madam,' said the woman closest to me.

'I'm wondering if you have seen this woman?' I placed one of the flyers on the table and they leaned in to take a look.

'Yes!' the one on the left said. 'I know her!' She was a slim woman with thick black curls.

'Me too!' said the one next to her. 'That is Nisha . . . I forget her family name now.'

The first, who had placed her cup of tea on the table, was leaning in, looking concerned. 'Well, that is my friend, Nisha. Sometimes we go to church on Sundays, when she is free; she meets me at the other café around corner from here, the one where all of us girls meet on Sundays, and we have a cup of tea together.'

'Nisha has gone missing,' I said.

'When?' asked the woman who hadn't spoken yet, startled.

'Two weeks ago. Do you know anything? The police said she might have gone to the north of the island.'

The first woman laughed now, but with a darkness that

seemed to extinguish even the dim light. 'They always think these things. They think we are thieves, too. My madam thought I stole her wedding ring. That's how I go fired. That's how I ended up here.' The woman shook her head and suddenly glanced down at Nisha's poster. She stared at it for a long time. 'I hope you find her, madam,' she said.

As I walked away, I realised that I had not asked the women their names. They had called me 'Madam'. From that point on, I held out my hand and introduced myself.

'Good evening. My name is Petra.'

I met so many women that night. Diwata Caasi, a sixty-one-year-old woman from the Philippines, who had been forced to drink water from a jam jar because she was only a maid, and the food was rationed so that she was eating less than the cat. She eventually left her employer and had nowhere to turn.

Mutya Santos, from the bay-side city of Manila, who used to be a midwife. She loved her elderly employer and had dinner with her every night, but when the old lady passed away Mutya was placed with a man who kept touching her, who walked in on her while she showered, who came to her room while she slept. She had complained to the agency who did nothing to help. When her employer found out, he fired her. Again, she was left with nowhere to go and huge debts.

Ayomi Pathirana, from Sri Lanka. Her parents were both farmers. As a child she would wake up early every morning to help her parents on the farm before going to school. Later, she left college as they were financially hard-up and

178

found a job in a bookstore for two years; but the money was not good, she could not progress and her parents were getting old. Her cousin encouraged her to apply for work as a nanny abroad. She went to Kuwait, where she was faced with difficulties. Eventually, she made plans to come to Cyprus, where she found similar problems. She was so young when she came here. Then she met a Cypriot man who promised to get her work, and though it was the wrong kind of work, she could not return to Sri Lanka because of the debts she had.

Etisha, from Nepal, who had to leave her one-year-old daughter, Feba, the source of her light, because she and her husband could not find work back home. Initially she came here as a student; she was promised work, but when she arrived there was nothing.

Every single one of them had a story. I could have sat there all night listening. But the bars on the windows, the flailing light, made me feel trapped. I just wanted to get out of there. But the women's stories . . . they moved me, they opened something inside me.

One of the girls I spoke to began to cry. She wasn't intending to. I showed her the flyer of Nisha. She didn't recognise her. Then I asked her where she was from, and instead of words, tears flowed out, down her cheeks, smudging her makeup. For a moment I slipped my hand in hers. She looked at me with black eyes that reflected the candlelight. 'I want to go home, madam,' was all she said. She did not tell me where home was.

'Can't you go? Just pack your bags and go.'

Through her tears, she laughed. 'It's not as easy as that. If only you knew.'

As I was leaving, I recognised a man at the bar. I was sure it was the guy who often visited Yiannis – Seraphim was his name. I assumed they worked together, as he sometimes dropped him off after they'd gone foraging in the forest for snails and mushrooms. He'd greet me politely whenever he saw me. Scruffy guy, uncombed hair. He sat at the bar on his own, drinking whisky. I was about to leave but I had a couple more flyers in my purse and decided to approach him.

'Good evening, Seraphim,' I said, standing beside him.

He glanced up. 'Petra!' he said, startled. 'What are you doing here?'

'I'm looking for my maid,' I said. 'Nisha. Do you remember her?'

'Of course,' he said. 'I know Nisha.'

'Have you seen Yiannis lately? Did he mention to you that she's missing?'

'I can't say that I can recall that conversation,' he said. 'But I am sorry to hear that.'

'Well, since you're here . . .' I handed him one of the flyers and he spent a long time looking at the picture of Nisha. The music seemed to go up a few notches, and the belly dancer was still twinkling and jingling in the candlelight.

'Very beautiful woman,' I heard him say, through all the noise. 'Don't you think? It's her eyes, isn't it? They seem to know a lot.'

I didn't reply. He handed the flyer back to me. 'I'm sorry,' he said. 'She must have been an asset to your household. But I suspect she will be back, and if she isn't, don't be surprised. These women come and go like the rain, you know?'

He grinned at me but I did not smile back. I didn't like this man. He was always so courteous when I saw him outside mine waiting for Yiannis to come down, but now I could see an intensity to him that I'd never noticed before. In fact, he seemed to be made of sharp edges – his nose, his cheek bones, even his elbows. There was a sharpness to his entire frame and bone structure; it was evident now in the candle-light. Or was it my mind playing tricks on me? I knew I was becoming more anxious, more unsettled with each passing day that Nisha was away.

'Hey, join me for a drink, won't you? You're lucky to catch me here tonight – I've been away for a few days, came back a bit earlier than anticipated.'

'I'm OK, thanks,' I said, 'so, when you're not away, do you come here a lot?'

He raised his eyebrows.

'I'm asking because I wonder if you ever saw Nisha here? You see, the old lady who lives next door to me told me that Nisha was heading this way the night that she vanished.'

'What night was that?' he said.

'Two weekends ago, on the Sunday.'

Again, he was silent for a while, thinking. 'I wish I could tell you that I've seen her, but I haven't.'

*　*　*

181

I inhaled the cold air out on the street. The night was fresh and I walked away briskly from the bar. I could still hear the voices of the women inside. I was eager to get home, but as I passed Muyia's workshop, I remembered the sculpture. Suddenly, I had to see it again. I felt compelled to go inside – the entrance, as usual, was gaping open. It was so dark in there I had to be careful not to trip over the debris on the floor. Slowly my eyes adjusted and I could make out the vague shape of the worktop, feeling with my hands to find the light switch on one of the lamps.

The sculpture of the mother and child had been covered in a white cloth. I lifted off the blanket and sat down on the stool opposite, struck again by the resemblance to Nisha. I could almost feel the energy emanating from her; so many emotions, she had a history, she had a whole life. And she had an enduring and powerful love for the child in her arms. A love that could not be replaced. Why had Muyia made this? It was Nisha, to be sure, her heart-shaped face, her fiery eyes. Even the tiny dimple in her right cheek. I reached out and touched her hand. I wanted her to speak. I was desperate that she would break out of her wooden case and speak to me.

'Nisha,' I said, gently. 'Tell me where you are.'

I waited as if I might hear her voice. I looked at her unmoving face, but I heard only the sound of the wind – nothing else, just the wind through leaves.

I covered up the statue and headed back home.

In the village there is a guest house: a small, rickety
building with brown shutters and whitewashed walls in the
back garden of a widow's home. There have been no
guests, though, for many years. Once in a blue moon,
someone will call from a distant land and make a booking
and the old woman will take down the details in a black
notebook she keeps by the phone. Then she will go to
great efforts to clean, and fluff up the towels and cushions.
She will place fresh tea-bags and honey and sugar on a
tray, and lay sugared almonds on the pillows and bake
pistachio cakes, which she'll display on the dressing table
wrapped in cellophane and decorated with paper daisies.
She will sweep the leaves and dust from the patio and
leave a tourist brochure by the bed.

It is dark when the phone rings. A young man, calling
from a hotel in Beirut, with one of those transatlantic
accents she has only ever heard on TV. He is travelling

around Europe with his new wife, they will be arriving next week, all being well. The old lady jots down his name and number and date of arrival in the black notebook beneath a doodle of a clown riding a donkey that her granddaughter has drawn.

The nights are getting longer and colder and she goes out to collect the washing from the line. The children across the street have gone in and their maid is out picking apples from the tree in the dark. A breeze blows. Good evening, she says, but her voice is carried away. Along the path a mist settles and darkness settles too, as there are no houses there to light up the way. Further along, there are only trees and clouds and sky, until the earth becomes jagged and dry and drops down to the red water of the lake, which is as black as the night and as the empty eye socket of the hare glaring up at the sky.

16

Yiannis

O N Saturday, before dawn, Seraphim picked
me up in his van. We drove to the Akrotiri base,
an hour and a half away. Our ride was mostly
silent: we were sleepy; Seraphim looked like he'd been out
late. I was biding my time. I wanted his full attention for our
conversation.

This time he'd bought with him four calling birds in two
cages: three blackcaps and a blackbird. These caged callers
would have been caught and kept in the dark for months so
that when they were finally taken out into the light, they
would sing their hearts out, unwitting decoys to lure as many
birds as possible into the trap.

The cages were in the back of the van with black sheets
draped over them. I dozed until we reached the wetland, an
area of 150 hectares known for its bird life and protected by

various agencies because of it. If we succeeded, it would be a good hunt, but we had to be careful.

With Nisha gone, however, and the memories of her tugging at my insides, I began to feel nauseous at the thought of killing all those birds, imagining them trapped in the mist nets.

They flap and they flap and they try to fly, but the sky has caught them.

I thought of the little bird back home, how it trusted me now.

If Seraphim smelt my apprehension, there'd be trouble, so I pushed these thoughts aside. There had been another arson attack a few days ago: a man named Louis, who had never been suited to hunting. They had set his car on fire, like the man before him, but this time Louis's teenage son was in there, apparently sneaking a cigarette. The boy had managed to get out, but with a badly burnt arm. It was all over the local news. There was an ongoing investigation, but, of course, Louis wouldn't let on what he knew. He would never tell the police anything.

I knew Seraphim had been the one to snitch on him. Well, of course he had. He is a weasel, this man: stealthy, sharp-eyed, cunning, shifty, sneaky, scheming. Above all, and this was the most dangerous part, he was loyal to the men in charge. I had met Louis – he came out with us a couple of times. He had still been learning the trade, and we introduced him to some good poaching locations. But then he wanted out, and Seraphim was pissed off – this Louis had been his next prodigy. 'Best to snitch before they snitch,' was his motto

– he'd said this with a wide grin and narrow eyes. The arson attacks were meant as a warning.

'You're even quieter than usual,' Seraphim finally said. 'Thinking about Nisha?'

'Yes.'

I could see the moon in the stretch of water outside the window.

Seraphim parked the van and we pulled the mist nets and poles from the back of the van, carrying them across the muddy terrain. We returned for the calling birds. There's a British military base there and the English are very strict about hunting, regularly searching the area for poachers, so we had to be extra careful. It was unlikely, though not impossible, that someone would be checking so early in the morning – it was 3.30 a.m., and because the land was so flat and open, we would see anyone approaching from quite a distance. If we stayed vigilant, we would not be caught.

Seraphim wore a head-torch and led the way. We put the nets up, securing them to eight-foot poles. Then he turned off the torch and carefully lifted the blankets from the cages. The birds were quiet, as it was still dark out. The blackbird's feathers were a deep ebony, like the night. I suddenly had the urge to open the door of its cage, to let it free so it could merge with the sky.

We placed their cages on the ground of the shimmering wetlands, just beneath the mist nets that hovered like ghosts above the earth, then we found a secluded spot nearby among some pine trees and rosemary bushes. Seraphim had bought a small gas canister and I took out from my rucksack bread, haloumi and olives. We toasted the food on sticks over a small fire. Shadows from the flames licked over Seraphim's face.

'That Sunday, when Nisha went missing,' I began, and he nodded, still staring at the olives on the stick that he held over the fire. 'Did she come to meet you?'

Seraphim looked at me now. 'Why would you ask me that?'

'I was chatting to someone, a friend, and they thought Nisha was on her way to meet you that evening. Around ten thirty.'

'Why would Nisha be coming to meet *me*?'

'I was hoping you would be able to answer that question.'

Seraphim was silent for a while. The darkness was thick behind him.

'Whoever told you that was not telling you the truth.'

'Why would they lie?'

'They might not be lying. They are just not telling truth. They may have had their wires crossed. If, on the other hand, they did lie deliberately, I assume they have their reasons for doing so, but I cannot possibly begin to speculate because I have no idea who this person is.'

Then Seraphim lay back with his hands behind his head, signalling that our conversation was over. He told me to stay alert and closed his eyes to nap. He fell asleep quickly, his mouth hanging open and emanating a faint snore.

The land stretched for miles all around, dark, with shivers of silver where the moon caught the water. I watched as a sliver of light emerged on the horizon, darkness becoming less opaque. At this first sign of day, the caged birds began to sing. Their voices rose in a swelling, melodic chorus – a burst of music after so much time in silence.

And that's when I heard it again: the voice of a woman, calling. Calling something which I could not understand, her voice mixed with the song of the birds

I stood up. Looked around. I shouldn't have left Seraphim alone, sleeping like that, but I instinctively followed the voice to the mist nets. When I got to the water's edge, it ceased abruptly. There didn't seem to be anyone there. In every direction, the land was open and empty.

Then the birds filled the sky – their music filled the sky. They swooped down in their thousands, their wings alight in the sunrise – gold and red and blue. They veered down sharply, diving towards the calling birds, to the song that was luring them to their death, down, down, down to the water's edge.

I stood frozen, watching them as their journeys ended, the mist net suddenly enveloping them. So many wings tangled, so many birds suspended mid-flight. Their song changed – from trills to shrieks, or so it seemed to me. But some, I thought, continued their melodic song, as if the sky might just open up again and release them.

'What are you playing at?' a voice said behind me. I turned. Seraphim was there, fire in his eyes.

'I thought I heard something,' I said.

'So you leave me sleeping on my own? What if somebody had come? I would have been done for!'

'I made a mistake.'

He stared at me without blinking. 'A mistake? A mistake is forgetting to bring the gas canister or the olives.' His eyes narrowed. The birds' cries filled the air around us. 'Well,' he said, 'let's not dwell on it now. We've caught enough.' He glanced at the net, sizing up the success of the hunt. 'Let's just take down what we have and head home.'

We brought the nets down and began pulling the birds from it, killing them one by one as we did so. We did this without speaking, in synchronicity with one another. I was freeing the birds from the net, passing each one to Seraphim so that he could bite its neck and put it into the black bin-liner. I could feel each one trembling in my hands, tiny heart racing, wings twitching and beating in my palms. The soft touch of feathers on my skin. There must have been twenty different species. But I was careful not to hesitate – I didn't want Seraphim to notice anything was amiss. The birds were still singing, though. That was what disturbed me the most. They sang until their last breath.

I got home around 9 a.m., fed the bird, and lay down. I was so tired. The conversation with Seraphim had been unsatisfying. Was he lying? Had Spyros been mistaken about what Nisha had said? Or was Seraphim trying to throw me off the scent of something else? I missed Nisha keenly.

I fell asleep with dreams of her in the wetlands. She stood in the water, which came to her ankles. A clear blue sky behind her. She was wearing her nightdress of beeralu lace with the garden of white flowers, the one Chaturi had made her. She was saying something to me, her lips moving, but I heard nothing.

'What is it Nisha?' I asked.

She pointed at something behind me, up in the sky. When I turned to look, the sky became black, it was suddenly night. When I looked back at Nisha, she was gone. In her place, the moon hung over the horizon, so big I thought I could reach out and touch it. I noticed its reflection in the water, painfully bright; a silver pool of light in the middle of black water. I took my shoes off and walked in: I wanted to find her, but when I got there, I saw that what I thought had been the moon's refection was in fact a deep well. A well that seemed endless. It was not a dark well. A bright white light glowed from within, illuminating its cobbled walls, spilling out onto the water. From it came immense heat.

I woke up drenched in sweat, a bright winter sun shining through the window, bathing me in its light. The little bird was sitting on my chest, chirping gently to itself. I stroked its soft feathers. Winter was coming. October had passed and Nisha was still missing. The bird sang to the sun and for the first time in many years, I began to cry.

I heard the sound again, the woman's cry, and I realised that this time it was coming from inside me, drifting around the dark corners of my mind. It was a pure and unpredictable sound: like the wind, it ebbed and flowed, it quietened down and came back with force. The sound was coming from a place that didn't belong just to me. It was such a strange and terrifying sensation that I jumped off the bed, the bird fluttering to the ground. And the sound of its wings, as soft as they were, startled my mind back to reality, back to the room I was in with the winter sun beaming through the window.

I felt nauseous, acid coming up from my stomach, burning my oesophagus. I went to the bathroom and vomited in the toilet. As I flushed it, I remembered the blood and grey tissue in the toilet bowl – the child that would never be.

I lay down on the bed again. After the night of the miscarriage, Nisha changed. She would come late at night, as usual, and lay down where I was lying now, hands crossed over her stomach, protectively – like the position in which one places a corpse, except her hands were on her stomach instead of her chest.

She would look out of the window and watch summer fade, each passing day an equation: 'On this day,' she would say, 'I would have been eight weeks pregnant, but instead I have been empty for seven days.' Or, 'On this day I would have been nine weeks pregnant, but I have been empty for fourteen days.'

At 3 a.m., she would wake up and speak to Kumari on the phone. It would have been 7.30 in the morning in Sri Lanka and Nisha wanted to catch her daughter before her school day. I would be half-asleep, the feel of Nisha's warmth still beside me on the bed. She would sit at the desk and her conversation and the light from the tablet would reach me. Sometimes my eyes would flicker open and I would see her silhouette, hear her words in Sinhalese and Kumari's response.

Though I didn't understand the language, I got to know their tones and rhythms. I could understand if they were having a joke, or an argument, or a light-hearted conversation about school or Kumari's homework or her friends. I could tell when Nisha was annoyed about something, or when she was firm and insistent. Sometimes I heard love in her voice; other times concern, joy, irritation, determination. Kumari was sometimes cheeky, sometimes agreeable, often so chatty that Nisha couldn't get a word in edgeways; other times quieter and solemn, moody. There were a few occasions when I could even hear the first signs of adolescent rebellion sneaking in. All the emotions that one would expect between a mother and a burgeoning teenager, but all of this was through a screen.

Many nights Nisha would teach Kumari English. They each had copies of *The Secret Garden* and they would take turns reading the pages aloud. They sometimes both got stuck on a word, but Nisha kept a dictionary by my bedside – a gift from her friend, Nilmini – and she would consult it for assistance. Their chatting drifted over my dreams like the echo of a birdsong.

One time, she said, 'Yiannis, come here. Kumari wants to say hello.'

'You've told her about me?' I mimed.

'Of course,' she said, her eyes bright and encouraging.

It was roughly a year ago, so Kumari must have been about ten at the time. She was wearing her uniform, ready for school, with a massive rucksack on her shoulders.

'Hello, Mr Yiannis,' she had said, smiling. Although she

had darker skin and eyes than her mother, her smile and expressions were exactly the same.

'Hello, Kumari, it's lovely to finally meet you!'

'Finally? Have you heard stuff about me?'

'Of course.'

'Good stuff?'

'Wonderful stuff.'

'That's OK then.' She scrunched up her face. 'So you are my amma's friend?'

'I am.'

'She said you feed the chickens in the garden downstairs.'

'I guess I do.'

'What else do you do, Mr Yiannis. Or are you just a chicken feeder?'

I laughed. 'I'm not *just* a chicken feeder. I go into forests and pick wild vegetables and snails.'

'Hmmm. What do you do with them after you pick them?'

'I sell them.'

'Hmmm.' She nodded. 'I guess that sounds all right.'

After that particular call, Nisha lay down next to me, entwining her limbs with mine. 'I have an extra hour or so before I should leave. Hold me really tight.'

And of course, I did. It was all I wanted to do. She would set her alarm for 5 a.m. I would drift in and out of sleep, and sometimes I would hear her crying.

'What is it, Nisha?' I would whisper in the dark.

'Oh, it's nothing, I just remembered something.'

'What did you remember? Tell me.'

During this time of grief for the lost child, Nisha told me

194

three stories of loss. The first was of her sister's death. The second of her husband's. The third of making the devastating decision to leave Kumari in order to come here. Her sister's death had coincided with the *Vesak Poya* festival of lights, on the first full moon in the month of May, when she was twelve years old and her sister, Kiyoma, had been ten. She told me about the white lanterns at night, hanging over the door of every home in the street apart from theirs. Her sister had died that morning. The year before her death, they went together to the Koggala lagoon and took a gondola to the tiny island where a Buddhist temple was located. There were hundreds of lanterns, and a thousand lights floating on the water as they glided across the lake. Her sister had called them *tiny moons in a starry sky*. Tiny moons that filled up the world.

The temple was covered in flowers, lights and incense; there were dancers and singers and firewalkers. Her sister's face was lit up by all the lights as she held onto Nisha's hand. Kiyoma was only a couple of years younger, but because of her heart condition she was small for her age and if someone didn't know they would think she was much younger. She had been named Kiyoma, which means *good mother*, because her own mother, Lakshitha, wished that Kiyoma would grow up to be a wife and a mother herself. It was the greatest wish that Lakshitha had for her daughter. But Nisha imagined her sister's heart like a tiny bird fluttering in her chest: she knew one day, before long, that it would break free of its cage and fly away. She knew because she could hear the changed rhythm of her breathing. It was so subtle, anyone else would have missed it, but Nisha could hear it because they shared a bed.

Kiyoma always wore a *panchauda* – a gold pendant embellished with five weapons: a bow and arrow, a sword, a disc, a trident and a conch, to ward off the evil eye. Lakshitha made sure Kiyoma never took it off and Nisha saw it glimmering in the light of the lanterns and the fires while they were on the little island visiting the temple. But when they got off the gondola on their return, the necklace had disappeared. It was Nisha who noticed. 'Where is your pendant?' she'd said to her sister with fearful eyes. Kiyoma had shrugged.

Later, their mother was beside herself. 'What could this mean? Nisha, did you see her drop it? Kiyoma, did you not feel it fall? Did either of you not hear it fall?'

Lakshitha had become obsessed with Kiyoma's heart condition. Some days she would be calmer and accept that her beautiful daughter might have less breaths to take in this life and in this world, which is really an almost impossible thing for any mother to come to terms with; other times, and most of the time, she would consult astrologers, or watch out for good or bad omens, such as who Kiyoma might have met at certain times of day, what somebody had said to her, or what they might have been carrying while they spoke to her. She bombarded poor Kiyoma with questions. Other times still, she used lotions, potions and oils on the scar that ran vertically down her youngest daughter's chest to her navel.

Kiyoma was a perceptive girl for her age. One day, while

they were walking back home from the paddy fields where their parents worked, she confided to Nisha that she had thrown the pendant into the lagoon while they were on the gondola on the night of *Vesak Poya*.

'Why, why, *why* would you do such a thing?' Nisha scolded.

'Because,' her little sister had said with candid eyes, 'the pendant felt like a chain around my neck.'

Exactly a year later, on the morning of *Vesak Poya*, just before light filled the sky, Kiyoma drew her last breath and her heart flew away out of the window. Nisha was fast asleep, but she dreamt of a bird with golden feathers as soft as waves that hovered over her for a while, and then flew out of the open window.

She woke up immediately and turned in the half-darkness to face her sister. She noticed that her chest was not rising gently, that her eyes were not moving inside her dreams. She leaned over her, placing her ear close to her mouth and nose. And that's when she heard and felt something that was, up to that point in time, completely unknown to her. The stillness and soundlessness of death.

Kiyoma's body was kept at the house for a few days in an open casket. Monks came to chant prayers and eulogise about the impermanence of life. Her body was placed facing west, and their mother stayed in the room with her day and night, to prevent evil spirits from taking up residence in the house. Pictures had been turned around on the walls, or placed facing down on tabletops; family and friends came to the house with offerings of white and yellow flowers.

Lakshitha did everything she could to ensure that Kiyoma's

transition to the next life was assured. She offered the monks white cloth to be stitched into monastic robes. Then relatives and friends poured water from a vessel into an overflowing cup while reciting prayers.

Nisha listened to the prayers and watched the water over-flowing – how it momentarily caught the light like crystals and seemed like the most beautiful thing in the world. And she understood for the first time that everything – everything – must come to an end.

17

Petra

THAT SUNDAY I GOT READY to go to Limassol. I had
arranged to meet Mr Tony at the Blue Tiger at
3 p.m. and I had about an hour's drive ahead of me.
After lunch, I took Aliki over to Mrs Hadjikyriacou, who
was sitting outside with the cats. It was a rather last-minute
plan, but when I had asked her the previous afternoon, she
seemed excited at the prospect of spending more time with
Aliki. 'She's a funny little girl. Watch her!' she said, beaming
from ear to ear, so that her paper-like skin had creased a
thousand times.

Aliki took her time to decide which shoes she was going
to wear. Eventually, she settled on one grey denim and one
bright blue with a flower pattern. Finally, she picked up
another odd pair: one with red cat paws and the other
bright red.

'You're taking a spare pair of shoes?' I asked.

'No.'

When we got to Mrs Hadjikyriacou's, Aliki placed the shoes on the floor beside her and the old woman looked down at them.

'They're for you,' Aliki said.

'For me?'

'They're a present. And, plus, I don't like your old-lady shoes. They won't do.'

Mrs Hadjikyriacou laughed out loud.

'Last time we learnt that we're the same shoe size,' the old lady said to me. Then to Aliki: 'Well, I must say, they are a perfect odd choice!' Then she called Ruba to come and help her change into her new shoes.

Ruba came out holding a tea-towel. She greeted us warmly before kneeling down by Mrs Hadjikyriacou's feet, pulling off her old-lady shoes and putting on the Converse sneakers.

The shoes were quite remarkable beneath her calf-length black skirt and against her dead-white skin. She leaned over herself with great effort and looked down at her feet, clicking her heels as if she were about to head to Oz. Aliki laughed. The cats ran off on some urgent business. At this, I quietly took my leave, hearing Aliki's laughter rippling behind me.

It was a bright and beautiful day. I rolled down the windows of my Range Rover as I drove southwest to Limassol. It was a bit chilly, but I welcomed the fresh breeze that came down from the mountains, which was soon replaced with a breeze from the sea, drifting in with the sound of the birds.

Everything seemed to melt as I neared the water. The salty air, the way it enveloped me, wrapped me up in a time long gone. *All the water on Earth once arrived on asteroids and comets.* Yes, that is what my father told me. He was a fisherman. He had a library of books in the cellar – where he also kept potatoes – and this was where he got all his information. During the war, the library was taken from him, but until the day he died, he could recall the title and author of every book. In the car, with the windows down and the sea opening up and glistening before me, I could almost hear my father's voice: *Since it came to Earth, the water has been cycling through air, rocks, animals and plants. Each molecule has been on an incredible journey. When you feel alone, try to remember that at some point the water inside you would have been inside dinosaurs, or the ocean, or a polar ice-cap, or maybe a storm cloud over a faraway sea at a time when that sea was still nameless. Water crosses millennia and boundaries and borders.*

For years, I'd forgotten my father's words, and they came back to me now. *Remember we all have something in common, and that is the water that runs through us.*

The Blue Tiger was not too far from the beach, just off one of the side streets that leads down to the sea. It was a dilapidated, double-fronted building, with colourful murals on its walls, mostly of sports scenarios: football players in a packed stadium, basketball players crouched on a court. Above these, on the concrete wall and continuing onto the concrete canopy, were painted vines, large and winding, with thick stems and giant leaves that climbed up to a bright blue sky. On the far left – just above a barred window and two air-conditioning units – looking out through the leaves, was a blue tiger with striking yellow eyes.

I looked at the time on my phone: 14.46.

Below the tiger was a sign that read:

DWA
DOMESTIC WORKERS ASSOCIATION OF CYPRUS
LIMASSOL
REGISTERED OFFICES

Beside the double doors of the entrance was a blackboard pavement sign, with a menu: BURGERS, HOT DOGS, SUPER DOGS, CHILLI CON CARNE.

Two men stood beside it, leaning on a motorbike, smoking. 'You are lost?' one of them asked, in a heavy, unfamiliar accent.

'I'm looking for Mr Tony,' I said, my voice croaky as if I had just woken up. 'I have an appointment.'

'You are not lost,' he said, smiling, 'He is inside the office. On the right.'

I could hear music coming from the depths of the place, and smell spices. I thanked the man and stepped through the open doors. I still didn't know what I was doing there or how this Mr Tony could help me, but by that point I was grateful to speak to anyone who might be able to offer a glimmer of hope.

In an open kitchen on the left, women were cooking in

large pans and woks; other women were scattered about, sitting at tables drinking hot tea or eating steaming dumplings that they dipped into a bright orange sauce. Most of the people were domestic workers from Nepal or the Philippines, Sri Lanka or Vietnam. A local man sat on his own, noticeable due to his bald head, white stubble and gleaming eyes – leering at the girls as they passed with trays of tea. He looked like he was about to drool. He glanced at me, smiling, and I turned away, disgusted. At the back of the kitchen was a set of doors that opened up to a large hall and stage. This was where the music was coming from. People were dancing there, men and women, beneath a canopy of multi-coloured flags.

I spotted what must have been Mr Tony's office: a rectangular glass booth on the far right of the dining area. A large man with broad shoulders and white hair sat behind a desk, a fan spinning above him blowing his hair while he spoke on the phone, a conversation that was clearly making him agitated. He hung up. I waited a minute, then approached the booth and knocked on the door.

'Enter!' he called.

He was sitting on a swivel chair in front of a computer. He smiled and raised his eyebrows. I went to close the door behind me.

'Leave the door open. We need some air in here.'

'Mr Tony?'

'Tony is fine.'

'I'm Petra.' I held out my hand.

'Ah, yes, of course.' He wiped his hand on his trousers and

shook mine; his grip was warm and sweaty. 'Take a seat.' He pointed at a plastic chair in the corner of the booth.

The entire place was awash in laughter and music and spices, and it all swirled around the little booth as it seeped in through the open door.

'What you have here is amazing,' I said. 'You run this organisation yourself?'

He nodded, smiled and said, 'Don't get me wrong – these Asians are ungrateful people.' But then his smile faded, and he glanced down at the ground.

'Really? So why do you help them?'

'I was married to one. Do you mind if I smoke?'

'Not at all.'

Taking a cigarette out of a box, he lit it with a large match, shaking out the flame and chucking it into a crystal ashtray that sat on a notepad.

'And plus, I found a lot of injustice around.'

At that moment the phone rang; he looked down at the flashing screen on his desk and sighed. 'Excuse me,' he said, and picked it up. 'Good afternoon, Mrs Kaligori, can I call you back in about—'

'No.' The voice on the other end interrupted. 'She's no good for me, Tony. She doesn't even speak any English.' The woman said a lot more but I turned my attention to outside the booth, where a beautiful young woman in a green and gold sari was passing by holding a bowl of steaming noodles. Beyond her, I saw the women in the kitchen still sweating and chopping, emptying the contents of their woks into large blue dishes.

'No problem, we'll sort this out,' Tony said loudly. 'I have someone here. Let me call you back in around thirty minutes.'

The woman seemed to acquiesce, although her voice was much quieter now and it was hard to hear.

'I don't work like the agents,' he said to me, when he had hung up. 'The employers come to me directly. They can try out the women, and if they don't like them they send them back. Like Mrs Kaligori. You're not getting some person from Nepal that you are tied to blindfolded. These people' – he waved his hand around him – 'need someone to help them. To the agents they are merchandise, not people.'

'So, the women aren't indebted to you?'

'No! That is the whole point. The agents are furious.'

I nodded and watched him as he sucked deeply on his cigarette, narrowing his eyes at a streak of light from the sliding doors at the front. I noticed on his desk, propped up on some paperwork, a tiny grainy photo of a woman in a bronze frame. He followed my gaze.

'Your wife?'

'Ex-wife. Vietnamese.'

It seemed to me that he was about to say more about this as he opened his mouth, but then he pursed his lips and took a long, hard drag of the cigarette, blowing the smoke in a straight line towards the fan.

'So, you're looking for a girl?' he said.

'Not exactly,' I said.

'On the phone you said you wanted to see me about an

205

urgent matter. In my experience most urgent matters come from women who are looking for a new maid because they are dissatisfied with the one they have.'

'I see.'

'So how may I be of assistance?' he asked, grinning even more broadly now. He was like a gambling saint – there was a disparity, a weird dissonance about this man.

'Well,' I hesitated, and he nodded, urging me on patiently and impatiently. 'I *had* a maid, and she has disappeared. She just vanished one day. I was told that you might be able to help.' I could hear my voice crack. Saying it out loud to a stranger, and a strange stranger at that, made it so much worse.

'Vanished?'

I nodded.

'When?'

'Two Sundays ago.'

'And you've been to the police.'

There was no question mark to this question. I told him I had.

'How did that go?'

'It was a useless waste of my time. They told me she must have run away to the north. I know she hasn't.'

He hastily grabbed the notepad that the ashtray was resting on and leafed through it. Without looking at me he said, 'What is her name?'

'Nisha Jayakody.'

'Where do you live?'

I told him and he continued to search his notebook, his

finger running along the pages. He took another deep drag of the cigarette and I watched him as the fan swirled the smoke around him, as his eyes skimmed over the words, as he turned the pages, flicking forwards and back again, as he placed the cigarette in the ashtray and ran his hand through his hair. I'm not sure what he was searching for but then he grabbed a pen and jotted something down.

'In the last month,' he said finally, 'two other maids have been reported missing to me.' He stressed the last two words and looked up with a deep frown, his eyebrows raised at the edges.

'Two?'

'Both Filipino. One worked in Akrotiri, the other in Nicosia. Where is your maid from?'

'Sri Lanka.' He jotted this down in the notebook too. I felt my body turn cold, despite the heat in the booth. Two other women had gone missing.

'What could this mean?' I managed to say. I found that I couldn't speak much, my mouth dry, my tongue stuck to the roof of my mouth. Perhaps sensing this, he called out to one of the maids who was passing the booth.

'Bilhana! Bilhana!'

A woman in an orange sari turned on her heel and arrived in the open doorway of the booth.

'Tell Devna – two coffees.' He spoke slowly, holding up two fingers. 'Sugar?' he said to me.

I shook my head. 'Do you think they are connected?' I said, once the woman had gone.

He responded by raising his eyebrows and opening both

of his palms – he was at a loss. 'I knew there was a problem when the first girl went missing,' he said. 'Rosamie. I placed her. She came here three years ago through an agency; she worked for a man who was no good to her. He beat her. God knows what else. She came to me for help. With some difficulty, I got her out of the clasp of her agent and found her a better home. She moved in with a British family in Akrotiri. They were good to her, and she was pleased with them. She would come here on Sundays, eat and talk with the other women. She was a good dancer too, loved the music here. One Sunday she didn't come.'

He paused there and stubbed out his cigarette. The phone rang again, but this time he turned it over and ignored it. 'Billie Jean' was playing in the back hall, and a couple of women were standing close to the booth chatting.

'The next Sunday,' he continued, 'she didn't turn up again, and I thought it was odd. The following one, her employer came here to tell me that she'd gone.'

'She'd gone,' I repeated. It seemed the only thing I could manage to say.

'Mrs Manning went to the police, but they convinced her that Rosamie had run away to find employment in the north of Cyprus. Poor woman didn't know what to believe. But I knew Rosamie. She came here beaming every Sunday because her bruises had faded, because she was happy with Mr and Mrs Manning. She would bring me a cake or biscuits, always thanking me. She said I had saved her life. Why would she run away? It doesn't make sense. You see, when you clump people together and don't understand their personal stories, you can make up any bullshit and convince yourself it's the truth.'

By now the ash from his cigarette was long and he threw it in the ashtray and took another out of the box, holding it between his fingers without lighting it. At this point Devna came in with a tray of coffee, two glasses of water and a plate of sesame fingers. She was a slim girl who looked like she could easily have been fifteen, but there was an assurance and confidence to her movements and posture which made me think she was older. I hoped she was, at least. She wore faded jeans with slits at the knees and a brightly coloured shirt. Large, silver, hooped earrings shone through her dark hair as she leaned over the desk, placing the tray on top of some paperwork.

'They don't know anything about life,' Tony said, looking at Devna. 'They've come from small communities, labourers in fields.' I watched Devna's fingers as she took the glasses and cups from the tray, placing them on the table – long, dark, beautiful fingers, her nails painted earth-green.

'They say they want to send money to their families, but a lot of them come to find freedom. They think they're going to be flying free in Europe. Back home they usually earn 200 euros a month; here it's around 500. But what do they do? They look at TikTok and photographs on their phones all day and think about which boys they like. Isn't that right, Devna?'

Devna laughed but said nothing.

'Don't you like boys?'

'I do,' she replied with a smile, 'but that is not why I am here.'

'So why are you here? Tell Petra why you are here.'

'Please, madam,' she said, smiling again with glistening lips, 'this is your coffee and water.'

'If they were clever,' Tony said loudly, more to Devna than to me, 'they would save!'

Devna turned her back to him and winked at me. There was a faint smile about her lips, a knowing in her pitch-black eyes. I took the wink to mean: *Don't listen to him, we know perfectly well why we are here.*

Someone called Tony from the kitchen. 'Excuse me a moment,' he said, leaving me in the booth with Devna.

'I'll tell you why I'm here,' she said; and now that Tony was gone her voice was sharper, louder. 'Tony is a good man, but he still doesn't really understand. I came because I saw no other way forward at home. There was no work, nothing I could do. I have a brother who is disabled, he can't walk or talk. My parents are old now. I have to send him money. Tell me, who will do this if I don't? I was working night and day at home and it wasn't enough. They say we have a better life here, but is that a reason to treat us like children, or worse, animals?' There was a fierceness to her words. 'Do you under-stand what I'm saying?' Her gaze was firm and penetrating.

'Yes,' I said, without looking away, feeling the full force of this woman's determination and strength. 'Yes,' I said, 'I do. Have you told Tony this?'

'Of course I have,' she said. 'He knows. He knows. He likes to tease me. The others don't know, though. They see me as a robot.'

I gulped down the water and placed the empty glass back on the tray.

Tony returned and Devna winked at me again, smiled and left.

'I can see that you're distressed,' he said. 'And I want to hear your story. But first, let me tell you about the other missing girl, Reyna . . . Reyna was a different matter altogether. She came here five years ago with her sister, through an agency. Her sister, Ligaya, was relatively happy with her employers but Reyna was miserable. She worked for an old woman who shouted at her and she felt pretty homesick most of the time. One night, she went out and never returned. Ligaya came here, a wreck, a week later. She was crying a lot and I had to calm her down before I could understand anything. Reyna's phone was switched off. She had left everything – her passport, other precious items, she went out with the clothes she was wearing and the shoes on her feet and never returned. The old woman wasn't bothered – she was advised to find another maid, and she did. Poor Ligaya got my details from some other girls and came to me because she was afraid to go the police.'

'Afraid? Was she an illegal immigrant?'

'No,' he said bluntly. 'She came here legally. She was afraid about how she would be treated.'

He struck a match on the box and it sizzled into a flame. He lit his cigarette and the smoke came out of his mouth in rings, which disintegrated and dispersed in grey wisps around the booth. He picked up his coffee and had a sip. 'Help yourself,' he said, signalling with his eyes to my coffee and the biscuits on the tray.

I took a sip. It was packed full of sugar, but I decided to

drink it anyway – I needed it in the heat and stuffiness of the tiny booth with the fan that circulated the same smoky air. Scenarios flashed through my mind. Had all three women got involved with something that had led to their disappearance? Could Nisha have known Reyna and Rosamie? A shadow loomed in the corner of my thoughts. Had something else occurred, something darker . . . I couldn't bear to think about it.

'So, tell me,' he said. 'What makes you think Nisha hasn't run away? Because I guess that is why you are here?'

I drank the rest of the coffee in one go, took a deep breath and told him the whole story: the trip to the mountains; her request to go out that evening which she hadn't mentioned again; the crash I heard in the garden that night; realising the following morning that Nisha had gone; that her bed had not been slept in; that she had left her passport, her locket, her daughter's lock of hair; and, most importantly, that she had not said goodbye to Aliki. I told him that she had been seen heading out at 10.30 on Sunday night, after I had gone to bed, and that she had been heading in the direction of Maria's, which was basically a brothel-type bar.

He nodded while I spoke, occasionally jotting things down in the notepad. Once again, his cigarette had turned to ash and it fell onto his beige trousers. He swiped at it, smudging it in.

'Where exactly is Maria's?' he asked.

I gave him the address and he wrote this down too.

Then I showed him the bracelet that I had been clutching in my hand the entire time.

'Some friends of Nisha's found this by the Green Line,' I said, 'not too far from Maria's. See how the clasp is broken?'

'May I?' he said, and opened his palm.

I placed the bracelet upon it. He looked at it closely, examining its every line, running his finger over Aliki's name on its underside.

'Who is Aliki?'

'My daughter. This bracelet was a present to Nisha from us for her birthday a few years ago.'

He gave me the bracelet and sat there, pensive. There was silence between us for a while. Ricky Martin's 'Livin' La Vida Loca' drifted in with the sounds of cutlery and conversation and laughter. Tony looked around the dining area through the glass of his office booth, like a captain at the bridge of a ship.

'Could there be a connection,' I said, 'between these three women?'

In response, he tore a piece of paper out of the notebook and wrote down the names of the women, including the date of their disappearance. 'I am assuming that you are in contact with some of Nisha's acquaintances?'

'Yes, of course,' I said.

He handed me the piece of paper. 'Please go back and ask them about these two other women. Had Nisha mentioned them? Are they known within her circle of friends? Once you start asking questions, I'm sure more questions will emerge. But you never know, there could be some answers in there, too.'

I stared for a while at the names of the women: *Rosamie Cotabu 12th October 2018* and *Reyna Gatan 23rd October 2018.*

What had happened to these women? How had they disappeared without a trace? And now Nisha would be added to this list: *Nisha Jayakody 31st October 2018*.

Tony asked for my details: my full name, Nisha's full name, my mobile number, my landline and my address. He took it all down in his notepad.

'I'm going to go back to the police,' he said. 'I'll write them emails, I'll visit, I'll camp out on their front step, if I have to. If a Cypriot woman had gone missing, they would have searched the Earth to find her. Why are they not bothering with these women? Because they are foreign. They are not Cypriot, they are not citizens. They just don't count.'

As I drove away from the sea, I could still hear the music in my ears, smell the food on my clothes. The road was almost empty on this Sunday afternoon. I was both reassured and troubled by my meeting with Tony. Most of the way home, the names and the dates flashed through my mind. Had Nisha ever mentioned these women? I really didn't think so. Perhaps their consecutive disappearances were mere coincidence. But something – something dark and sinking and sinister – told me this wasn't the case.

It was just before 6 p.m. when I arrived home. In front of her house, Mrs Hadjikyriacou had her black skirt hitched up to her knees, teaching Aliki a dance move, kicking about in her new red and cat Converse. Aliki was taking the lesson very seriously. Ruba had opened a foldable wooden table in the front yard and was bringing out bowls of steaming food.

When Mrs Hadjikyriacou saw me, she beamed. 'We've had the most fantastic time,' she said. 'I'm getting rather tired though.' She let her skirt drop down to her ankles and insisted that I join them for dinner.

We all sat together around the table. Aliki must have been starving because she was already holding her knife and fork, eager to start eating. She eyed the food in the bowl – a Nepalese dish of fine noodles and vegetables that instantly reminded me of the smells at the Blue Tiger. There was a jug of bright, freshly made lemonade, bowls of creamy white goats' yoghurt and warm bread.

'I was going to ask you how it went, but you look famished, so let's eat first.'

Ruba lit the outdoor heater and bought out some colourful crochet throws for Aliki and me to wrap around our shoulders; they were of the softest wool and smelt of jasmine. 'I made those after the war,' Mrs Hadjikyriacou said, 'when I first came to live here. Each is a flower that used to grow in my garden back home.' And as we ate, she listed the flowers in alphabetical order.

Aliki liked this game because she challenged Mrs Hadjikyriacou with ever more obscure flower species.

'How about the cyclamen Cyprium?'

'No, they only grow in the mountains.'

'How about the Cyprus bee orchid? They are very pretty. Our teacher likes flowers. He teaches us all about them.'

'No. They usually grow in grasslands and open pine woodlands.'

'How about the tulipa Cypria? My teacher, Mr Thomas,

told us they are so hard to find, and they are the colour of deep red blood. Did you have any of those in your garden?'

'No, but I'm pretty sure that my Auntie Lucia had some of those in her garden. She had three thumbs. Talking about three thumbs . . . have you heard of the monster that lives in the underwater caves near Cape Greco?'

Aliki shook her head, eyes round.

'Some people say it has several heads and numerous limbs. But everyone who talks about the creature speaks of its friendliness. It is said to appear from the deep sea, attracted by fish caught in a net. Some people think it is a giant sea snake or a large runaway crocodile, but I have seen it with my own eyes and I can tell you that it looks like a prehistoric Plesiosaur. It was many years ago, when I was exactly your age, Aliki, that I went with my parents and my seven siblings on a summer trip to the sparkling waters of the east coast . . .'

I listened to the story and devoured the food on my plate. Ruba ate with us and was vigilant should we need anything – occasionally refilling our glasses with lemonade, or passing around the bread and yoghurt. Her eyes darted about the table; from time to time she smiled at me or Aliki and gave a slight nod, but she never spoke.

There was a light on above my flat. Yiannis was sitting on the balcony looking out across the street. I knew that I would need to speak with him, tell him about the Blue Tiger and share the information that Tony had given me. I prayed that he would know something.

The man with the army boots and the windbreaker is
sitting on a rock. He drinks some hot tea from a flask and
stares without blinking at the still water of the lake. Beside
him is a black suitcase, lying on its side. After a moment,
he straightens his posture, focuses his eyes, looks around
and places a hand on the case.

Five or more beetles are crawling over the hare's fur.
Some feed on fly eggs, larvae and maggots; others devour
its flesh. They like the dark, the time when they feel most
free. With their flat bodies, they crawl into the empty
socket of its eye, feeling their way around with long
antennae. A black whip snake glides past, raises its head
and continues to the edge of the crater. It trickles like a
shining stream down to the lake, but it does not enter.

There is no breeze tonight and the sky is full of stars. A
half-moon gleams, dropping its bone-white light upon the
pecan trees and fruit trees, down upon the distant river

where dragonflies swarm, down upon the sunflowers and the dirt path, leading to the homes in the village, where most people are asleep. A TV flickers in one of the bedrooms; a night light glows in another. In the guest house, a cockroach, enticed to the room by the sugared almonds, feeds on the paper of an old book of fairy tales resting on a wooden shelf. The widow is snoring. She has left the washing out on the line. A cat, with the stripes of a tiger, watches from behind a rosemary bush, planning to catch a lone dragonfly that has found itself far from the fresh water of the river – a scarlet dragonfly with ghostly, red-veined wings.

When the breeze picks up again, the man with the army boots and the windbreaker and the suitcase is no longer there.

18

Yiannis

THERE WERE FLYERS OF NISHA all over the neighbourhood. On every corner, there she was. Even
from my balcony I could see her, glued to the pole
of a street lamp outside Yiakoumi's antique shop, and on my
walk, hanging from the canopy at Theo's, stuck to the wooden
pillars and walls of the restaurant. Passers-by glanced at them
but mainly took no notice. Only the other maids paused,
contemplating Nisha's picture, with something in their eyes
like fear – or perhaps it was recognition, a fearful look in
the mirror.

The birds from the hunt in Akrotiri had filled the fridges
in the spare room. I needed to clean them, but I couldn't
find the discipline to sit down and focus.

Felling uneasy, I grabbed my coat and headed downstairs.

Crossing the street, I pulled off one of the flyers from a lamp-post and headed to Lakyavitos station.

I was kept waiting for forty-five minutes before I could see the chief constable, Vasilis Kyprianou.

'I understand you're here to report a missing person,' he said, opening a notebook and clicking a silver pen.

I nodded and placed the flyer on the desk.

He glanced down at it briefly, then up at me, 'I see. Can I get you a coffee?'

'No, thanks.'

He picked up the phone and asked for one coffee and some biscuits. I proceeded to tell him about Nisha and how she had disappeared without her passport.

'I know that her employer came to report her missing but had no success,' I concluded.

He put his pen down now and with a gesture that seemed to suggest that he wasn't fussed, he closed the file. 'And who are you to her?' he asked, tapping the flyer roughly with a finger.

I hesitated.

'Her lover?' There was a slight smirk on his face.

'Well, I wouldn't put it like that.'

He smiled now. 'I don't blame you, a lot of them are extremely beautiful. I wonder sometimes, though, if they really are as beautiful as they seem or if it's because they look different, exotic, if you know what I mean?'

I didn't reply. I could feel my neck and face heating up.

'So. How would you put it then?' he asked.

'I care about Nisha very much. She has been working hard for nine years to send money to her family . . .'

His smile broadened and he started waving his hand, as if he couldn't be bothered to hear the rest. 'These people don't care about their families. They have no real roots. They would throw their families away at the drop of a hat! That's why they are able to come here, or travel even further to countries in Europe, or to the Arabic Emirates and God only knows where else. You wouldn't see a Cypriot lady making that sort of decision now, would you? Leaving her children behind? That would be unheard of, no matter the circum-stances. But then again, their lives are so shitty back home. They are peasants. No prospects. They come over here and we give them more than they could have ever imagined – good accommodation, good food, higher wages. But they have no gratitude – some steal, some sell their bodies, others take off. You'd think they'd appreciate being here more. Don't make the mistake of thinking they are like us. They are made of different stuff, mark my words.'

'Whatever you say, she is missing, and I would like you to launch an investigation.'

'Look, I'm not here to be chasing after these women. They come here. They don't find what they are looking for. They run away to avoid the debts they owe to their agents. Don't you think we could put taxpayers' money to better use than launching an investigation which will inevitably be a complete waste of time and resources?'

This guy was an arsehole. His skull an impenetrable wall.

I focused on the blue veins that ran down from his receding hairline, the steep bridge of his nose, his yellow teeth. I clenched my fist beneath the table to trap the anger.

A woman came in with a coffee and a plate of biscuits, which she placed in front of him. He took a sip and sighed with contentment. I got up to leave, leaning over to take the flyer from his desk, but instead deciding to leave it. Let him throw it away.

At home I cleaned the birds. Mechanically, systematically. I needed to get the job done. I defeathered the blackcaps, song thrushes and chiffchaffs. These birds would be pickled, roasted, fried, eaten whole in secret. The tiny blackcap sat beside me, chirping now and then, struggling to flutter up onto the table in order to eat some berries. It succeeded, then clumsily wafted back down again to give itself a bath in the bowl I'd set out for it. It was getting stronger, its wing clearly mending, but it needed more time. I'd purposely put its food on the table and the bird bath on the floor so that it would exercise its wings, test its strength.

When I first starting poaching, I did some reading on avian intelligence, hoping to confirm the bird-brain theory, so that I would feel better about what I was doing. Instead, I learned that certain bird species were so smart that they were considered 'feathered apes'. For decades, scientists believed that birds weren't capable of higher thinking because they lacked a cerebral cortex; however, now they knew that a different part of the brain – the pallium – evolved to fill its place.

In my heart, this revelation was not surprising. I had known since I was a child – and had held that dead golden bird – that they had an inner life. Throughout my boyhood, I had known birds solve problems with cognition beyond instinct, their minds flexible and sharp. I even had a crow-friend I called Batman, whom I'd watch make tools out of twigs and wood. Sometimes I would offer Batman some metal wire and create sort of a problem – a puzzle as such – and sit beneath a tree and watch it work out a solution.

Seraphim killed Batman during one of his visits. He shot the bird with a pellet gun. His dad had given him the gun to practise aim control so that he could go out hunting with the men. He was using figs as targets. He was pretty good: I remember him scrunching up his left eye, holding the gun steady on his right shoulder. Aim. Fire. Aim. Fire. He became more proficient by the second. Then, while we were having our lunch one afternoon, Batman flew down from the sky through the pines. Seraphim swiftly put the gun to his shoulder, aimed, and fired. The bird didn't die straight away, and Seraphim held it by its legs upside down, the bird squirming in his grip, and took his trophy down the mountain to show his father.

As I made my way through the bin-bag – an indistinguishable mass of bodies, feathers and beaks tangled together – my eyes fell upon an owlet. I reached down for it. It was smaller than my palm, but its body carried heft, its feathers impossibly soft and fine. I wondered if it had flown into the net while following his mother on a night hunt. Its oversized opaque black eyes in its pale, heart-shaped face looked up at me without seeing.

I thought of Nisha's story of the owl, of losing Kiyoma, and I almost dropped it on the floor. How did I not notice this bird in Akrotiri when we were sorting the birds? Did Seraphim see it and let it pass into the bag on purpose? I can imagine he would have bitten into its neck indiscriminately. To him, a bird was a bird was a bird. To me, I worked like a machine. A hunt was a job was money.

Not knowing what to do, I covered the owlet gently with my other hand, making a cocoon. I thought of Nisha's first story of loss and how she had felt and heard for the first time the stillness and silence of death. I considered the other birds. The ones I had trapped, killed and defeathered. The ones that were soaking now in the basin and the bath, and all the other species that I had discarded in a bin-liner because they would not sell. This is where the baby owl would end up. I could not bring myself to throw it in there. So I sat. I sat there on the stool with the owlet nestling between my palms and I did not move for what must have been more than an hour.

Music drifted in through the open doors in the other room. It was the woman again, at Theo's. Her voice pure gold. After a while I heard Aliki laughing out front; she must be home from school. I heard Mrs Hadjikyriacou's voice. It sounded like they were playing a game.

I thought about how simple everything used to seem. How I used to sit out on the balcony, after these sounds of the neighbourhood had ceased, when most had gone to bed, and waited for Nisha. Those nights after the miscarriage, she came to me with eyes carrying pain. But she still came. Because that's what we do. When there is love, there is a safe place for sadness.

Nisha told me told me another story of loss the second night after her miscarriage. She lay down on the bed and placed her hands over her stomach in the corpselike manner she had done before. She inhaled deeply and her chest trembled. She wanted to cry, I was sure, but she held it in.

'What's your favourite colour?' she asked.

'I don't know, I've never thought about it.'

'But what if you were given a choice, the last colour you saw before you died, what would it be?'

'I'm still not sure. It's hard to choose.'

'You have to choose one!'

'Maybe this is a game Aliki would appreciate.'

'Yes, she loves these games. But choose.'

She tilted her head in my direction, staring at me with wide eyes, as if she'd asked me the most important question in the world.

'Amber,' I said.

She nodded to herself.

'I don't know what colour Mahesh would have chosen,' she said. I held my breath at the mention of her husband – she very rarely mentioned him. 'I never got to ask him that question.'

225

Then, in a soft, faraway voice, she told me the second story of loss.

Nisha's parents had worked in the paddy fields. They rented a plot from a rich landowner, ploughed the earth, grew rice and sold it at the market. They lived in a simple house, not quite a mud hut, but with makeshift walls of asbestos sheets. There was a well in the back garden that brought forth cool and fresh water from the dark veins of the earth, even in the heat of the summer. They had a jackfruit tree as well as papaya, mango and passion fruit. Trellises of jasmine flowers separated their garden from the neighbour's. Nisha's father grew yams and mace in the yard. He was a tall man with lighter skin – it was well known that his ancestors had joined the Dutch East India Company fleeing Catholicism in the seventeenth century, and that was why her family carried the surname Van de Berg, which meant *from the mountains*. Her mother's colouring was rich and dark, like Nisha and Kiyoma, but Nisha had her father's amber eyes. The kids at school called her 'mango-eyes'.

Their house was at the end of a long road that divided the paddy fields from the sea, overlooking a coconut plantation on one side and the Indian Ocean on the other. From her bedroom window, Nisha could see the fishermen take the boats out in the night. She'd wake up early to watch them cast the nets in the water just before dawn and then pull them in at around nine o'clock, before it got too hot. On Saturdays, she would go with her father to buy fresh fish.

She liked the silver scales, but she didn't like the sea. It wasn't a friendly sea, rough and unforgiving, and most people in Sri Lanka had never learned how to swim because of it.

Rice-growing was a family affair. Husband and wife worked together, the children expected to follow in their footsteps. However, when Nisha had reached her teenage years, an increasing number of people were leaving the farms to work in factories – garments, ceramics, gems and jewellery. With Kiyoma gone, Nisha's father encouraged her to find a job where she could be independent and not owe rent money to the rich landowners. The country was changing. Since the 1960s, the Sri Lankan government had imposed much control over trade, with heavy tariffs for imports, even banning some imports entirely. But in 1977, a new government came into power, which introduced trade expansion under new policies. Nisha's father would sit with her in the garden and explain all this; he would bring her books and articles to read – he wanted her to understand, he wanted her to understand life, the economy and people, and how these were intertwined, so that she could make productive and logical decisions.

In 1995, when she was sixteen years old, Nisha left Galle for the alluvial gem fields in Elahera. Along the banks of the Kalu Ganga river the land was luscious and green, but the foliage had been stripped away, exposing the muddy, red earth. Men climbed down deep mine shafts in Rathnapura, hoisting gravel into baskets to the surface.

In a large reservoir next to the mine, workers washed the gravel in wicker baskets, swishing them in the water a few handfuls at a time. This was Nisha's job, and it was hard work. She spent most of the day in the sun bent over the reservoir, or wading in the cloudy water, until she would see a crystal sparkle in the light amongst the dirt: blue, yellow and pink sapphires; rubies; topaz; chrysoberyls. Nisha loved finding the blue sapphires: they were her favourite. They reminded her of the colour of the early morning sea from her bedroom window, with the silver fish that twitched in the nets.

Mahesh worked in the mines. He noticed Nisha immediately. He thought her eyes were like yellow sapphires. This is what he said during a lunch break when they sat beneath the canopy of trees drinking hot tea, looking out at the arid land where the mine shafts were, where the workers cleaned the gravel chest-deep in brown water. She laughed at him and told him that his comment was cheesy, but that made him like her even more.

They became frequent lunch companions, and Mahesh told her about the journey down the shaft and along the dark tunnels of the earth, the unbearable heat, the humidity, and the fear he had of being buried alive. He was a small, gentle man with a smile that was bigger than his face. He would sweat in the mines and nearly hyperventilate, but he gritted his teeth and kept going. Nisha admired his strength, his character and determination. She told him this and he'd said that he would remember her words, that they would give him courage. Every morning, from then on, when she saw him descend into the mines, she prayed for him.

He would descend fifteen or so metres beneath Rathnapura, looking for topaz and sapphires. He would push a metal rod into the porous mine walls and listen to the sound it made, try to feel the vibrations of the earth along the rod. He could normally tell when he hit alluvial gravel or sapphire, but sometimes he would inspect the rod after pulling it out as harder gem material would scratch the metal. He was good at his job, fast and agile; he hoisted more sacks full of good, gem-filled gravel than any other worker there.

They were married in Galle the following year and bought a house in Rathnapura, which was bigger than the house she had lived in with her parents.

She loved him with all her heart. He was kind. He never raised his voice, like the neighbour who shouted at his wife day and night. He cleaned his own shoes and always put his dirty clothes in the laundry basket. He had a high-pitched laugh that made Nisha laugh. No matter how tired or wary or fed up he became, she could always see the child in his eyes. That was what she liked about him. It is possible to love someone without really liking them, but she liked Mahesh a lot.

Every night he'd have sore, swollen hands. After dinner Nisha would rub them with cream. 'You don't have to do that again,' he would say, with his huge smile. 'You are tired too. How about I rub your feet?'

But Nisha wouldn't have it. 'What, with those crusty things?' She'd point to his hands and pull a face. 'Besides, I can rub my own feet. Now lie back and think of the open sky.' He liked the open sky. It was the opposite of the mines.

He didn't like coffee, he drank sweet tea. Every Sunday they went down to the market to eat *kottu* with spicy curry sauce, a flat crispy fried bread made with *godamba roti*. Some evenings Mahesh would make a delicious green jackfruit curry with pandan leaves and coconut milk. He would climb the tree himself to get fresh coconuts. He was sexy when he chopped vegetables because his thick fringe would flop down over his eyes. Nisha would call him a shaggy dog. He would laugh and lick her face from chin to brow.

When she found out she was pregnant, Mahesh ran around the neighbourhood calling out, 'I'm going to be a father!' Then he came home sweating, beaming from ear to ear, pacing the kitchen, making plans.

One day, months later, after she had just given birth to Kumari, Nisha was in the kitchen breastfeeding the baby. Hearing a noise, she looked up and saw someone through the window, running and tripping as she went. It was one of her neighbours, a woman named Shehara, running through the fields, shouting something that at first Nisha could not understand. Then her voice flowed in through the open doors: 'It has caved in! It has caved in! It has caved in!'

She shouted this over and over again, until the words lost all meaning. *It has caved. In it has caved. It has caved in it has caved in it has caved in it has.*

Nisha understood immediately what had happened. The very thing her husband had always feared. It was why Nisha had prayed every night from that very first day when they spoke in the shade of the trees. Mahesh was stuck down there in the deep, dank well with no way out. She knew him so well that she could almost hear the beat of his heart, feel the blood pumping in his veins. She could hear the dripping water, see the dripping walls, the shimmering crystals in the light of his head torch. She could smell it – the earth. The earth that produced such beautiful gems, the earth that held such brilliant colours, had now swallowed him up.

Nisha stopped her story there. She could not go on. She sat up and began coughing, as if she was the one trapped in the mine, struggling for breath.

I got up and bought her a glass of cold water. She took a few sips and handed it back to me.

'I can't tell any more,' she said, eventually. 'My tears are going into my throat and choking me.'

It was so hot that night. We were on the bed with the fan blowing on us and the patio doors wide open. Once again, Nisha lay on her back, placing her hands on her stomach. All the lost futures drifted through Nisha into me. I felt sorrow for the lost child. I had a feeling of crying internally; I recognised it from when I was a boy, when my father had returned with blood in his eyes trapped in the visions and sounds of the war, never seeing me again. He made me a desk with fresh oak from the woods. He placed the desk away from the window so that I couldn't look out. He became obsessed with my education. I was no longer allowed to roam around and look at the birds and wildlife. I could no longer go with them to the market. He wanted me to study. He checked in on me. If he saw me standing by the window, he closed the blinds.

It was this thought: that loss cannot be reversed, that I

could not bring back my father's lost mind, or the child that – this lack of control, this helplessness – made my hand tremble over Nisha's.

'I wish it could have been safe inside me,' she said.

'You know it was not your fault,' I said.

'I *do* know.'

She looked up at the night sky, through the window. The moon was not visible, only stars. I placed my palm over her hands and we stayed like that for a long time.

I thought about the dying man in the gem-filled darkness of the mine. How long would it have taken him to die? Did he have time to sit in the dark and think about his life, his wife, his baby daughter up above, about all the things he loved and those that he hated, about his triumphs and regrets? What would he have felt, meeting the inescapability of death before it had arrived? What kind of hunger did he feel? What thirst? What pains plagued his body? What memories his mind? Or was he so panicked that his death came faster?

'But I didn't know what his favourite colour was,' I heard her say.

Still cradling the owlet in my palms, I went to the balcony and saw that Petra and Aliki were having dinner with Ruba and Ms Hadjikyriacou in her front yard. This was a good time for me to go to the garden. I took a spade and buried the owlet in the soft soil beneath the orange tree. I buried it deep so that cats and wild animals could not get to it. Then I sat on the balcony holding the little bird, who had nestled deep into its feathers, and I listened to the laughter and endless chatter down below.

At exactly 3 a.m. the iPad rang again. I answered it. Kumari stared back at me, confused. Once again, she was in her school uniform, purple rucksack on her shoulders. This time her hair was down, straight as needles.

'Hello, Mr Yiannis,' she said.

'Hello, Kumari.'

'Can I speak to Amma?'

I paused for only a second: I didn't want her to pick up on my anxiety.

'I'm sorry, Kumari, your mum is at work again.'

She thought for a moment, clearly sceptical. Her eyes were round and severe. 'But it is very late in the night there. Why she is working now?'

'She had extra duties to do.'

'With the chickens?'

'Erm, yes. With the chickens.'

She nodded, thoughtfully.

'She told me to tell you that she loves you so much, more than anything in the whole world, and to be really good at school.'

'OK, Mr Yiannis. You be good at work too.'

Once again, she smiled and she was gone.

19

Petra

THE NEXT DAY, AS I drove home from work, I decided to speak to Yiannis again. As I parked, I noticed the flyer of Nisha just outside the house was no longer on the lamp-post where I had put it. But her smiling face stared at me still further along the street.

Going through the garden and up the stairs, I knocked for Yiannis. It was the first time I had been in the flat since I had rented it to him. He kept it neat and tidy and so sparsely furnished that it looked as though he was only staying for a couple of days. He kept the patio doors in the living room wide open so that the winter light and wind flooded in. He pulled the doors closed when he saw me shudder, and offered me a hot drink, which I accepted.

In the kitchen he brewed coffee in a stainless-steel pot on

the stove. On the windowsill were two plants: a small cactus and a jasmine flower, whose summer scent reminded me of the old man on the bus to Troodos.

'*I spy with my little eye, something beginning with N.*'

'*Hm, that's a hard one.*'

I could almost hear them now: Aliki's laugh, Nisha's mock concentration, as she searched out of the window.

'I went to the police,' Yiannis said.

'Oh?'

'I couldn't sit around and do nothing.'

'What did they say?'

'Basically nothing.'

He watched the coffee brew on a low flame, making sure that it didn't boil and spoil the *kaimaki* – the marbley film of creamy froth on its surface.

'Look,' I said, 'I know about your affair with Nisha.'

'Affair? Why, who am I cheating on?'

'What would you call it then?'

'I love her. We have a relationship.'

He said this matter-of-factly, as he poured the coffee into cups and placed them on a heavy oak table, which looked more like a desk than something one might find in a kitchen. One chair was made of the same wood by the same hand, and opposite was a black plastic chair that had nothing to do with the table. I sat down on that one.

Yiannis took a sip of coffee, glancing at me momentarily over the rim of the cup.

At this point I heard a chirp and saw a tiny bird beneath

the table by his feet, one of those songbirds that sweep in from the west in the winter. I used to hear them over the sea, when I went out with my father in his fishing boat.

Yiannis reached down so the bird could hop onto his hand. He bought the bird up onto the table and it settled beside the coffee cup.

'That's an odd choice of pet,' I said.

'It's not a pet. Its wing was damaged. I'm taking care of it until it's ready to fly again.' He was silent for a moment, looking at the bird. Then he said, 'Do you have any news about Nisha – is that why you're here?'

I took the note that Tony had given me, and Nisha's bracelet, out of my pocket and placed them on the table.

'What are these?' he said, going very still.

'Two other women are missing.' I said, trying to keep my voice steady. 'These are their names and the dates when they disappeared.'

Yiannis stared at me without looking down at the paper.

'And this is Nisha's bracelet, as I'm sure you recognise. It was a gift from Aliki, and Nisha never took it off. Another maid found it on the street near Maria's.'

I could see the fear in his eyes. His hard silence reminded me of Muyia's wooden sculptures, frozen in time.

I told Yiannis about going to the Blue Tiger, how I had met Tony and what he had told me about the other two maids. While I was talking, he sat with both hands on the table, a deep frown between his brows. It was only when I finished talking that he moved, bringing his hand up to his face, pressing his temples with his thumb and finger, creasing his face in the way that he had when he'd downed the *zivania* at my apartment.

I expected that he would speak but he said nothing at all. We sat there in silence for a long time, Yiannis with his fingers pressed against his temples, me with my hands in my lap. The kitchen window was open a crack and a cold breeze drifted through the jasmine flowers, riffling their smell.

'*Aliki, this is too difficult.*'

'*Keep going!*'

'*Nylon? And before you ask, the woman who is reading the novel – to your right – is wearing nylon tights.*'

'*That's very good. But no.*'

'*Necklace.*'

'*No.*'

'*Neck!*'

'*No.*'

'*Nun?*'

'*Nisha, where do you see a nun?*'

'*We passed a church and a nun was outside in the garden.*'

'*You see everything.*'

'*You should be more observant.*'

'*OK, do you give up?*'

'*Let me try one last time . . . nostril!*'

'*The answer is Nisha.*'

'*Me? That's cheating! I can't see me!*'

'*Why? I see you!*'

'*I would never have guessed that! I could have gone all week and I would never have guessed that.*'

'*Isn't it funny that you saw everything but yourself?*'

'Something is really wrong,' Yiannis said, eventually.

'I know.'

'Something is really wrong,' he repeated, this time more to himself, as he scratched a knot in the wood of the table with his nail. His foot shook intermittently underneath his chair, which made the table tremble and the coffee cups rattle in their saucers. He seemed to be thinking, thinking, thinking. I imagined his mind spinning and I tried to keep mine still.

'At first I thought I might have scared her away,' he said.

'Why?'

'The night before she went missing, I asked her to marry me.'

'You wanted to marry her?'

The table stopped trembling. He exhaled deeply and bought his hand up to his face again, this time rubbing his thumb and forefinger towards each other across his eyes, as if he was scooping up tears before they fell.

'I found a ring on her dressing table. So that was from you.'

He nodded and glanced up at me, as if he was now worried about my reaction.

I wondered what conversations they may have had: the discussions about Nisha losing her job, just like other maids who had become embroiled in relationships. They were meant to be working and even when they were resting, we owned them. This was the unspoken truth.

Had his proposal scared her away? Was this a possibility? It would have been simpler and much less frightening to cling to this thought, but the piece of paper in front of us fluttered slightly in the breeze as if it was trying to take flight.

'Please,' I said. 'Have a look at these names. Do you recognise them?'

He picked up the piece of paper and read it. 'No. She's never mentioned them to me.'

'You're sure?'

He nodded. 'I would have remembered.'

'Mrs Hadjikyriacou told me she saw Nisha the night she went missing, at ten thirty, heading north up towards the buffer zone.'

'That's the street that leads to Maria's,' he said, nodding. 'Yes.'

He thought for a while. 'Spyros – the postman – told me he saw her rushing along the street. Apparently she told him that she was going to Maria's to meet Seraphim.'

I frowned. 'Seraphim, your colleague?'

'Yes.'

'I bumped into him at Maria's on Friday night. I stopped in to leave a flyer and talk to the manager. What connection does Seraphim have with Nisha?'

'Nothing, as far as I know. She'd met him and his wife a few times, that's all.'

'Have you spoken to him?'

'He denied seeing her or arranging to meet her.'

'Do you believe him?'

He didn't reply.

'Something's not right there,' I said.

Yiannis went into the living room and returned with a handful of red berries, which he placed on the table. The bird ate them one by one. I watched Yiannis as he watched the bird eat. There was a softness to this man; he seemed to have a gentle and troubled soul.

'What about Kumari?' I said. 'Won't she be trying to contact her mother? The girl must be beside herself with worry now, if she hasn't heard from her.'

'Nisha used to speak to Kumari at my place.'

I nodded, not knowing what to say, feeling ashamed that I had not known this.

'I've spoken to Kumari,' he continued. 'I'm trying not to worry her too much until we know more.'

I nodded again, concerned.

'Leave it with me,' he said. 'Kumari knows me. I'll deal with it.'

'Thank you,' I said.

'At least we can agree that she was heading in the direction of Maria's.'

'Yes. That is one thing, at least.' But it felt like nothing. 'Can't we check her bank account,' I said, 'to see if money has been taken from it?'

'It's not possible to check her account without the police.'

He offered me another coffee, but I declined. I had left Aliki alone and I needed to make dinner; it would be getting dark soon.

'Listen,' I said, as I headed to the kitchen door, 'this guy – Tony – he's going to call me to arrange a meeting with

240

the employer and the sister of the other missing women. Would you come with me?'

'Of course,' he said, immediately. 'Thank you, Petra.'

'Thank you, too,' I said.

As I walked back down the stairs, my feet were heavy and I felt tears begin to well in my throat. I wasn't ready to face Aliki yet – I didn't want her to know I had been crying – so I made my way over to the abandoned rowing boat and got in. Clutching my sweater around me, I sat on the rough wooden plank and thought about the day that Nisha had first arrived from Sri Lanka.

It was spring, a week after Stephanos had died; I was thirty-two weeks pregnant. I had prayed that he would live to meet our baby. Before his illness, I'd envisioned our future like a storybook: we would have a beautiful garden full of fruit and flowers; Stephanos was going to build a small BBQ out of brick, on the far right by the cactus; we would have two children. We'd made these plans before I even got pregnant. If someone had told me then that soon my only hope would be that my husband would live long enough to see his only child just once, I would never have believed them. We didn't understand how bad things would get: neither of us had any experience with cancer. We had assumed that things would be tough for a while, and then return to normal. Treatment. Remission. Like so many others.

Then, one day, I had had to carry my husband to the car. With the help of a neighbour, we lifted him into the seat and we drove in silence to the hospital. My husband's eyes were yellow and his hands black, and we carried him, twelve

241

months pregnant with bile, over the threshold to no man's land.

That Christmas Eve, when he could not lift his arms or his eyelids or his lips to smile, I kissed him. I fed him and brushed his hair and filled the creases around his eyes with cream, then I folded the white sheet beneath his chin and tucked it in around his bones and waited for him to say, 'I'm here.'

He lay in his faeces with a catheter and a keepsake from the church, and drank soup through a straw. He had no voice and no hope and no more days left.

After he was gone, a blur of people came. My mother was still alive in those days and she and my father would turn up together, at any time of the day, with shopping bags and oven-dishes of warm moussaka – which they knew was my favourite. They tried so hard to keep me from sinking. Later, after my mother's fatal stroke, my father bought a boat and moved to Greece, finding his solace on the sea where he always belonged.

Friends and neighbours visited. They would ring the doorbell, come and go like ghosts. I had hot food and hot cups of tea. They tried to keep the house tidy. They made sure I ate and bathed and slept. They bought gifts for the baby: yellow gifts – candy yellow, sunshine yellow. Life-before-death yellow. Stephanos and I had chosen the room facing the orange tree for the nursery, so that's where I stored the gifts in a pile, like a castle, on top of a changing table.

I drifted through it all, but I was not there. My mind was stuck in the life we had planned; it could not fathom this new reality. All the evidence was that Stephanos was still there. His clothes and military gear were in the wardrobe. His aftershave and cufflinks on the dressing table. His razor by the sink in the bathroom. The canister of his shaving foam still had froth on its tip. His hair was still in the comb. His shoes in the wardrobe. Our bed still held his smell.

Nisha arrived soon after. She was dropped off by the agent's representative. She had one small suitcase and copper eyes. She wore a black dress, the material too fine for the cold weather. She stood by the door behind the agency woman, looking around, then her eyes settled on me. The woman – Koula or Voula – wore a grey suit and had a blonde bob and was talking, but I wasn't really listening. I remember signing the contract on the dining table, while Nisha stood watching by the door.

'You've got a good one,' the woman said. 'She speaks English. My girl is from Nepal and doesn't know a word. It's a nightmare, I'll tell you.'

Thankfully, that was the end of the conversation.

When the woman left, I showed my girl to her room. She put her suitcase down by the bed and asked me if she could open the blinds. For the first time in a long time, the sun came in.

Dust floated about in the light. I hadn't been in this room for ages. My girl walked around touching the bedcovers and dressing table and armchair with the tips of her fingers.

'Madam,' she said, 'thank you for this beautiful room. You are very kind. Some of my friends said that I might have a dark room sleeping on the floor.'

'I don't think that's true,' I said. 'We look after our maids here.'
She nodded.

'When is the baby coming?' she asked.

'In a few weeks.'

'I have a little girl in Sri Lanka. Her name is Kumari. She is two years of age.'

I didn't know what to say. I had no energy and no desire to hear about her life, or anybody else's, for that matter. There were no questions inside me.

Her eyes flitted to my stomach and then she glanced again around the room.

'You can have a rest,' I said, 'after your long journey. Settle in, unpack, have a good sleep and start work tomorrow.'

'Thank you, madam.'

'Then you'll be working from 6 a.m. to 7 p.m. Monday to Saturday, with a two-hour break in the afternoon. You'll have Sundays off. When you're not working in the evening, I expect you to rest in your room so that you are fresh for work the next day.'

She nodded and said nothing.

'You have very unusual eyes,' I said.

'Thank you, madam. At school my friends called me "mango-eyes".' She smiled now, and her face was radiant. I left the room and closed the door behind me.

From then on, Nisha slowly brought the house back to life. She made me fresh eggs with toast and tea every morning. She cleaned until the marble floors sparkled, the kitchen spotless. On the mantelpiece, the photo of Stephanos stood polished in its silver frame.

244

Mostly I stayed out of her way. The baby was due soon, and I was working as much as I could, putting in extra hours at the shop. I came home at night exhausted and falling into bed, barely eating the dinners Nisha would prepare.

But, one evening, I looked up at Nisha and smiled at her. 'Thank you,' I said. 'You've done a fantastic job.'

She nodded and smiled. 'I'm glad you're happy, madam,' she replied. Then, after a moment's hesitation, she went on: 'But there is something I need your help with.'

I followed her to the nursery. She had folded all the yellow clothes and put them away, in the drawers and cupboards. She had washed and ironed the bed sheets and throws, and made up the cot.

'It's very nice, Nisha.'

'But it is not beautiful yet,' she said.

On the changing table were ornaments and toys, gifts I barely remembered.

'I wonder, could you help me to decide where these will go?'

She picked up a snow globe and shook it – white glitter swirled around a cat with four suckling kittens at her teats. 'Where shall I place this?'

'Anywhere you like.'

'I think it's the job of the mother to decide.'

'Fine,' I said. 'On the dressing table.'

She went over to the dressing table and placed to the left of the mirror. 'Here?' she asked.

'That'll do.'

'Or how about in the middle?' She pushed the snow globe over a few inches and turned to look at me. I said nothing.

Then she picked up a string garland for the wall. White fluffy clouds and wooden stars. 'And this, madam? Over the crib, or on this wall on the other side?'

'Either will be fine.'

She contemplated for a moment and held them up over the crib and finally decided to place them on the wall adjacent to the patio doors. I watched her as she did it. Concentrating, making sure they all lined up neatly. Then there were fairy lights of moons and stars, a bedside lamp of a cottage where the windows lit up, rainbow building blocks, a family of teddy bears, cactus ornaments, a yellow pillow with the word Dream embroidered on it, and some tiny animals made of felt – a bird, a hedgehog and two bears. She placed each item with purpose and care and soon the room had been transformed. The bedside lamp glowed in the darkening evening light, a beautiful, welcoming little house.

Then she took me to my room. The bed was neatly made, the mirrored wardrobes had been cleaned and the room smelled of polish.

'I will leave all your husband's things until you tell me.'

I was grateful for this.

But, eventually, I let her clean out my husband's belongings. I felt a throb of shame that I could not bring myself to do the task, but by then I had become so used to letting Nisha do everything for me – and for the baby, when she eventually arrived – that it took almost nothing to turn to

246

the window and sip my coffee, Aliki asleep in her bassinet, while Nisha removed every trace of my marriage from the room.

I suddenly noticed that Aliki was standing in the garden looking at me. She was holding Monkey.

'Does that cat belong to us now?' I asked, pretending to be cross.

'Ask him,' she said. At that, she released Monkey, who took the opportunity to spread out on the ground and set about licking himself. Then Aliki stepped into the boat with me.

'I'm hungry,' she said. 'Are you going to make supper?'

'Yes. Yes, my baby, I will make it in a moment. I'm sorry it's gotten so late.'

'That's OK. But I am hungry.'

'I know,' I said. 'But first, would you tell me about the Sea Above the Sky? I'm feeling sad. I'm missing Nisha and I think I would like to hear a story.'

She looked at me for a moment, then said, 'OK, then. Close your eyes.'

I did as she said.

'You mustn't peep. I can tell if you are peeping!'

I scrunched up my eyes, to prove that I wouldn't cheat.

'Most boats go forwards and backwards, but this one goes upwards,' she said. 'Into the sky. We have to go through the layers of sky and then we get to the sea.'

'Isn't the sea on the ground?' I asked.

'No. And don't interrupt. Just be patient,' Aliki said.

247

I smiled at the scolding. *Just be patient.* Those words reminded me of Stephanos. I was always more eager than him to get on with things, to make plans, to get married, to get pregnant. *Chill out, Petra. Just be patient.* It's not because he didn't love me, I had no doubt about that, but he was a man who wanted to take everything a step at a time, slowly, as if we had all the time in the world. It was also how we made love, so unrushed, so slow, and it made me go crazy for him.

'We're there,' Aliki said. 'But don't open your eyes.'

I nodded and kept my eyes closed.

'Up here it's eight hours ahead,' she said, 'so the sun is coming up. But *just* coming up, so it's still kind of dark. The sea is shiny, all silver and gold. The sea is as wide as the sky, it never ends, so you can sail above any country in the whole world. When you look down through the water, you can see the earth, all the trees and rivers and houses. And the people.'

'Are there people up here, too?' I asked.

'Sometimes, but not today. There are plenty of birds, though. They are birds that have died and now they are here and they make promises to each other. Some of them used to be human and they came here to find each other again. But not all – some of them were birds before.'

I opened my eyes now and looked at my daughter. Her hair was wild about her shoulders, and shining a deep glossy brown. She was wearing her pyjamas and her wrists and ankles seemed to be bursting from them. How had she grown, this child of mine? I could see the past in her eyes, Stephanos looking out at me, just for a second, before the memory of him vanished and then there was only Aliki. Aliki. Aliki in her own right. With her beautiful almost-translucent skin and silver veins on her lids and flushed cheeks and soft ridge in her brow and cheek bones like half-moons. She took my breath away.

The cat jumped on my lap and rubbed its head against my arm, my shoulder and my face, its soft purr close to my ear.

'Can we have dinner now, Mum?' she asked.

Mum.

'Yes,' I said.

'Mum?'

'Yes?'

'I miss Nisha.'

'Yes,' I said. 'So do I.'

'Is she coming back?' Aliki asked.

'I don't think so, but I don't know for sure.'

'Are you trying to find her?

'I am.'

Aliki was quiet for a while and then in a very serious voice she said, 'She was worried about the birds.'

'The birds?' I said.

'The ones that get trapped on the lime sticks by their feathers and legs. She was going to tell the man to stop stealing all the birds from the sky.'

'What man?'

'He's called Seraphim.'

I tried not to react. I chose my words carefully. 'Did she go to speak to him?' I said, as gently as I could.

'Yes. When we came back from the mountains. When she tucked me into bed, she told me that she was going out to talk to the bad man about the birds and that I should be a good girl and stay in bed. You know, because sometimes I need to wee and I knock on her door because it's too scary at night for me to go to the toilet all on my own.'

I didn't know that, but I nodded.

'I think we should go back now,' she said. 'The waves are getting bigger. We can come again another night.'

I nodded.

'Would you like to come up here again?' she said.

Once more I nodded, but I found that I couldn't speak.

The man with the army boots is walking out of the water, wet to his ribcage. He is completely dressed in black, with a windbreaker that has an orange trim around the lapel. Guided by the light of the moon, he bends down to pick up his phone, which he has left on the yellow rock by the side of the lake, and makes his way up the crater until he comes across the decomposing hare. He flashes the light of his phone over the corpse. A beetle climbs out of the empty eye socket.

The man walks away from the lake, picking up a black rucksack that he's left beneath a wild thyme bush; he catches the smell as he bends, and he pauses for a moment and inhales the scent with closed and distant eyes. Perhaps he is trying to replace the smell of death, which is clinging to his nostrils. With the rucksack over his shoulder, he walks a few yards to his car. He does not turn on the headlights as he drives away.

20

Yiannis

EARLY IN THE MORNING, THERE was a knock at the door. I jumped out of bed thinking it was Nisha, but Petra was standing there, looking pale as the moon.

'Can I come in?' she said.

'Sure.'

She was wearing pyjama bottoms and a white T-shirt. She had dark circles under her eyes. 'I haven't slept,' she said.

I led her into the kitchen and put the coffee on the stove. She looked up at the wall clock.

'My god, I didn't realise it was that early.'

She seemed disoriented in the chair, trembling hands in her lap, shoulders sagging. She reminded me of a moth. Usually she was so put-together. This wasn't a woman who cuddled or cried. She did not fall apart. Her name, Petra, means 'stone'. I'd never really liked her, to be honest. She was the wall that stood between Nisha and me. Her, and the whole damn system.

The little bird hopped around on the windowsill, bobbing its head, looking at the world outside.

'It wants to fly,' she mumbled.

'Yes. But it's not quite ready yet. It won't survive if I release it now.' I placed the coffee in front of her and she took a few large gulps. 'Watch it,' I said, 'it's scorching,' but she didn't seem to hear.

'I have some more information,' she said.

I sat down opposite her. My heart beat fast but I tried to keep calm.

'I was talking to Aliki last night. She said that on the night that Nisha went missing, she had put Aliki to bed and told her that she was going out to meet a man about birds.'

I straightened, heat creeping up my neck. 'Who?'

'Seraphim. According to Aliki, he was stealing birds out of the sky and Nisha wanted to make him stop.'

I felt sick.

'The thing is,' she continued, 'I've been up all night thinking, trying to work things out, but I'm missing all the pieces. If there is something you're not telling me, Yiannis, I think now is the time to do it.'

She said my name with bitterness, as if she knew I was guilty of something. And I was. I could tell she knew by the way she had drawn her shoulders back now, challenging me. This was the Petra I knew.

'*Is* there something I should know?' she said.

I instinctively looked over to the spare room.

'Look, I'm not messing about.'

'Neither am I,' I said.

'What is this thing with Seraphim and the birds? I know you know something.'

I got up and asked her to follow me to the spare room. I unlocked the door and we went in. She looked around at the fridges, the lime sticks and the hunting gear.

'Right.' She opened the fridge closest to her, looked inside, turning her face away immediately, closing it. 'So this is what you do.' It wasn't a question.

'I got involved when I was made redundant. I got in and couldn't get out.'

'Nisha knew?'

'Eventually, yes.'

'She was trying to get you to stop?'

'Yes.' I felt a wave of guilt surge through me. So big that warm liquid came up to my throat, and I remembered again Nisha's flesh and blood in the toilet.

'And Seraphim?'

'He's above me. The middle man.'

'How do they stop you from getting out?'

'Usually arson. They come at night. That's the first warning.'

'And the second?'

I didn't reply.

She nodded now and looked around the room, thinking.

'So, Nisha went to talk to Seraphim. She wanted to help to free you. Could he have hurt her?'

'I don't think so.'

'You don't sound too sure.'

I stood up and opened all the windows; my neck and face were on fire.

'She went to speak to him, then she vanished. She went to speak to him, then she *vanished*. Do you understand that?'

'Of course I do.'

'We can't go to the police.'

'No.'

'You need to find out what happened, Yiannis.'

'Yes,' I said. 'I will.'

I called Seraphim and arranged to meet him that night. He told me he would be at Maria's from 10 p.m.

'Join me anytime you want,' he said. 'I'll be there. I'm always there.'

In the meantime, I couldn't sit down, I couldn't eat, I couldn't think about anything else. I was supposed to be putting the birds in their containers and sorting them for delivery, but I spent the whole day sitting on the bed where Nisha and I used to talk and make love, staring out of the window at the street below and trying to piece the story together: I asked her to marry me. She left holding the ring. She went to speak to Seraphim. She wanted to free me. She was not seen again.

That night, I walked passed the flyers of Nisha posted around the neighbourhood. Nobody had called Petra. I watched people walk by and Nisha's smiling face looking out at them. They did not see her.

I found Seraphim sitting at a small round table near the

bar. There was a young woman sitting with him, petite with large, brown eyes – like that of a child – hair as black as coal, leaning into him, smelling his neck.

'Off you go,' he said to her, when I arrived. She obeyed. I watched her as she walked over to another table where two old men sat smoking. One of them removed some food from his tooth with his finger. The other stubbed out his cigarette. Whose fag-yellow breath would she be inhaling tonight? I hated these men. I was not one of them, I was sure of that. Had Nisha become involved in sex work? Had she got herself trapped? Maybe she was desperate to make extra money, desperate to get out of here, to get back to Kumari. There was desperation everywhere in this place: it dripped from the windows in condensation, it made the tables wet.

Seraphim clicked his fingers. A sound so sharp that I turned to face him. A waitress glided towards us with an empty silver tray.

'Two whiskies, my dolly,' he said.

'No, I don't want to drink.'

He ignored me.

'I was with her last night,' he said, flicking his eyes towards the woman sitting with the old men. 'She's lovely.'

I looked away. His face was making me feel sick.

'You've been jittery lately,' he said. 'I hope you're well.'

He didn't hope I was well. He hoped I wasn't bailing out. I'd heard him say the exact same thing to Louis before they'd burnt down his car – with his son in it.

The waitress returned with two glasses of whisky. She placed them on the table, one for me, one for Seraphim.

'Go on,' he said, 'you look like you need it.'

I downed the whole glass in one without flinching, just to get the damn thing out of the way. 'Seraphim,' I said, 'I miss Nisha, and I need to know what happened to her. Two people have confirmed that she was coming to meet you here the night she went missing. Please. Tell me what happened that night.'

I didn't know how else to put it. I could hear the desperation in my voice, see my pathetic self in his eyes.

He glared at me. He smiled. Deep lines around his mouth.

'This is the problem with being *in love*,' he said. 'It always creates a mess, and I like to keep things tidy, if you know what I mean?'

'So she came to see you?' I persisted.

He glanced around, over his shoulder. 'I'll tell you what,' he said. 'I don't like talking about these things in public. How about we go to mine, have a drink there?'

He downed his whisky and stood up before I replied. He left some notes on the bar, winked at the barmaid and I followed him outside and along the street to his car.

We got into his Jaguar, doors opening like wings. The interior, soft leather. He had a top-of-the-range sound system and the engine purred like a tiger. I turned my face towards the window as he goosed the gas pedal and we flew into the night.

I'd never been inside Seraphim's house before. It was a gated, white monstrosity with pillars and blue-tinted windows that looked like the sky. It was on a hill and looked down on the Famagusta Gate. It seemed to jut out of the earth at a strange angle; it reminded me of a huge cruise liner on a choppy sea.

When we stepped into the living room, a maid was standing on a chair in the middle of the room. She looked like she was in her fifties, a short woman with enormous breasts that she seemed to be carrying like an extra weight. A few lamps were on in the room and she was cleaning the chandelier – a huge crystal eyesore. When she saw us, she climbed down and turned on the main light. The crystals shimmered, the light sending thousands of orbs around the room.

'I have finished, sir,' she said, looking at Seraphim.

'Good girl. Did you do all the other things on the list?'

She nodded.

'You didn't leave anything out like last time?'

'No, sir.'

'OK, go and get us some nuts and a couple of whiskies. Put them in the back room.' He turned to me and said, 'You should always keep your lights clean.'

The maid gathered her cleaning supplies and shuffled out of the room.

'We have a dinner party tomorrow – my niece is christening her first child and the whole family is coming here. My wife is probably in bed. Let's go to the garage, we can talk privately in there,' Seraphim said.

We walked through a hallway of white marble – it was everywhere: the floors, the walls. Vivid paintings lined the walls, so extraordinary they were almost alive. Images of Troodos, orchards, streams, farms. One in particular grabbed my attention: an old man with a white goatee, large hands and black trousers, a deep crease in his brow, carrying what looked like a bag of wool across a field.

'Is that—?'

'Yes,' Seraphim said behind me.

'Why?'

'These are my memories.'

I looked at the man's face more closely, remembering my grandfather. I could almost smell the funk of sheep coming off him. Then I noticed the background, the landscape stretching out behind him, green and luscious with vegetation, but down in the valley a fire, raging, and threatening to grow and expand up the hills. There had never been a fire like this as far as I could recall.

'Why is there a fire?' I asked.

'It's the war,' he said, matter-of-factly. 'And other things.'

'What other things?'

'The things that threaten all that is natural and beautiful and right with the world.'

It was then that I noticed for the first time a sadness in his expression. It reminded me of Seraphim as a boy, before the rifles, before the black crow. Something came back to me, a boy with sad eyes standing on the trunk of a fallen tree, pretending it was a mountain, saying, 'Look down there, Yiannis!'

The past echoed along the corridor. Seraphim placed a hand on my shoulder. 'Now take a look at this one,' he said.

The next painting was simply of an apple tree full of ripe

fruit, a blue sky behind it. Bright greens, yellows and blues contrasted with shadows of deep red and purple.

'That's the tree outside my house, back in the day, isn't it?'

'Yes.'

'These are phenomenal.' I could feel myself being sucked back, drawn to a time almost forgotten. I found myself surrounded by my past.

'You painted these?'

'Of course,' he said.

Then I remembered Seraphim's father. A prominent heart surgeon and hunter. Always suited and booted, even when he had a gun in his hand. He had hard eyes, that man, and a quiet but harsh tone that left Seraphim and me trembling.

Before I could say anything more, Seraphim continued on down the hallway. At the end of the long corridor was a wooden door that he unlocked with a silver key. The door opened up into a large garage, which looked more like a showroom. Three beautiful cars gleamed like water beneath halogen lights.

'Extraordinary,' I said, in spite of myself. I hadn't come here to see his cars. I wanted to talk about Nisha. He was distracting me, I could tell. He had a habit of doing this, throwing you off course.

'This one is a Lamborghini Miura. A mid-engine supercar.' He waved his hand at the nearest car, and beamed. I decided to humour Seraphim in all this, to get him in a good frame of mind.

'Metallic green,' I said, 'with tan leather seats. Very stylish.'

261

'Now take a look at this one,' he said.

'Wow. The Porsche 911.'

'Magic! Special order Lava Orange.'

I looked inside at the black leather interior with orange stitching and seat belts.

'This beauty has a 7-speed PDK transmission.'

'And a switchable sports exhaust system?'

'Of course.'

'Impressive,' I said.

We walked around to the silver Mercedes SL 300 Gullwing. It was beautiful. He put his hand into his pocket and pressed a fob, the lights flashed and he opened the doors on both sides, asking me to step back as if it were about to explode.

'Now, look at it,' he said. 'Didn't I tell you? Doesn't it look like it's about to fly?'

'Higher than an eagle. This is a car dreams are made of.'

He smiled in the way he had when he was a boy, after he killed Batman.

'Now the ice will be melting.'

'The ice?'

'Our whiskies. We almost forgot them.' He closed the doors of the car and clicked the fob in his pocket to lock it.

'I want to talk about Nisha.'

'Sure,' he paused, waiting. When I stayed silent, he said, 'Go ahead.'

'She came to see you the night she vanished?'

'She didn't arrive.'

His evasiveness was making my blood boil. He was playing with me. 'But she'd arranged to meet you?'

'Yes.' His eyes remained fixed on mine.

'Why didn't you tell me this, when I asked you this two weeks ago?'

'She's got guts, your girl, I'll tell you that. She called me, said she'd got my number from you. Said she needed to speak to me about you – she wanted me to let you go. I told her, of course, that that wasn't possible and reminded her kindly to mind her own business. That this was not the kind of thing she should be getting involved with, that she'd get herself into trouble. She insisted – she doesn't give up, your girl, I'll tell you that. She said she had something to offer me that I wouldn't be able to refuse.'

'What?'

'I have no idea. She never showed. She was meant to meet me at Maria's late that night. I waited. She never showed. I didn't mention it because your loyalty to us is solid, is it not? I didn't want to open up a pointless conversation, you know what I mean? I expect your girl will turn up in no time.' Before I could say anything, he waved his hand and smiled like nothing fazed him. 'Now, which is your favourite car?' he asked.

'Excuse me?'

'Which of these three cars do you most admire?'

'I don't have a preference' I said.

'Choose one, will you?'

'The Gullwing.'

'It's yours.'

I remained silent.

'Stunned, huh? Never thought you'd be in possession of such a beautiful specimen? Now look, if you exceed your target before the end of the season, it's yours.'

'I don't want your car,' I said.

'Consider it yours already. You've never let me down.'

'Seraphim,' I said, fixing my eyes on his, 'I'm telling you now that I don't want your car. Or any other reward, for that matter.'

'I see,' he said, nodding, and I saw a slight twitch beneath his right eye.

I glanced at my watch.

'I've got to go,' I said.

'There's whisky and snacks,' he said, but I told him that I had to get going. I needed to get out of there.

When I got back to the neighbourhood, it was just past midnight. I was about to go upstairs to my apartment, but something stopped me. I looked about the street almost as if I could see Nisha's footsteps, as if she'd left prints in the sand for me to follow, or crumbs for a little bird. I started walking down the street. This is the way she would have gone, heading toward Maria's.

Silver moths flew below the street lamps. Theo was just closing up for the night. He lifted his arm to greet me; I nodded. I watched the road ahead, imagined her walking. What had she been wearing? Would she have held a handbag? Hair up or down? Why hadn't I asked Spyros? I painted a picture of her for myself. Nisha in jeans and an orange jumper, the one with the sunflower on the front. She was wearing her new black trainers, the ones Petra had bought her. Hair in a ponytail. She was concerned, serious, on a mission to sort my life out. I saw her walking ahead of me, turning right onto the street where I had seen Spyros; the street lined with lemon trees where corrugated metal sheets spilt the island in two. There weeds grow. There is a dead apple tree. There is a row of mostly abandoned shops and workshops, shutters always drawn, doors bolted, some don't have doors or front walls – they were once cloth and carpet stores; some sold copper, and now they are empty.

Then Muyia's studio, dark, no one in there, his sculptures covered in white cloth. It had been a while since I'd spoken to Muyia. Could he have been there that night?

And there, at the end of the street, Christos lived in his old shack – might he have seen her? Could he have been outside? Would she have waved or stopped? The windows were dark now. I knocked. Nothing. I knocked again. Then footsteps, shuffling around. 'Who is it?'

'Yiannis!'

He didn't hear. 'I said who is it?' The door opened and he stood there in boxer shorts, pointing a hunting rifle at me. When he saw my face, he lowered it. 'What the fuck are you doing? Fuck you!' The few hairs he had stuck up on his tanned head.

'I'm sorry, Christos. I know it's late, very late.'

He narrowed his eyes at me. 'Come in,' he said.

The living room and kitchen were one room. There were

doilies everywhere – on the coffee table, the mantlepiece, the back of the sofa. People in black and white photos stared out at me from all directions. We'd spoken many times in the front yard, but I'd never been inside.

'Take a seat.' He pointed at an armchair next to the unlit fireplace. It was cold in there, but he didn't seem to notice.

'I'm sorry I woke you.'

'I'd just gone to bed. No big deal. Can I offer you a drink and a sweet?'

'Just some water,' I said. I was parched after the whisky.

'When did you take up smoking?' he asked, filling up a glass from the tap. 'You fucking reek.'

'I was at Maria's.'

'Oh, yeah?' He raised his eyebrows, placing the glass on a doily on the coffee table.

I gulped it down.

'Still poaching?'

I nodded. Christos was a hunter, not a poacher. He followed the rules of the hunting seasons, was respectful of regulations, and made a measly living.

'I need to ask you a question,' I said.

'Go ahead. Figuring it's as important as fuck for you to knock after midnight.'

'Can you think back to three Sundays ago. Were you home?'

'Well, let me see.' He rested his glass of water on his huge hairy gut. 'Last Sunday I was in Larnaca, I know that. The Sunday before I was cleaning the car.' He leaned forward, placed the glass on the table and picked up his phone. He

266

scrolled through. 'So the one before that would have been the thirtieth?'

'Yes.'

'I was home that day.'

'Are you sure?'

'Yes. I have here: *Loula visiting with lunatic kids.* Yes. My sister came to visit with her crazy grandkids. I made us all lunch. She left around eight o'clock that evening.'

'After that?'

'I sat outside with Pavlo from down the road. I remember it well because it was the night he'd got the all clear. He had cancer, poor chap. We played backgammon for a couple of hours.'

'Did you see Nisha that night?'

'Who?' Christos asked.

'Oh, um, Petra's girl. Her name is Nisha.'

'Well, let me see . . .' He glanced up at the ceiling. 'I'm pretty sure I saw Spyros with that stupid dog of his, because he stopped to ask Pavlo about his results. It was a quiet night, not much going on. Then there was the maid. Yes, it was Petra's girl, I think. She was rushing past here like she'd missed an appointment.'

'Before or after Spyros?'

'Actually, just before. By a couple of minutes. Pavlo commented, I remember – he called out, "Come here, my little girl! You're a stunner! I'll do you when my dick works again." He'd had too much to drink. Way too much.' He laughed, his belly shaking under his T-shirt.

I paused for a moment and tried to empty my head of

those words, but they'd already gotten under my skin and I could feel my palms sweating.

'Did she say anything?'

'Nothing.'

'Do you remember what she was wearing?'

'I seem to recall black . . . Yes, a black dress. When she left, Pavlo said he wanted to get under it. Unzip it like the night, see the light underneath – those were his exact drunken words.' I flinched. Christos laughed even more now, rubbing his stomach, a throaty phlegmy laugh.

'Was her hair up or down?'

'Down. Ahhh, that thick, long hair. Who could not notice that? Imagine rubbing your face in it. I bet it smells like apples.'

I felt the anger again. I got up, apologised for getting him out of bed and quickly took my leave.

On my way home, I retraced Nisha's footsteps again. I could see her more clearly now. Black dress, hair down, the way it would have shone under the streetlights, light waves. I could see her rushing, turning the corner . . . Pavlo calling out, *Come here, my little girl! You're a stunner! I'll do you when my dick works again.* Then laughter. There must have been laughter. And Nisha's eyes, narrowing, lips tight, head up, thinking she wanted to belt him. That's how I imagine her. And let's take Seraphim's word for it and assume she didn't make it to Maria's. Then what? What happened to her between Christos's and Maria's? Could she have climbed over the fence? Gone into the buffer zone? But why? There was no reason for her to do this.

I could see her fingers now, dangling by her side. Calf

muscles, lean and strong as she walked. I could smell her, the faint whiff of gardens and spices and bleach.

Then she might have seen Spyros, greeted him, bent down to pet the poodle. Probably laughed at whatever silly outfit Spyros had put the dog in that night. Maybe he'd hummed the theme from *Raiders of the Lost Ark*, maybe she'd hummed it back. Perhaps she'd had it in her head as she turned the corner.

I could hear her heart beating. A clear and cold night with a full moon. Just like tonight. Why was she rushing? Seraphim wasn't the type to have left if she was late. Unless there was another reason.

When I got home, I put all the birds into their rightful containers for the last time. I worked like a madman. I would never do it again. I should have stopped the moment I had promised Nisha and faced the consequences. She had been trying to help me, she had been trying to free me and then she was gone. If I had stopped like she'd asked me to, Nisha would have still been here. I was sure of that. My body felt heavy; I felt like there were weights on my wrists and ankles.

It took me a few hours to complete the job, working through the night. The entire time my mind retraced Nisha's steps, over and over again. I saw her in her black dress. Every time, at the end of Christos's street, she vanished. I couldn't place her after that. I couldn't imagine what had happened. It was like the ground had swallowed her up, and I remembered again Nisha's retelling of her husband's death: *The earth has swallowed him up the earth swallowed him up he has been swallowed whole by the earth.*

As soon as the tablet rang I jumped up to answer it. The sight of Kumari in her uniform, hair tied up in a ponytail like her mother, purple rucksack on her shoulders, sent a sharp pain through my head.

'Is Amma looking after the chickens again?'

'That's right.'

She looked up at the sky. I could see that she was outside this time. She took a sip from a drink with a straw.

'Are the chickens sick?'

'Yes. They seem to be.'

'Mr Yiannis, you are lying!'

'No, I'm not.'

'Yes. I know when a person is lying.'

'How?'

'Because they say silly things that they don't realise are silly things.'

'What did I say that was silly?'

'You said Amma was looking after the chickens.'

'That's because you asked me if she was.'

'But my question was a lie. Because I knew you had a lie in your sleeve. It is three o'clock in the morning where you are. I know that Amma wouldn't tend to the chickens in the middle of the night!'

I couldn't help laughing. 'Your English is very good.'

'I know. Amma teaches me on the iPad and I learn at

270

school too. And I have an auntie who is married to an Englishman up in the cold mountains and they teach me too.'

'Well,' I said, 'that's excellent.'

'Today I have my favourite subject at school.'

'What's that, then?'

'History.'

'Lovely. What do you like about it?'

'I like it because I see how people were silly in the past.'

'Like my lie with the chickens?'

'Yes.' She smiled that cheeky smile again. Then her face became serious. 'So, where is my amma?'

'I don't know, Kumari.' I couldn't lie to this girl anymore. 'I'm not sure. Usually she speaks to you on my iPad from my home, but she hasn't come to see me for a while.'

'That's unusual.' Though her voice was light, her eyes were suddenly heavy and dark.

'Why is that then?'

'Well, because you are Mr Yiannis and my amma said she loves Mr Yiannis very much because he is such a good and kind man. Why would she not come to see you if she loves you very much?'

I couldn't answer her question. In spite of her confusion and anxiety her eyes sparkled once more.

'I will call again tomorrow and I hope that she is there. You be good at work now, Mr Yiannis,' she said, and then she was gone.

21

Petra

'STILL NO SIGN OF NISHA?'

Keti was leaning on the counter, staring at me.

I filled Keti in about Nisha's relationship with Yiannis, about our discovery that Nisha had been going to visit Seraphim, and how Yiannis was going to confront him.

'Gosh,' she said. 'That's a lot to take in. So, she was on her way to meet this man, Seraphim, about poaching birds and she disappears into thin air?'

'Exactly.'

'I don't like it.'

Her words made me sink into a nearby chair.

'And Yiannis – can you trust him?'

'I think so.'

'You look exhausted,' she said.

272

'I couldn't sleep last night.'

She examined the bracelet so closely, as if she was determined to find an answer within it. Then she sighed, seemingly at a loss. She placed the bracelet in my palm and squeezed my hand. 'Go home,' she said, 'get some rest. If you burn out it won't be helpful for anyone.'

My head was pounding with a dull ache, my eyes bleary. I needed to sleep. Aliki was still at school for a few hours, so I could get in a good nap before I had to go and collect her.

But after I parked the car, my feet wouldn't carry me to my front door. Instead, I found myself walking in the direction of Muyia's workshop.

'Hello?' I called, but no one answered. As I'd hoped, Muyia wasn't there. People in Cyprus used to leave all their doors open in the past, and it was as if Muyia was stuck in those bygone days. But that was good, as it wasn't him I was here to see: it was Nisha. I quickly headed over to the sculptures next to the worktop. I pulled the white sheet off and there she was, the mother and child. I put my hand on her hand and leaned my head on the worktop. Nisha had sacrificed so much to come here and I had never allowed myself to know that. Now she was gone.

I imagined the wood being hollow, and her trapped inside. I thought that if I found the seam in the wood that I could lift it and open it up like a Russian doll, and find her there.

'Petra,' a voice said, sharply.

I opened my eyes to cold light, a breeze and a person standing above me.

'Petra. What are you doing here?'

I straightened up. Muyia was staring at me, perplexed.

'How long have you been here?'

I stood up and backed away from him. His eyes were fixed on me.

'Not long,' I said. I glanced at the statue and he followed my gaze. 'Is that Nisha?' I managed to say.

'Yes. And the little child is her daughter, Kumari.'

'Why?'

He blinked a few times but said nothing.

'How did you know we were going to the mountains?' I asked.

'What do you mean?'

'The other week, when I passed here you said, "How was your trip to the mountains?" How did you know?'

His brow creased and I saw something moving at his side: he was scratching his arm.

'Nisha visits me a couple of times a week. You know, on her way to the grocery store – that sort of thing. She brings me fruit from your garden, whatever's in season. Until recently she bought me oranges. Still a bit bitter, but they were fine.'

I stared at him.

'She says I'm a lonely man who needs a woman in his life.' He laughed. 'And besides, she likes to tell me stories.'

'Stories?'

'You know, about Kumari and her life back in Sri Lanka. Also about her sister and the owl.'

The owl. I had no idea what he meant about her sister and the owl.

'I make sculptures of people and animals that leave an impression on me. Nisha has told me so many stories about her life, she has bought me so many oranges and grapes and prickly pears, tomatoes . . . and, let me see . . . oh, eggs and sometimes wild greens. She says I'm too skinny, that I look like a lizard, that I need to keep up my strength if I'm going to capture the beauty and sadness of the world. So, I wanted to do something for her.' He paused. 'But what are you doing here?'

'When was the last time you saw Nisha?' I said.

'Oh, weeks ago. It's been a long time! I thought you were keeping her busy. Tell her I miss her stories and her oranges, will you? And don't work her too hard – she'll do everything to please you, it's the kind of person she is.' He smiled and the cold morning light lit up the deep creases of his face.

'I haven't seen her for three weeks,' I said.

'How come? Gone away?'

'I don't know.'

His smile vanished.

'She went out three Sundays ago and never came back.'

'And you haven't heard from her?'

'No, I haven't.'

'Well, that's unusual.'

He sat down on the stool and remained quiet, pulling at his beard. He seemed anxious, agitated even.

'I thought she was busy,' he said. 'I didn't realise. So there's a chance I might never see her again?'

He looked up at me, waiting for an answer that I couldn't give. There was something childlike about him, as if this question had been living inside him forever, and it had finally emerged from his soul.

'She's such a good person,' he said. 'Bad things always happen to good people.'

'We don't know that anything bad has happened.'

'Sorry, don't mind me.' He stood up, as if waking from a sort of stupor. 'I tend to think the worst – always have. I am sure she is just fine. At the end of the day there will be a reasonable explanation.'

His words followed me like a shadow as I walked home. I kept my eyes on the road so that I wouldn't have to look at Nisha's flyers.

When I got home, the house was empty and hollow. I collapsed onto my bed. I imagined I was inside a seashell. The past echoed in its chamber, a far-away sea, long ago, my father's voice clear and warm above blue waves: *Look at that, Petra, look at that jellyfish, look how luminous it is, look how beautiful! No, don't reach out to touch it, baby. It will hurt you. Sometimes the most beautiful things can hurt us.*

And Stephanos, his laughter. That's what I could hear – Stephanos laughing about a cake I had baked that was as flat as a Frisbee. We spread jam on it, we ate, we made love. Then Nisha, crying in her room night after night when she first arrived. Me, stopping outside her bedroom door and listening. 'Can you hear that baby crying?' Nisha had said one night, leaning out of the window. 'I can hear a baby crying, as if it is crying for me.'

And Aliki.

Mum.

The word had disappeared. She had swallowed it up inside her. She knew, didn't she? She knew that I was far away, from the day she was born. I heard it now, that single beautiful word; I heard it inside the hollow shell over the sounds of the sea and my father's voice and Stephano's laughter and Nisha's tears.

I saw it like a jellyfish floating away in the water, and I wanted to reach out and touch it.

Mum.

And that's when I understood Nisha's tears. That's when I finally knew about her pain.

Mum.

I woke up to Aliki patting me on the cheek.

'Mum, Mum, Mum, are you awake? What are you doing home?'

'Oh, stop now, shush, girl. Do not wake your mother.' Mrs Hadjikyriacou appeared in the doorway, motioning for Aliki to come out of the room.

'It's OK,' I said. 'I'm awake.'

I thanked Mrs Hadjikyriacou, letting her get back to Ruba, and suggested to Aliki that we cook together.

'How about we make moussaka?'

Aliki's eyes lit up and she nodded. This was her favourite

Greek dish too, and she had always loved helping Nisha fry the aubergines and make the béchamel sauce.

I was in bed and just about to drift off, when my phone rang. I looked at the clock and my heart dropped. It was eleven o'clock. No one called with good news this late.

'Is that Petra?' a male voice said on the other end.

'Speaking.'

A short silence followed before he said, 'Petra, this is Tony from the Blue Tiger.'

I sat up in bed. 'Yes, Tony, hello.'

'I'm wondering if you might be able to come and see me. I have some information, but this is not a matter I can discuss over the phone. I would prefer to see you face to face.'

I ran a hand through my hair, the better to wake myself up. 'I'll come tomorrow,' I said. 'I might bring someone with me this time, if that's OK with you?'

'As long as you're certain this person is trustworthy.'

'He is. Don't worry about that.'

The following morning, I took Aliki to school, and once again called Keti and asked her to cancel my appointments for the day. Back at home, I went straight up the iron stair-case and knocked. It took a while for Yiannis to come to the door. He was unshaven and dishevelled. His stubble had a hint of silver.

'Did I wake you up?'

'No,' he said. 'Come in.'

In the kitchen, morning light fell through the shutters onto the table, and the bird was hopping amongst the rays. In the middle of this large table was a bowl of water and a handful of seeds.

This time Yiannis put the coffee on the stove without asking, and I sat on the plastic chair. The bird fluttered from the table to the kitchen worktop, close to Yiannis. He put his hand out to protect the bird from the flame and left it there as a barrier.

'The bird's even better today,' I said.

'Yes.'

'You'll set it free soon?'

'Of course.' He stirred the coffee gently. Then he opened a jar of *karydaki glyko* and placed two fresh, whole walnuts, husk, shell and nut, leached and soaked in honey syrup on small plates with tiny silver forks. I hadn't had one of these for years, and even the smell reminded me of this very flat, many years ago, when my aunt lived here. I suddenly remembered the lime-green curtains that had hung from the wall, embroidered with peacocks and lime trees. What had happened to them?

'So, you have more news?' Yiannis said, placing the coffee in front of me and sitting down.

'I received a call from Tony – the guy I told you about.'

He nodded.

'Late last night, he called to say he has some information that is troubling.' I swallowed hard, trying to hide my panic from Yiannis; I thought I would start to cry.

Yiannis sat up, a deep crease forming in his brow.

'He wouldn't tell me over the phone. I'm going to see him this afternoon. I thought you would want to come with me.'

'Of course,' he said, gently, but I noticed that his fists were clenched and his knuckles were white. He caught my eye. 'I'm scared,' he said.

'What of?'

But he didn't reply. We ate the *karydaki glyko* and drank our coffee in complete silence, while the bird hopped about in the rays of light between us.

'There's something else,' I said.

'Yes?'

'Kumari, Nisha's daughter. I've been thinking about her. Have you spoken to her again?'

Here he sighed deeply. 'I have,' he said. 'But I just don't know what to tell her.'

A taxi drives into the village. It stops outside the widow's
house.

There you go, the driver says, glancing with a yawn out
of the window.

The woman in the car double-checks the address on her
phone.

It's coming up to midnight and the widow has been
waiting up for them. She comes out onto the patio and
raises her thumb. Yes, she says, welcome. This is the right
place.

The taxi driver opens the boot and carries two medium-
sized cases, one in each hand, up to the front door of the
widow's home.

Round the back, she says. That's a good lad.

The widow leads the couple through the courtyard to
the guesthouse and shows them around. The man picks up
a sugared almond from the pillow and sucks it and says it

reminds him of something, though he can't for the life of him remember what.

Tomorrow we will visit the Byzantine Museum and the Museum of Barbarism, the woman says.

They are both equally illuminating, the widow says, before she leaves them alone.

I like the word Barbarism, the woman says to the man. It strips violence of ideologies – leaves it bare, don't you think?

The other houses in the village are dark by now and so is the road leading out of the village, once the taxi has rumbled away.

Down by the lake, flesh has been removed from the head of the hare, from its abdomen and its hind legs. There are three mice feeding upon it now: one scuttles across the body as if it is running over a small hill.

The sky is dark. Clouds have gathered, thick and heavy, as a storm is brewing.

22

Yiannis

'YIANNIS, MATE. I WANT YOU to go on another hunt this weekend. We've had a number of huge orders come through. Christmas parties coming up and all that malarkey. It's gonna be busy again, like it was last year, remember?' Seraphim said, over the phone.

I was in the bedroom with the windows closed, shutters down, keeping out the winter and the light, agitating about what news this Tony guy might have about Nisha.

What exactly was Seraphim asking me to remember? How I did everything without questioning it? How I had killed inside me the boy I used to be? How I had lied to Nisha?

I remained silent.

'So,' he continued, 'this time, let's go to the west coast of Larnaca. You had a great catch there last month. I'll come with you this time, we'll be even more productive.'

I remained silent.

'We'll go this Friday,' he continued. 'I'll pick you up as usual, at 3 a.m., so be outside waiting, with all the gear.'

I remained silent.

'I gather you've lost your tongue.'

'I'm just looking at my diary. I still need to do all the deliveries from the last hunt.'

I saw myself in my childhood room, sitting at the oak desk, my father hovering over me. By then, I no longer called him 'father': he was *He*. My father had died in the war. I didn't know this new man, whose eyes were unfocused. He ranted. He wanted me to study, to get out of the village, to make something of myself. Was that so unreasonable?

Well, I did. Look at me. Didn't he tell me to chase money at any cost? When he died, he no longer remembered my name. But he walked the same, in the care home, along that green corridor, up and down, hovering over green lino, not knowing who he was or who I was. I guess we can die many deaths.

Seraphim cleared his throat. He'd allowed me the silence, but it had gone on too long.

'That's fine,' I said, 'I'll see you on Friday.'

I lay in the dark thinking about Nisha, the way she had held on to me in the night, grieving for the lost baby. There are many ways to lose a person, that was something Nisha had taught me. It was then she told me the third story of loss.

After her husband died in the gem mines of Rathnapura,

Nisha decided to move back to Galle to stay with her mother, in the house between the sea and the paddy fields, where she had lived as a child. By that time, her father had passed away and her mother had retired and was able look after Kumari while Nisha worked.

She found a job as a street vendor in Galle Face Green – an urban park in the jumbly city by the beach – making *kottu*. Sometimes there were rallies there and parties, and, back in the old days, horse races that she had attended with her father. Along the green now was a sizzling rainbow of street food. Every day she made the *kottu*, adding *roti*, meat, vegetables, egg and a spicy sauce called *salna*, prepared on a hot plate and chopped and mixed with silver blades.

The man who owned the stall was fat and dark. For the first few weeks, he watched over her, especially during the final step of preparing the dish, where she mashed and chopped all the ingredients together with the blunt metal blades. He wanted to make sure she got the process 'just right'. Once he was satisfied – 'This is the fucking best *kottu* in Galle. I grew up on this stuff and know what's good' – he more or less left her to it, and went off to manage his other stalls. He paid her hardly anything, but it was the only job she had been able to find: she'd walked up and down the streets practically begging for work. All day long and late into the evening, she was bathed in aromatic spices, and her sweat and her tears dripped into the food, for she did not, for a single day, stop crying and longing for her husband.

There was a carousel a few stalls down, whose music never ended, and opposite an old woman sold colourful saris. Next

285

to her, a middle-aged man had a cart selling nuclear-orange *isso vadai* – spicy lentil cakes with prawns – and next to him a young woman who made luminous desserts with shredded coconut wrapped in betel leaf.

The park was ringed with food vendor carts lit by small puddles of electric lights at night. There were colours and smells and sounds everywhere, and Nisha was exhausted. Her mother's pension was measly, so Nisha was keeping them all afloat. When her husband had been alive, they had worked together to pay the bills, and although it had been tough, at least she had been in it with someone else, with both their wages helping them get by. They had also managed to put a bit aside for Kumari's education. It was Mahesh's wish that his daughter would be educated, and be the first in the family to attend university.

Once Nisha left for work, Kumari would cry. In fact, she cried until she turned blue. Her grandmother could do nothing to console her.

'Your daughter is a crazy genius,' Nisha's mother would say to her. 'She knows too much. I can't distract her like I could with you. She's bloody minded. Where did she get this from?'

'You, Amma!' Nisha would say, remembering her mother's obsession with her little sister's heart all those years ago. Remembering the pendant that Kiyoma had thrown into the river to free herself.

Kumari was always awake when Nisha came home from work. There was nothing Nisha's mother could do to get her to sleep. She tried everything. She sang to her, she walked her along the beachfront. Nothing – Kumari looked at the waves and laughed. Nisha's mother changed the songs to prayers, chanting beneath the hush of the trees in the garden. At one point she thought of organising a *thovil*: 'Nisha, I'm at my wits' end. This child of yours is possessed.' She was joking, of course; Kumari still smiled through it all.

Whenever Nisha came home, whether it was 9 p.m. or 11 p.m. or 1 a.m., Kumari would begin to cry. It seemed to Nisha, on reflection, that these were tears of immense relief. She would pick up her daughter, sit on the bed, and make a little nest by crossing her legs. Kumari would cluck and mutter, while Nisha put her baby to her breast. Kumari would suck vigorously, resting her left hand under Nisha's breasts, her right hand holding Nisha's fingers. When Kumari had finished, Nisha would take off her sweat-drenched clothes and lie on her back on the rug with her baby on her chest. She liked lying on the floor, feeling the firm ground beneath her: it made her feel safer, held by the Earth. And then, finally, Kumari would sigh and drift into a soft sleep.

At these times Nisha was happy. This was when her tears stopped, when she had her baby in her arms. On warm nights she'd lie like that in the garden for more than an hour and think about the world from the womb to the stars. She thought about time and space and existence and how some-where between birth and the heavens we all exist, and that somewhere out there was her husband's energy-force either waiting or being reborn.

No matter how much Nisha worked, however, her income was never enough. They had already started eating into the education fund, which left her feeling mortified. Within just a few months, there was nothing left. The three of them were surviving pay-check to pay-check.

One day, the young woman across the street who made coconut sweets with betel leaf, didn't turn up. She was replaced by an older woman with dappled skin who always wore the same purple sari. For so many months, Nisha had watched Isuri as she delicately wrapped the sweets – dark eyes down, flicking up occasionally to take in the passing crowd. Nisha and Isuri would exchange *kottu* for sweets, pleasantries for smiles, and eventually grievances for hugs. Isuri wasn't yet married and was looking for a suitable match and was progressively getting fed up with her life; she could never earn enough to support her ailing father and two much younger sisters.

Nisha and Isuri had become close, and Isuri's sudden departure had had a profound effect on Nisha. Isuri had been talking about leaving Sri Lanka, hoping to go to Europe and work as a maid. 'So many women are doing it!' she told Nisha one morning, with sparkling eyes. 'I could earn double what I'm earning here in one month! I could send money home and still have enough for myself. I'll be given nice accommodation and food. And imagine having all that freedom too! Imagine being able to go out, to be free, and not have to answer to anyone. I will be my own woman.' She had been so excited, and Nisha would never forget how Isuri looked that morning with so much hope in her heart.

At home in the evenings, with Kumari sleeping peacefully on her naked chest, drenched in drying tears, she felt her body begin to ache and her mind spin. How could she ensure that Kumari had a good life? How could she fulfil her husband's wish and send their daughter to university one day? Staying in Galle was a dead end. She had three mouths to feed and she had to do it all alone. The flour was running out in the cupboard, as was the rice. Her mother had started to ration the portions. Kumari was wearing hand-me-downs from the neighbours – this wouldn't have been a problem in itself, had Nisha been able to put money aside for Kumari's education and make sure that she was well fed, but no matter how careful she was, no matter how much overtime she worked or tips she earned, she still could not afford to buy all the food they needed for the week, let alone put money aside for the future.

Nisha felt her baby's tiny fingers, soft and warm as she slept; she gently squeezed her chubby thighs and placed her little feet in the palms of her hands and held them. Kumari sighed but did not move and did not wake. Nisha inhaled her sweet breath. Then she exhaled her decision. 'Yes,' she said out loud. *Yes. I must sacrifice these beautiful moments for Kumari's future.* And then she kissed Kumari's hands a hundred times while she slept and resolved to give her everything she could, every chance in life.

It took more than a year before her plans came into fruition, but eventually Nisha had found an agent, had filled out all the relevant paperwork and when all that was done, which took a few months in itself, she waited patiently for a suitable placement.

There had been a few opportunities that fell through –

289

one with a large family in Singapore, another with an old man in a village in Saudi Arabia, another with a young couple in a town in Cyprus. Then came Petra: a pregnant business woman who wanted help keeping the house and looking after her baby once it arrived. Nisha felt that this was perfect for her – not that she really had a choice. She would have to take what was offered or else she would have to wait longer. The island of Cyprus seemed small and homely, and she had been told that there were many women from Sri Lanka who had already made their way there, and that everyone spoke English, and that the weather was good.

The agent's fee was astronomical to Nisha, the equivalent of 10,000 euros. Of course, she couldn't afford to pay it upfront, so she would pay the debt in instalments, commencing with her first pay-check. She calculated that this would still leave her enough money to send home, and to also put aside for Kumari's education.

Meanwhile, Kumari would no longer settle on Nisha's chest when she returned from work. She would writhe and mutter and claw at her skin, then cry inconsolably, as if it was herself she had hurt. Nisha was convinced that Kumari understood on some instinctive level that her mother's heart and mind were somewhere else. Nisha couldn't bear it. She knew that Kumari knew. Kumari grew each day and became a force to be reckoned with. The muttering turned to actual words. 'No!' she would say to her grandmother when she didn't want to sleep, and 'No!' she would say to her mother when Nisha wanted a hug and a kiss on her return from work. By the time she was two and could string sentences together, there was no arguing with her. 'No, Amma! You go back to work now!'

'But you were waiting for me all this time, and now you don't want me?'

'No. Not waiting. Kumari playing with Ziya. Ziya hungry.' Ziya was Kumari's favourite doll that her grandmother had made with old rags.

Kumari watched Nisha as she packed.

'Big bag, Amma?'

'I'm putting my clothes in, ba-baa.'

'Why?'

'Amma is going away.'

'Kumari going?'

'No.'

'Ziya going?'

'No, ba-baa.'

Nisha arrived in Cyprus late one Sunday night, with a small suitcase, wearing a black linen dress that a neighbour in Galle had made for her. She was picked up at the airport by the agent's representative, and taken to an old dark house in an old dark city where a forlorn pregnant woman greeted her with a broken smile and distant eyes.

Isuri had been right about one thing – she was given a lovely bedroom with antique furniture that backed onto a garden full of plants, chickens, a cactus, a fig tree and an orange tree. There was a small fishing boat in this garden, which reminded her of the fishermen in Sri Lanka – those she had seen from her bedroom window – and Nisha knew she had come to the right place.

That night, she was awakened by the sound of crying. She got out of bed and held her ear to the closed door. It was a child, very young, probably around Kumari's age. It was as clear and present as the darkness. She walked along the corridor, following the sound, and it led her out into the garden through the communal door. There the sound was louder. She thought that it might be a neighbour's child, but it seemed to have no direction. It was coming from every-where, or so it seemed to her. She sat in the unused boat in the garden and tried to understand where the crying was coming from. It came from the earth and the trees and the sky. She sat there until she fell asleep and woke at dawn to the sound of a cockerel crowing in the distance. The crying had stopped.

She only had an hour before she needed to begin work, so she decided to start straight away. She cleaned and scrubbed every surface until it shone, until the memory of the night's disturbance began to fade.

Petra was happy with Nisha's work. It was the only thing she seemed happy about. She appeared to live in a constant state of despair and she carried her stomach like an object, as if she was carrying the earth.

The following night, when she was tucked up in bed after a long day, Nisha again heard the crying. Once again, she got out of bed and followed the sound out into the garden, through the glass doors in her bedroom. It was a clear night, frosty and cold. Stars in a dome above her. The air was still, no wind, and she listened, alert as a cat, in order to locate the source of the sound. But once more it came from everywhere: from the leaves on the trees, from the branches and bark, even from the roots – it seemed to run like rivers beneath the earth, like the deep song of the trees. Equally, it came from up above, from the fabric of the sky, from the waves and particles that make up our existence; it was carried on the wings of bats and owls, and higher still, much higher, it came from the stars.

At this point in her story, Nisha paused. She stopped talking and looked at me right in the eyes, then she ran her hands along my arms as if to clarify my existence, to ground herself in the present.

'Did you find out where it was coming from?' I had asked.

But instead of replying she drew her body close to mine, so that there was no space between us; she moulded herself onto my body, she tucked her head into my neck and for the first time since the miscarriage, she had begun to cry.

23

Petra

'S O, WHEN DID IT ALL begin?' I said. 'You and Nisha? If you don't mind me asking . . . ?'

Yiannis and I had set off for Limassol. I had the radio on low. It was raining hard, so we drove with the heat on, windows up. We were passing an orchard of orange trees and then a farm. I opened the window a crack and breathed in the cold air; the smell of earth and manure rushed in.

'Two years ago,' Yiannis said.

'When you first moved in?'

'Yes. Well, that was when we started talking. It took some time after that, to get to know each other.'

I thought he might say more but he was staring into the distance, at a village on a hillside.

'How did you keep it a secret for so long?'

'She would come and see me a few nights a week. She'd

speak to Kumari at 3 a.m., always on Sundays and Tuesdays, sometimes other nights too, and then get up at 5 a.m. so that she could get back to her room before you woke up.'

I kept my eyes on the road but I could see in my peripheral vision that he was looking at me now, perhaps waiting for my reaction.

'I see,' I said. 'I wish Nisha had told me.'

He didn't respond to this. I mean, what could he say? I would never have accepted it then. I was too greedy, I needed Nisha for myself – and for Aliki.

I never would have considered her right to her own life.

I was embarrassed and ashamed, because I had been so self-absorbed all these years, and I hadn't noticed. I wondered – would I have been different if Stephanos had still been alive? Would he have kept me in check? My world had become so narrow it hardly even included our daughter. I had missed so much of Aliki's life, and it was right in front of me. What had she been showing me that I couldn't see? What had she been saying all these years that I couldn't hear?

And then there were the birds. Yiannis bringing thousands of songbirds back to his apartment, selling them on the black market, being involved in what I knew to be a highly criminal organisation. Ahead, the sea was agitated by the rain. A blurry horizon revealed a washed-out sunset. We were nearly there.

Tony was sitting in his glass booth. The atmosphere at the Blue Tiger was different today, perhaps because it was a weekday. There was a Cypriot man behind the counter making sandwiches. A few customers were dotted about at various tables and there was no music blasting from the back hall, no one walking around with trays of food and drink. It was as if the other Blue Tiger had been something I had seen in a dream. But then I spotted Devna, coming out of the kitchen area towards us. This time she had on bright red lipstick. She was wearing a different pair of dark blue jeans with a pink and white checked shirt that revealed a soft cleavage.

'Madam,' she said. 'And sir.' She nodded at Yiannis. 'Very nice to see you here again, madam. Mr Tony will be ready in only five minutes. I will bring you both a drink?'

Yiannis shook his head. He looked yellow. 'I'm fine, thank you.'

I asked for a black coffee with no sugar.

Devna went off to fetch the drink while Yiannis and I stood there awkwardly, until Tony lifted his arm and waved us in.

Yiannis shook his hand and introduced himself, simply with his first name. He looked like he was there to close a business deal, with his crisp white shirt and grey twill trousers. He was even more handsome now next to Tony, whose white hair was wild and uncombed, while large sweat marks drenched the material under his armpits. A cigarette smoked on its own in the ashtray.

He shook my hand too and we all sat down. Tony eyed Yiannis and picked up his cigarette, taking a long drag of the stub, a long stem of ash falling to the floor by his feet.

He stamped on it as if it might cause a fire and said, 'So, Yiannis, right? What brings you here today?'

'Nisha and I are close friends.'

Tony raised his eyebrows. At that moment Devna came in with a tray of coffee and biscuits. She had made one for Yiannis too, and he took it out of courtesy. Tony turned the fan on and the smoky air circulated in the booth.

'Is that a new pair of jeans, Devna?' he said, and Devna smiled at him with bright red lips. She placed the plate of biscuits on some paperwork on the desk, winked at me and left.

'They never learn, these girls,' he said to us now. 'Her employer is a middle-aged widower who treats her like a princess. He's bought her a car, he buys her new clothes every week, he's now given her a credit card with unlimited funds. So, tell me, why do you think that is?' He smiled, revealing yellow teeth, but his eyes were attentive and sharp and he fixed his gaze on Yiannis, who shifted in his seat and took a sip of coffee. 'Anyway, I trust that you are both here because you care about Nisha. I have some rather troubling news.'

Yiannis placed his coffee on the desk and sat upright. I saw that he was gripping his knees with his hands.

'Since you came to see me, Petra, two more people visited me. One was a Romanian maid, who works on the outskirts of Nicosia. She came here to tell me about a childhood friend of hers, Cristina Maier, also Romanian, who has disap-peared with her daughter, Daria, who is five years old. The young girl lived here with her mother. As a Romanian citizen she was able to do so. It turns out that mother and child went missing two months ago. The friend has tried everything to raise the alarm, but her employers and police are not interested. The second is again a woman from Romania, Ana-Maria Lupei with her daughter, Andreea. They were reported missing last Wednesday, exactly a week ago, this time from another town near Nicosia, and again she had her young daughter with her. Her employer, an old veteran, came here with his son to speak to me just yesterday. Apparently, she had popped out one evening to meet a friend. She took her daughter with her – and they didn't return. The old man was beside himself with worry. He is very fond of them both. He went to the police and found the encounter futile.' Tony shrugged. 'In both cases, the women disappeared without warning; in both cases, friend and employer insist that it was out of character, that they left without belongings or passports, and in both cases the police were not interested in pursuing an investigation. The only difference here, however – and what is even more disturbing – is that these two women have disappeared not on their own, but with their daughters.'

Tony was silent now, letting his words sink in. He held his cigarette with his elbow on the table, looking from me to Yiannis and back again.

Yiannis inhaled deeply and his breath came out in fragments. I did not turn to look at him. I couldn't. Any hope I might have had drained out of me: the disappearances wove together now in a complicated web. It had become so much bigger; something dark and wrong clawing at the edges of the booth.

Tony threw his cigarette butt in the ashtray and lit another. The flick of the lighter was loud, the flame cracked into existence, the smoke travelled around us.

Yiannis suddenly stood up, bought his hand up to his face, bought his palm down over his eyes and mouth.

'Are you OK, Yiannis?' I said.

'I'm sorry,' he said. 'I just don't understand.'

'Clearly,' Tony said, 'they must be connected. It's too much of a coincidence. There has to be one person or a group of people behind this. It's transpired that one of the women was going out on a date. I have no information about the person she was intending to meet –I'm working on that – but she let one of her friends know before leaving home. This confirms, more so, that the police are wrong. These women did not just decide to run away to the occupied territory in the north. I'm going to go back to the station tomorrow with all the facts I have here before me.' He placed his hand on the notepad. 'And I'm not going to leave until they agree to take this seriously.'

Yiannis was still standing, his head bowed as if he was praying. Without saying anything, he sat down again and placed his hands on his knees, as before, except this time the anguish was evident on his face.

'Do I have your permission to share the information that you've given me about Nisha?' Tony now asked.

'Of course,' I said.

'Do you have anything that you could add?'

There was a pause. Then Yiannis spoke, his voice gaining strength as he did so: 'We now know,' he said, 'that Nisha was heading out to meet a colleague of mine. His name is Seraphim Ioannou. He and I are involved in an illegal network involving poaching. Songbirds, specifically. Nisha had found out and had arranged to meet him. Apparently, she never turned up for the appointment.'

Tony's eyes turned to slits. He opened the notebook and asked Yiannis to repeat the name. 'Do you have proof that she was going to meet him?'

'Yes, Seraphim has confirmed it to me.'

Tony nodded and scribbled down a few more notes. Then he closed the pad, leaned back in his chair, looking now for the first time through the glass at his restaurant that had begun to fill up, considerably.

We drove back in complete silence. The sun vanished into the sea as the afternoon turned late. Aliki would be home from school by now. Mrs Hadjikyriacou was collecting her and probably keeping her company with her stories, while Ruba made them something warm and fragrant for supper.

Yiannis stared at the rain ahead beating down on the windscreen and only spoke when I turned into Nicosia.

'Do you mind if I turn the heating off?' he said

'No, of course not.'

I flicked my eyes towards him and noticed that his neck and face were red. I wanted to ask him what he was thinking but no words escaped my lips.

It has been raining so much that the lake has overflowed. The tunnel of the mineshaft has started filling with water.

The rain has washed away the ants and the maggots from the hare, and the mice have run for shelter. Along its hind legs there are tufts of rain-drenched fur, but mostly the skin has been stripped away. The rain falls onto its open wounds, it falls into the open space where its eye once was, into the open space where its heart once was. A part of the ribcage is visible, like a new moon.

The rain continues to fall into the red water of the lake, it pounds down upon the yellow stone, it slides down the rusty skeleton of the gallows frame and into its deep mineshaft. There, on the surface of that dark water, is the white shimmer of material – drenched linen – wrapped around something unknown. Only a tiny bit is visible, like a small, white mountain rising out of darkness, like the tip of a glowing iceberg.

In the guest house, the man and the woman lie side by side on the double bed: she is on her side, facing the window where the rain streams down; he is reading the news on his phone. Its light illuminates his face. He is young still.

The woman reaches for the brochure on the bedside table and flicks through it.

Let's go to the red lake tomorrow, she says.

The red lake? he asks, distracted.

Yes, I told you about it. There was a copper mine there once. There is a red lake there now, as red as Mars, and people say it is very strange and beautiful and otherworldly. We can see the gallows frame too. What do you say?

Yes, the man says. Sounds wonderful.

24

Yiannis

SERAPHIM PICKED ME UP IN the early hours of Friday morning, while it was still pitch-black out. The streets glistened from the past few days of rain. I had all the gear ready and was waiting for him out front, as usual.

Without a hello: 'Did you complete the deliveries?'

'Yes,' I said, getting into the passenger seat and clicking in my belt, after I had put all the stuff in the back of the van.

'When?'

'Last one yesterday afternoon.'

'Good.'

The road ahead was dark, lit only by the moon. There was a fine layer of frost in the fields, luminous in the night. It reminded me of the unusually cold late October morning, not so long ago, when I had seen the mouflon in the woods, when I had rushed home to tell Nisha.

Eventually we turned onto a dirt track and the road became darker, shadowed by trees. It was so dark I felt like we might be heading off a cliff and into the sea, but the sea was miles away. The van kept rumbling on until we came to an abrupt stop in a clearing beneath a huge oak tree.

Seraphim got out without saying a word and opened the doors at the back of the van. I followed him and he handed me the shoulder bags holding the lime sticks, calling devices, three covered-up cages with sleeping birds, one large mist net, and finally a rifle.

'A rifle?' I said.

'It's hunting season. I thought we could hunt some game. We're allowed on Wednesdays and Fridays in November.'

I took the rifle from him and he turned to me and smiled with his over-stretched grin. Since when did Seraphim care about hunting regulations? I knew that November was a good time to hunt hare, chukar partridge, black francolin, wood-pigeon and woodcocks, but there is a limit on the quotas that hunters are allowed to take – something like two hare and two partridges per hunter per hunting day. But I felt like a hypocrite thinking about the quotas when on the ground by my feet lay the rolled mist net – non-selective and indiscriminate of quotas.

We carried the gear into the woods. As we unrolled the mist net and secured it on poles between two junipers, I remembered walking with my grandfather through the forest, and how he had explained that in ancient times the island was almost completely covered with impenetrable forests.

'Imagine what it would have been like back then!' he'd said. 'For wildlife to be undisturbed by human hands that take so much more than what they need.'

'Where are you?' Seraphim called out, sharply.

'Right here.'

He shook his head, pushing the pole deeper into the earth. 'You're miles away. Focus, man. Imagine you have fourteen pairs of eyes. Be alert.'

I nodded and he signalled for me to lift the covers from the cages. I did so. The birds remained true to the darkness and kept their songs to themselves for the time being.

'Oksana is pregnant,' he said.

I forced myself to sound happy. 'Wow, that's great news! Congratulations, my friend.'

'We had the first scan the other day. You should have heard the heartbeat. You know, it's the most amazing thing in the world, that this little human is growing inside her. I'm going to be a father.'

His eyes shone, but his smile held a hint of fear or apprehension and I saw in this the boy I once knew.

'You'll be great,' I said.

'I've started to do up the nursery. I'm painting murals on the walls.'

'What are they of?' I asked.

'Oh, kids' stuff. You know, a waterfall, mountains, hot-air balloons, that sort of thing.'

'Sounds nice.'

We proceeded to place the lime sticks on the bushes and trees in the dark. We didn't use torches in case the area was being patrolled. We worked in silence, listening carefully for any unusual sounds or movement.

So, Seraphim was going to be a father. Seraphim. It made my intestines turn. A flash of blood in the toilet bowl. Nisha with her hands crossed over her stomach. I watched Seraphim's movements in the darkness – they were fluid and discreet, like a shadow. I wanted to ask him again about that Sunday. Had Nisha really not turned up? Did he have something to do with her disappearance? He couldn't. I mean, he couldn't. Seraphim was an arsehole, the lowest of the low when it came to certain things, but he couldn't possibly be involved in something as sinister as a missing person, or even five missing women and two children, if they were connected. I could see the fuzzy outline of his mouth and eyes. He seemed to be smiling. He was pleased with himself.

Seraphim, of all people, was going to be a dad. The prick.

When we finished setting up, we lit a small fire and waited for dawn, for the birds to descend into the trees. The calling devices sang in the dark in preparation and the mechanical but beautiful song reached us as if in a dream. The caged birds wouldn't sing until the sun rose. We toasted olives and haloumi on skewers over the fire. Seraphim had his rifle close to him.

'What are you hoping to kill?' I said.

'Maybe some hare, that sort of thing, after we've collected the birds. Wait for the wildlife to wake up.'

I nodded and removed a warm olive from the skewer with

my teeth. A black olive, bitter and grainy. There was not much conversation between us. Seraphim was alert all the time, his head darting about whenever he heard a sound. I kept my eye on the rifle. It bothered me, the way Seraphim fingered the trigger, the way he kept it so close.

It was the moment when the light of dawn cracked through the darkness and the birds in their cages and all the free birds began to sing, that I heard the crunch of leaves. Of course, Seraphim heard it to, and he was up immediately, gazing into the dawn light. I thought that was it, finally we would be caught, and more than anything I just felt relief.

But what appeared seconds later in the clearing beneath the trees was not a man in ranger's uniform, but the mouflon ovis.

I stood up too and it peered at me as it had that day, with weary, amber eyes. Once again, it stood straight and strong and its fur and horns shone gold.

'Look at that,' Seraphim whispered. 'Extraordinary!'

He gently crouched down, levelling the rifle, without averting his eyes from the animal.

The mouflon, following his movement with its eyes, took a step back so that it was now directly in a pool of light in the rising sun. And, just then, birds came in their thousands, cutting across the sky.

'Seraphim,' I said, urgently. 'Don't shoot!'

'Don't be stupid! This is a prize!' His raspy whisper was full of excitement.

He nestled the gun more securely on his shoulder, preparing himself, watching the creature.

'It's protected,' I said.

He chuckled, a low soft sound, but it came from deep in his chest. The animal took another step back, now into the shadows beneath the trees, and it seemed to be looking straight past Seraphim, at me.

I moved closer and grabbed Seraphim's elbow. He pushed me with so much force that I stumbled sideways.

'What the hell are you doing, man?' His voice back to normal. The animal shuffled back further into a darkened, shrouded space, but its fur and horns caught the light.

I straightened up and quickly positioned myself between him and the animal, while Seraphim repositioned his gun.

He held the rifle steady on his shoulder, left eye squinting hard, right eye aiming through the muzzle. 'Come on now,' he said. 'Get out of my way.'

Seraphim tried angling to the left and to the right, to get the mouflon from a different angle.

And then I saw his finger begin to tighten on the trigger.

In the next second, without thinking, I rushed into his line of fire, and before I could think another thought, he fired.

There was a searing pain in my arm, as if it had been scorched with fire.

Even through my pain, I heard the animal behind me fall. I heard its collapse, meeting the earth among the fallen leaves. Although I had my back to it, I could see its rapid decline in my mind's eye – and I still see it, time and again.

Seraphim lowered his gun. 'Fuck,' he said.

I had grabbed my arm and could feel warm blood leaking

through a huge tear in my jacket. The bullet had sliced through my skin on route to the mouflon behind me.

I turned to look. It was lying on its side, a hole in its chest, a gradually expanding pool of blood on the ground beside it. Its eyes were open. It was still alive. I crouched down beside it and placed my bloody hand on its back, stroking its fur. 'It's all right,' I whispered. A stupid thing to say.

It glanced at me sideways, its amber eyes now pools of liquid gold. I stroked its head. It was all that I could do. Its breathing was shallow and strained. Finally, it took its last breath and its eyes lost their focus.

Crouching down on the ground beside the dead animal I began to cry in a way that I had not cried since I was a boy. I cried for loving Nisha, for missing her, for being afraid for her. I cried for this beautiful creature whose life had been cut short so senselessly. I cried for the way it had looked at me as it lay dying, and I cried for the needless deaths of so many animals.

Seraphim moved behind me, and, remembering that he was there, I turned. He had lowered his gun now and was holding it loosely at his side.

I got up. I'm not sure what expression I wore on my face, but whatever it was, he took a step back, in spite of the fact that it was he who was holding a weapon.

'Are you all right?' He seemed shaken and smaller.

'Tell me what you did with Nisha.'

He stared at me without speaking. I took another step forward; he took another back and tightened his grip on the gun.

'Where is she?'

'I don't know.'

'Seraphim!'

'I'm telling you the truth! She never came to see me. I promise you on my mother's grave.' He crossed himself and held my gaze. 'I'm sorry. I apologise, you're bleeding. Let's get you to the hospital.'

Maybe it was my face, my eyes, or maybe something had happened to him when he heard me cry, because his eyes were wide and alarmed, and now in front of me stood an uncertain man, apologetic and confused to his rotten core.

I saw that his hand was shaking and he dropped the gun as he held his hands up. 'I promise you,' he said again. 'If you still don't believe me, let me show you something.'

He glanced at me tentatively, waiting for me to respond and I nodded. He reached into his back pocket and retrieved his phone, then he scrolled through it and held it out for me to take from his hand.

He'd opened up to a series of messages between him and Nisha.

31/10   22.16

Dear Mr seraphim I am running a little late because it was difficult for me 2 leave but I will be at Marias bar in half an hour.

31/10   22.19

Ok. Please don't be too late as I need to leave earlier this evening.

31/10   22.21
Dear Mr seraphim I will try my best to get there as soon as possible Thank you for meeting it is very important.

31/10   23.15
I am still waiting. Are you on your way?

31/10   23.43
Hello Nisha?

01/11   00.01
I'm afraid I will have to leave now.

Then he took back the phone and scrolled through again. This time he wanted me to look at a series of text messages between him and his wife.

31/10   22.10
Please come home early tonight? Been a long day. Need a hug.

31/10   22.18
I will. Don't worry. Love you

31/10   22.22
I won't be too long. Waiting for someone, have a meeting, shouldn't take long. Hug is coming! Love you

'What does this prove? Someone else could have been involved,' I said.

Seraphim blew out a puff of frustrated air. 'What do you think happened? What are you imagining? You can go through my entire phone. Go ahead! I've got nothing to hide from you.'

Still holding the phone, I turned back to the mouflon. It lay there peacefully, unmoving, its right horn digging into the earth at an odd angle. Its eyes were still open, one looking straight up through the leaves of the trees at the morning sky, which was still half-dark. I stared down at it through watery eyes.

I sat down beside it again. I put my hand on its chest, and, as the sun rose further, the morning seemed to draw the gold from the mouflon's body and eyes.

Then I saw it. I saw the gold evaporate and merge with the air and rise into the sky. I saw the gold rise from its body like light, like one might imagine a soul leaving a body. The gold became part of the sunrise before me. The fur on its underbelly was pure white now, its body and face a soft chestnut-grey. Its beautiful curved horns were an off-white that reminded me of stone.

My hand shook on its chest. My breath shook with more tears, a fierce sadness that was tearing itself upwards from deep inside me.

Seraphim remained silent behind me.

'Did you see that?' I asked.

'See what?'

'The gold, the way it left its body; the way it dissipated into the sky.'

He didn't respond immediately, and after a few deep breaths he said, 'You haven't been right since Nisha left.'

'She hasn't left. You're an asshole, you know.'

I faced him again and I remembered everything that Nisha had wanted from me, the things she had said, the way she had cried over the photograph she had seen of me as a boy. *You were just so beautiful and so sweet.* Had those been her words?

'Seraphim, I'm out,' I said. 'From now on, you leave me alone. You don't have to pay me for this hunt or the last one, for that matter. I want nothing more to do with any of this. You can burn everything I own for all I care, but if anyone gets hurt, I swear I will kill you.'

The caged birds were still singing their hearts out.

The sun rose higher still. Time seemed to be moving faster. How long did we stand there staring at each other?

'What will you do for money?' was all he said.

I didn't bother replying.

The iPad rang at 3 a.m. I was wide awake. My arm had been stitched and bandaged and I had said nothing to the doctors about what had happened.

When I answered the phone, both Kumari and Nisha's mother stared back at me.

'What happened to your arm, Mr Yiannis?'

'I fell over, Kumari. Don't worry, it's nothing.'

She squinted her eyes at me. She wasn't convinced.

The old woman began to speak to me in Sinhalese. Her face was as smooth as a stone, her large eyes fixed on me.

Her fingers opened and closed as she spoke. 'You tell me!' she said finally, in English. Then she nudged Kumari.

'My grandmother is very worried,' Kumari said. 'She want to know where my amma is. She says that never has she not called her beloved daughter and beloved mother. She is asking what have you done with her?'

I realised my hands were shaking as I held the tablet.

I was silent for a while and they both waited. The old lady with the smooth face had her hand on Kumari's shoulder. She gripped it tightly.

The young girl glared at me from beneath a newly cut fringe.

'Kumari.' I took a deep breath. 'Kumari, I'm sorry. Please tell your grandmother that I don't know where your mother is. She went out one night, nearly three weeks ago, and she hasn't come back.'

The girl paused for a moment and opened her mouth to say something to me, but then changed her mind and turned to her grandmother to translate.

The old woman was besides herself. She began to cry and speak so fast that the young girl waved her hands before her grandmother's eyes to stop her, to make her see her perhaps. The old woman continued to speak, breathless now, and Kumari, above her grandmother's voice, began to translate: 'She is asking where is she? Why would she leave? Why would she not come back? Did something happen?'

'I don't know, Kumari,' I said. 'But we are doing everything we can to find her. You must know and understand this. Everything.' My voice broke on the last word.

'She wants more information, Mr Yiannis. She says that what you have told us is not enough. She needs to know more.'

'All I know and all I can tell you is that four other women, all of them foreign maids, and their two children, have also gone missing.'

Kumari translated for her grandmother, and the old woman began to speak faster. There were questions I could tell, so many questions, but the young girl turned to face me now with a solemnity and sudden seriousness that reminded me of her mother.

'Mr Yiannis,' she said, softly, 'why didn't you tell me this? You knew for a long time, yes?'

'Yes,' I said.

'Why did you not tell me?'

'I was afraid.'

'What were you afraid of, Mr Yiannis?'

'I was afraid to break your heart.'

As soon as I said this the screen went black and she was gone.

I sat there staring at the tablet, wondering how Nisha had managed to have an entire relationship with her daughter through this tiny screen. I wanted to break through the glass, reach Kumari, pull her into a hug and tell her not to worry. I wanted to reassure this young girl who reminded me so much of her mother, but I couldn't. Not only was there so much distance between us, but also because I really didn't know what to say to comfort her.

Two vultures are gliding and sailing beneath the clouds, wings held in V-shapes. Far below, the empty eye socket of the hare stares up at their two-toned underwings of black and silver.

What a beautiful morning it is. As blue as a sapphire, with wandering winter clouds. Years ago, vultures flocked like herds of sheep or goats in this area; now these two are a rare sight. They swerve down towards the hare, the shadows of their wings lengthening across the lake as they descend. They will clean up the dead. They land on the yellow rocks of the crater, their tiny red unfeathered heads perched upon their spindly necks. Together they inspect the hare.

They begin to feast on the flesh that's been left, soft and liquified by the rain. The lake is brilliant beneath the midday sun.

In the mineshaft, white linen has unravelled in ribbons

and the overflowing rainwater moves gently over the blue and purple flesh of a breast.

At the guest house, the man and the woman tie up the laces of their hiking boots.

It's going to be a nice day, she says, as sunshine beams into the room through the slits of the shutters.

I've been reading up on the old mines, he says. I'll tell you on the way.

He speaks about the ancient history of copper and bronze as they walk past the barley and wheat fields. As they walk past the sunflowers, he tells her everything he's read about the old mines and how the men died of silicosis, and eventually they are on the arid plane where the earth stretches lonely to the horizon. The sun is strong and she holds her hand over her eyes like a sailor setting out to sea.

Seeing the couple, the vultures abandon the corpse of the hare and flap lazily away.

25

Petra

THE PHONE RANG WHILE I was collecting grape leaves from the vine in the garden. I wanted to cook something nice for Aliki. We had spent a quiet Saturday playing board games, pretending to read, but really worrying about Nisha.

I was planning to make stuffed vine leaves for a picnic on Sunday, wrapping them in foil so that we could eat them with our fingers beneath the Famagusta Gate.

Tony's voice at the end of the phone changed everything: 'Petra, I would tell you to come but this can't wait. A body has been found in the mineshaft by the red lake of Mitsero.'

I started shaking. I managed to hang up the call, then quickly gathered up Aliki and walked her over to Mrs Hadjikyriacou. The moment she saw my face, Mrs Hadjikyriacou took her in without asking any questions.

When I turned to leave, Aliki called out, 'What it is? Where are you going? Is it about Nisha?'

I couldn't find the words to answer her, but I met her eyes and nodded, then rushed off.

Taking the stairs two at a time, I ran up to Yiannis's apartment, pounding on the door.

He opened the door with red eyes, and I saw that his arm was in a sling. It looked like he had spent the night crying.

'What happened?' I said.

'It's nothing at all to worry about.'

He looked horrified when I told him about the call from Tony. He grabbed his keys and slipped on his trainers without saying a word.

It takes twenty minutes to get Mitsero from where I live. The whole time I thought about that water, with the rusted structures of abandoned mines guarding it like ghosts.

We drove to the end of a paved road that passes by the village of Agrokipia. I left the car on the side of a cracked pavement as we had to walk from there along the dirt path, to get to the lake.

A small crowd had gathered, eager to see.

These things don't happen here!

This kind of thing – never.

I wonder who they found?

I tried to block out the voices of the crowd.

The area surrounding the lake and gallows frame had been roped off. Helicopters circled above. We were on the slant of a jagged hill of yellow rock that dropped down to the water. I could feel Yiannis standing beside me, but I didn't dare to look at his face. If I saw fear there, it would have broken me; I was just barely keeping it together myself. But I could hear him breathing, I could hear his breath shake.

The body was bound in white cloth.

Tourists, they were hiking.

The mineshaft filled up with water after the rain.

Yes, that's what I heard too!

And it bought the body up.

Yes. The body came up.

I could see Nisha as if she were standing in front of me: in flip-flops and shorts; a soft sprinkling of dark hairs on her thighs; the plait that reached the base of her spine; beads on her wrist – bracelets that her daughter had made and sent in a tattered envelope. My thoughts expanded: Nisha pulling off yellow rubber gloves, spreading orange marmalade on toast for me, stirring coffee on the stove with a long spoon, questioning me with eyes that were always curious, always sombre, dark with the past.

Far away, across the land, church bells rang. They rang again and again, but I could still hear the voices of the crowd.

The body is decomposed.

They will have to do DNA tests.

I didn't dare to say the thing that was on my mind, but I knew that Yiannis was thinking it too, because when I finally turned to look at him, he was pale and shaking.

The next moment, he had left my side. I saw him slip through the crowd, heading towards the gallows frame. I lost him for a while, then I heard a commotion. I pushed my way closer to the front and saw Yiannis having an argument with a police officer: he had managed to get over or under the rope into the investigation zone. The officer was holding his arms out, creating a barrier; another was approaching from the right. This second officer placed a hand on Yiannis's shoulder and gestured for him to calm down.

'Hey!' I shouted. 'Leave him alone! It's OK. He's knows her. It's OK, he knows her.'

It wasn't until they all turned to look at me – the police, the people in the crowd – that I understood what I had said.

We left the lake without knowing. The police told us to go home, they would have to do tests, something about DNA, testing the bones – I could barely distinguish the words.

We were driving now, and I looked over at Yiannis. He looked like the shell of a man. His eyes were sunken, his lips pressed in. He was a shrivelled bird, something featherless and old.

I was just about to take the turn off for Nicosia, when he spoke, his voice dry and hoarse, as if he hadn't used it for centuries.

'Petra,' he said.

'Yes?'

'Will you go somewhere with me?'

'Where?'

'I can't go back yet.'

'But where?'

'To the woods.'

'Why?'

'I have to check something. Will you come? Will you drive me there?'

'Of course,' I said.

Following Yiannis's directions, I drove us to the west coast of Larnaca, near the village of Zygi. I was hit by the smell of wild thyme and rosemary. In the distance I could see the beautiful oranges and yellows of the citrus plantations. He directed me to a sheltered spot by the side of the road and I parked the car. He got out and headed down a narrow path through the trees, motioning me to follow him. We were walking into a dense and dark forest of eucalyptus and acacia trees. We walked for a few minutes, picking our way among the brambles, until we came to a clearing.

There, swarming with flies, was a mouflon ovis. I took a step closer, but Yiannis grabbed my arm with his good hand.

'No,' he said. 'Not this.'

I followed him further into the woods and began to hear a cacophony of birdsong. I'd never heard anything like it, so many songs overlapping. There were thousands of them, above our heads, surrounding us, thousands and thousands of birds writhing in nets that stretched the length of the glade.

'What is this?' I asked, in horror.

'The mist nets,' he said, in a hollow voice. 'Yesterday we were hunting—'

I shot him a sharp look.

'Yes,' he said, turning down his eyes. 'We were hunting.

Seraphim and me. We left so quickly after my arm was injured. I didn't know if Seraphim had come back. It looks like he didn't.'

I looked up again. It was a cacophony. The song of thousands of birds trapped in one place. I wanted to throw up. Thousands of birds stuck in the net, trying to fly away.

'Will you help me?' Yiannis asked, 'to release the birds?'

With one hand, he began to yank at the net until each side dropped gently to the earth. He knelt down and tended to each bird, one at a time. He was struggling, working with only one arm, so I went to help him.

'My god,' I said. 'My god.' Some were dead, but those still living, I cradled in my palms, stroking the birds' feathers with my fingers, placing them on the ground, waiting to see if they would move. Some hopped away, others flew up into the leaves of the trees or into the sky. One by one. One by one. Yiannis worked beside me, though clumsily and mostly ineffectually. I saw his frustration in his failed attempts, but I knew better than to tell him to step aside.

We worked for nearly an hour, releasing the birds together. There were so many that were migrating birds, and residents of the island too. Amongst the blackcaps were grey herons and blue rock thrushes, and beautiful tiny wallcreepers with their crimson flight feathers.

By now, I was crying, my sobs mingling with the birdsong.

'There are crossbills and coal tits, jays and tree creepers,' Yiannis said, as if he was seeing them properly for the first time. 'And black kites,' he continued, 'and steppe buzzards and honey buzzards. And look . . . hundreds of finches.'

'Isn't it sad that they are still singing?' I said.

'They would have sung until they died,' Yiannis replied.

'Just listen to their music,' I said. 'Oh, look at that!'

In the middle of the mist net, tangled up with pulsating wings, was a kestrel.

'It's still alive,' I said. Its wing was stuck in the net, but I tugged at the filaments with my fingers, tore at it with my nails, careful not to scare the kestrel, not to hurt it more.

'It would have died slowly,' Yiannis said.

I held the kestrel on my lap, while working on disentangling it from the net. It lay still, looking up at me with its large, beady eyes. Above us and around us flew the birds that had been rescued. On the ground beside us lay the birds that had died.

Finally, I released the kestrel from the net and Yiannis and I both stopped to watch as the kestrel opened its spotted wings and launched into the sky. I said: 'Nisha was always smiling, you know, in spite of everything. She brought up my daughter and cleaned my home and always smiled with all of her heart. Did you see that?'

'Nisha once told me,' replied Yiannis, tracing the kestrel's path in the sky with his eyes, 'that she wanted to protect Aliki from her pain. She carried much of it – pain. I don't know if you knew that. But she wanted Aliki to see her as happy, so that the child could feel that the world was full of joy. Nisha said, "Children search our eyes to discover the world. When they see happiness or joy or love there, then they know that these things exist."'

I knew instantly that this was the gift Nisha had given to my daughter – that Aliki had learnt to understand the world through Nisha's eyes.

Two nights later, I was tucking Aliki into bed. 'Do you remember you told me about the birds stolen from the sky?' I asked her, as I pulled the sheets up to her chin, then folded them back and patted around her arms, pulling the fabric tight as she liked it.

She nodded.

'I rescued them. Yiannis and I, we went to rescue them. We released them from the nets so they would be able to fly again.'

'So now they can carry on with their journey?'

'Yes.'

She nodded again, her eyes wide and watery in the light of the bedside lamp.

'Did some of the birds die?'

I paused. 'They did,'

'Nisha will be sad.'

On Thursday, Tony rang and asked if he could come visit that evening. He didn't sound OK.

'Is there something wrong?' I said. I had become accustomed to the tone of his voice, but today he sounded apprehensive, tentative. He called nearly every day to check in, give any updates, to see if Yiannis or I had any news.

'It's best if we talk when I see you,' he said.

I went up to tell Yiannis that Tony would be visiting at 7 p.m., but I did not elaborate on the nature of our conversation.

I took Aliki over to Mrs Hadjikyriacou's.

'Someone is coming to tell you something about Nisha, aren't they?' Aliki said, as we knocked on Mrs Hadjikyriacou's door.

'I think so,' I said.

'Hm,' was her response. A small sound, like a mouse.

Yiannis arrived first, just before 7 p.m. He was holding his tablet in his hand in case Kumari called: he was worried about her. His hair had grown, he was unshaven, there were dark circles under his eyes and he looked as though he'd been wearing the same clothes for days. His arm was still in a sling and I didn't bother to ask him again about it. He sat down on the sofa close to the fire. Neither of us mentioned the afternoon of the songbirds, and neither of us mentioned Nisha.

'How is Aliki?' he said.

'She's fine, thank you. She's with Mrs Hadjikyriacou.'

He nodded.

'Can I get you a drink?'

'Just water.'

I went off to the kitchen and heard the tablet ring.

'Why aren't you at school?' Yiannis said.

'I couldn't go in, Mr Yiannis . . . feel too worried. I make up stories of what has happened to Amma. Maybe she is trapped underground like my baba was. Amma told me the story about Baba. Will you tell me true things from now on, Mr Yiannis, because then my brain make up other things?'

'Of course,' he said.

'My grandmother want to know any more information. She is in the other room on the bed. She has been crying.'

'OK, Kumari,' he said. 'Listen to me carefully and remember that I'm here any time if you or your grandmother need to speak to me.' Yiannis hesitated as I returned with a jug and three glasses on a tray, placing it on the coffee table. 'A woman has been found in a lake here on the island,' he said.

I stood behind him out of the glow of the screen. Kumari remained silent at first, then with a shake in her voice, she said, 'Is the lady in the lake alive?'

'No.'

'Could the lady in the lake be my amma?'

'I don't know. I don't think so. I'm sure it's not.'

Once again there was no response for a while.

'You think it might be Amma. I know you do,' she said. 'Because if you thought it was definitely not Amma you wouldn't tell me this information. You are telling me to . . . prepare me. Isn't that right Mr Yiannis?'

'Yes, Kumari.'

Then she was gone.

Yiannis sat without moving, staring at his own reflection in the dark screen. I took a step forward and placed my hand on his shoulder.

The doorbell rang.

I left Yiannis sitting there and went to let Tony in. It was strange to see him out of the booth. He was much taller and

328

wider than I realised and he walked slowly and heavily, like a bear.

He sat in the armchair opposite Yiannis and I poured him a glass of water.

'Can I get you anything else?' I asked. 'A coffee or tea? It's quite a long journey from Limassol.'

'No, thank you, Petra,' he said. 'And thank you for your kind hospitality.'

I smiled faintly and sat down. We both stared at him and he hesitated before speaking.

'I wanted to come and tell you before it comes out in the news.'

'They've identified the body?' said Yiannis. He was perched at the edge of the sofa and I noticed a tremor in his hands as they rested on his knees.

'Yes, they have.'

'It's Nisha?'

'No,' Tony said, and I heard Yiannis exhale. 'Allow me to finish,' said Tony. 'The woman has been identified as Rosamie Cotabu. Petra, you might recognise the name. She was one of the women I told you about during your first visit.'

I nodded and glanced quickly at Yiannis, who was looking more agitated than ever, rhythmically rubbing his right temple.

'Rosamie Cotabu,' Tony repeated slowly. 'Would you mind if I light a cigarette?'

'Not at all,' I said, and got up to bring him a saucer that he could use as an ashtray. By the time I returned from the kitchen he had lit the cigarette and the smoke was swirling amongst the light of the fire. I could see that Tony's hand was shaking too as he held the cigarette up to his lips, taking three long, hard drags so that the ash drooped from it. He moved his hand carefully to the saucer and allowed the ash to drop in there.

'I have a friend in the police force,' he said, glancing at me. 'He's junior in rank so he had no power to launch an investigation, but he's been useful in getting information.'

I nodded and sat down.

'Rosamie Cotabu,' he said, 'I told you about her didn't I? The one who worked for a man who was physically abusing her.'

'Yes,' I said. 'I remember.'

'She went to the police for help, but they told her to leave Cyprus if she wasn't happy. Nobody helped her.' He paused and with heavy eyes took another drag of smoke before stubbing out the cigarette. 'I knew Rosamie wouldn't run away. I knew something was wrong. Why didn't I do more?' He lifted his arm and dropped it down onto the arm of the sofa like a dead weight. He took another cigarette out of the box and held it between his fingers but did not light it. 'Oh,' he said smiling now, 'What a joyful girl she was! She had so many friends. She said I saved her life.' At this point Tony began to cry, like a sudden storm; tears broke out of him and he apologised again and again through stifled sobs.

'I'm sorry, Petra. I did not come here to be a burden on you,' he said, composing himself, lighting the cigarette, taking in the smoke as if it would save his life.

'Don't worry, Tony,' I said. Yiannis was so quiet, I almost

forgot that he was there but when I turned to him, he was alert and present and trembling inside. I could see it. He reminded me of the way wheat stalks shake in the breeze in the open fields.

'The police went through her phone, which they recovered in the nearby field.' Tony continued. 'They discovered that she had communicated via text with a man whom she had met on a dating site. She had gone out that particular night, the night she went missing, to meet him for the first time. He was the last person she texted. The police discovered that his dating profile had a fake name but they managed to trace the details back to a thirty-five-year-old Greek Cypriot soldier serving at the national guard. They have taken him in for questioning. The autopsy showed that she had injuries on her body and marks around her neck.' He shook his head. 'I'll tell you, this doesn't look good.'

'No,' Yiannis said, and his voice came out hoarse and unfamiliar, as if he hadn't spoken to a soul in many years. 'But I know for a fact that Nisha wouldn't have gone on a date with anyone. I know that for sure. She loved me.'

Tony nodded sympathetically. 'It will become clearer in time,' he said, 'but for now we must wait.'

After the men left, I felt frightened and cold. A strong wind rattled the windows and bent the olive tree out front. I went into Aliki's room. She was fast asleep. I crawled into bed with her and curled up around her, smelling her hair, giving her soft kisses while she slept.

26

Yiannis

THE MURDER OF ROSAMIE COTABU had been
announced on the news. People were restless. The
Vietnamese maids with their rice hats kept their
eyes fixed on passers-by. Downstairs, at Mrs Hadjikyriacou's,
Ruba stood out front holding a broom, looking frightened.

This time I called Kumari. Once again, she was alone.

'Good morning, Mr Yiannis, do you have any more information? My grandmother is making me breakfast and she is
crying all the time. She is wiping all her tears on her sleeve
and cardigan.'

'Have you been crying, Kumari?'

'No. I don't cry until I know all the facts. Are there new
facts now?'

'They know who the woman in the lake is and it is not
your mother.'

Kumari let out a huge sigh as if she had been holding her breath and her words came out shaken and broken: 'Thank you. Oh, my! Mr Yiannis. It is not my amma.'

She left her tablet on the table with me staring up at the ceiling, and I could hear her saying things to her grandmother, who once again seemed to be asking many questions through her tears.

Kumari picked up the tablet again.

'What is the lady's name that they found inside the lake?'

'Her name is Rosamie Cotabu.'

'Was she one of the missing ladies that you told me about?'

'Yes, she was.'

'One of the five missing ladies.'

'Yes.'

'Was she a maid like my amma is?'

'Yes.'

Kumari was silent now. I could hear the old lady in the other room, still talking.

'You think they will find Amma like they did this other lady, don't you Mr Yiannis?'

'No,' I said, 'I don't think that.'

'But she was also a missing lady, like Amma. Isn't that right, Mr. Yiannis?'

It turned out that Rosamie Cotabu was Christian and church bells rang for her departure to the next world. Meanwhile, anger was brewing. The maids were not just scared, they were livid. Rosamie Cotabu had, after all, been reported missing and the police had ignored her employer's pleas and concerns. Then she had been found in a mineshaft, wrapped up in white cloth.

The women walked by on the street below, always in pairs now, keeping their heads close together in muffled conversation, but their eyes were always roving, on the lookout for the next threat. It felt like the hours and days after a massive earthquake, where people walk around expecting it to happen again at any moment, where the walls and the ground beneath one's feet no longer seem solid and there is no certainty of safety anywhere.

A man was in custody but his name had not been released to the public and Tony had no idea of it either.

During that week, at some point one evening, Seraphim knocked on my door. This was the first time he'd ever come to my place and the first time he had arrived unannounced.

I opened the door for him and without saying anything I stepped aside to let him in.

'How is your arm?' he asked, glancing at the bandage. I'd released it now from its sling.

'Better.'

'I heard about the woman found at the Mitsero mines,' he said.

I nodded and offered him a seat.

'Have you heard from Nisha?'

'No,' I said.

He looked out of the balcony doors but said nothing.

Then he unzipped a rucksack that he'd placed by his feet and took out a wad of money. From the look of it, it was much more than what he owed me for the previous hunt.

'That looks around 10,000 euro,' I said.

'You're spot on.' He put it on the coffee table between us. 'It's yours,' he said.

'A bribe?'

'Why would I need to bribe you?'

'To keep my mouth shut.'

The little bird hopped up onto the table now and inspected the wad of notes that lay upon it. Seraphim frowned and glanced at me straight on.

'You have a pet bird now?'

'It's not a pet,' I said. I had no energy to say more.

'The money is to help you get by, until you figure out what you're going to do.'

I just stared at him blankly.

'We go a long way back, don't we?' he said.

I nodded, apprehensive, wondering what dirty plan he had up his sleeve this time.

'I remember when I used to come visit your farm with my dad, do you remember?'

I just shrugged, but he went on.

'I loved being there, getting out of the city. I saw the kind of life you had and I was jealous. I was always so jealous of you and all that freedom you had. The only time I got to be out in the open was when I had a rifle in my hand.'

His eyes had drifted away for a while and they flicked back to me now.

'The other day, when I saw how you reacted to the death of the mouflon, it . . . it reminded me of . . .'

I waited, but the sentence was never finished.

'I'll tell the bosses that you've been badly injured in an accident and won't be able to work anymore.'

'Thank you,' I said.

'I'll reassure them that we won't need to keep you quiet.'

I nodded.

'You know, I wasn't always such a pig. Don't you remember?'

What I remembered was Seraphim running down that mountain holding the crow he'd killed by its feet.

He must have seen the doubt on my face as he said, 'Come on, Yiannis! Don't you remember? It was as soon as they placed that gun in my hands, that's when I changed. Before that we played in the woods. You showed me all those creatures that crawled amongst the leaves. You showed me how to catch a snake and release it. We played dominos in the olive orchard. We made an igloo out of twigs and explored the North Pole! We fought sharks in the Pacific Ocean!'

He was right, of course. I remembered all of it. Those memories were exactly what had stopped me from despising him completely. I had a sudden image of him now, standing on the fallen trunk of a tree, encouraging me across a treacherous river of grass.

'We made a catapult to knock the ripe apples off the trees,' he said, 'so that we could eat and survive in the Amazon.'

'Yes,' I said.

'You do know.'

I nodded, slowly.

336

'Take the money,' he said. 'Please.'

'OK.'

I didn't thank him and I didn't offer him a drink.

'I have a new apprentice,' he said, as he made his way to the door. 'Young lad, very sharp. Exactly what I need. But, you know, Oskana wants me to stop all this stuff. She doesn't understand there's a huge price to pay. We are expecting a child. I cannot take risks.'

His eyes were so sad, so full of anguish.

'How *is* Oksana?' I said.

'Very well. I finally finished painting the nursery and revealed it to her, grand opening, that sort of thing. She was beside herself.'

'I'm so glad,' I said, and for a brief moment I genuinely was.

'If I'd really hurt you, I would never have been able to live with myself,' he said.

'I know.'

Then he was gone.

I glanced down at the money and I knew what I wanted to do with it. I would send it to Kumari, along with everything else I had saved.

As for me, I would start again. I'd get a job at a restaurant somewhere, maybe even at Theo's if he needed any waiters. I would do this and start over again, and when Nisha returned, she would see that I had let go of my old life, that I had understood.

There was not going to be another earthquake. One was enough. But I could hear my grandfather's voice in my head:

'The truth is in the earth, in the song of the birds, in the rhythms and whispers of the animals. If you want to see and hear it – only if you want to – it is there.'

It had been nearly a week from his last visit when we heard from Tony again. Petra knocked on my door one evening to say that he had called and he was coming late that evening. She asked if I could come down at ten o'clock, after Aliki was asleep.

I arrived early and Petra offered me a seat by the fire. I took the same armchair I had occupied before, and placed my hands on my knees. Petra kept glancing over at me, as if I were a stranger, and I smiled to myself. My hair and beard had grown even more and I was sure I looked something like a bear. A friendly one, I hoped.

'I've stopped the poaching. I should have listened to Nisha from the start,' I told her, and waited for her reaction.

'Yes, you should have,' she said and then seemed to regret her words, the heat of them. They were true, however. Fair and true. I lowered my eyes to the ground.

'I'm sorry,' said Petra. 'I'm sure Nisha will be very relieved and happy when she returns.'

I glanced at her sharply and was about to speak, but the doorbell interrupted us.

A moment later, Petra ushered in Tony. He remained standing for a moment, taking us in, before taking a seat.

'Can I get you anything?' Petra offered.

'No, nothing,' he replied, bluntly.

'So,' he said, 'I will come straight out and say this. The man they have in custody, the soldier, he has confessed to the murder of Rosamie Cotabu.'

'Why?' I blurted out. I wasn't quite sure what I was asking. Perhaps I needed quickly to see a motive for this murder so that no one could, even for a second, be able to link it to Nisha's disappearance.

'Because he is a mad man!' Tony's eyes were alight with fury. He looked as though he was about to stand up, grab something and dash it at the wall, but instead he collapsed back into the armchair, and for a moment he seemed deflated, defeated even. Then he took a deep breath, leaned forward, clutching his hands tightly together over his thighs. 'This monster is apparently devastated by what he has done, as if all he had done is steal something. He has decided to help the police. He said it's the least he can do.' Tony's voice was harsh, it shook with anger, he spat out the last sentence with venom.

He glanced at Petra, then he looked over at me and held my gaze. 'He has subsequently confessed to the murder of four more women and two of their children. The women were all foreign maids. He met two of these women on dating sites – those two he knew their names, though the police won't release the other, not yet, not until they have recovered the bodies. The rest he captured as they were walking; for them, he said he never asked their names. He is a lunatic. He needed to kill. He killed foreign maids because it was easier, he knew that nobody would search for them, he thought he would be able to get away with it. What does that tell you, huh? Tell me, what does that tell you about the shitty world we live in?'

Neither Petra nor I seemed to be able to speak.

'He threw two of the bodies into the mineshaft,' Tony said. 'The other two women and the children are in suitcases in the red lake. He put them in suitcases, he threw them away, as if they were not human.'

Tony stopped talking. He pressed his temples hard with his fingers, scrunching up his eyes. I could feel a burning sensation in my chest, fire burning. I couldn't move. Petra quietly began to recite names, ticking them off on her fingers:

'Rosamie Cotabu,

Reyna Gatan,

Cristina Maier and

her daughter, Daria,

Ana-Maria Lupei and

her daughter, Andreea.

And Nisha Jayakody.'

Petra stared at her hand, all five fingers stretched wide. She looked over at me, as if still trying to comprehend, put together the pieces of everything she had just heard.

'The search is beginning tonight,' Tony said. 'Soon, everything will be certain.'

27

Petra

WHEN I WOKE UP, I thought I had blood on my hands. I felt it, sticky and warm. When I opened the blinds, however, and held my hands up before my eyes, they were clean and white in the morning sun.

I remembered the blood of the birds. The way it had felt and smelt, the way it had stuck in my nails.

It was a cold winter Saturday and the house was silent. The dust had gathered. I sat down by an unlit fire.

'Mum, Nisha isn't coming back, is she?' Aliki was standing in the doorway, looking at me with sombre eyes.

'You're awake, baby. I was hoping you would sleep longer.'

'She's gone,' my daughter said, simply.

'I think so,' I said. 'I think she might be gone.'

'She made my heart be full of stars, now it's just dark inside me.'

I reached out and Aliki came to me. I pulled her into my lap, her gangly legs barely contained on my knees, the fug of sleep still clinging to her sweatpants and T-shirt. I stroked her hair, pulling it back from her face, and she closed her eyes.

And then we both heard it. Shouts. Cries. A murmur that was growing, beginning to swell. Aliki sprang off my lap and ran to the door. I followed her. We both stood in the doorway, watching people pass by.

First, we saw the two Filipino maids who always walked with the young girl between them, the pretty little girl with pigtails, holding each of their hands. But this time they were without the child, and heading down the street with a solemn determination. Then we saw Nilmini stepping out of Yiakoumi's shop, untying her apron and leaving it by the front door as she headed in the same direction.

When I looked back at Aliki she was crying. I put my arms around her and she cried into my chest; I felt the weight of her on me and I embraced her, tighter. Then she held herself upright and watched the maids pass by. There were so many now, all heading in the same direction. I held Aliki's hand tight. Her tears fell down her cheeks and dropped onto the cobbled street. I imagined a stream, flowing, a stream of tears flowing in the direction that the maids were heading.

The two maids at Theo's abandoned their tasks and followed the crowd. Finally, Ruba from Mrs Hadjikyriacou's house next door stepped out, closing the door behind her.

I stopped her. 'Where are they going? What is happening?'

'Come and see,' she said.

Aliki shoved her feet into the nearest Converse and we followed the maids.

Women that I'd never seen before in the neighbourhood were joining in. They watched from windows and came out as the women passed, without a second thought joining the rest. Most were immigrant workers and there were children, too, some Aliki's age, some even younger, who held the hands of their nannies as they followed the crowd. We walked along the backstreets from the Famagusta Gate until we reached the Cyprus Museum, then we took the main road all the way down to the Presidential Palace. There, a crowd of thousands, dressed mostly in black, spread out across the street below the palace holding lighted candles with their heads bowed in prayer. Others held banners reading 'Misogyny and Racism Must Stop' or 'End discrimination towards women and foreigners' and 'We sacrifice our lives'. I saw Soneeya and Binsa in the crowd, standing close together with candles in their hands, directing their shouts at the white palace. In her hand, Binsa held a banner that simply said: 'Where are they?'

We stayed out for hours and the sun began to set as the afternoon turned late. Someone handed Aliki a candle and she held it high above her head, joining the shouts and demands. She was still crying, but kept the candle aloft. As the darkness gathered the candles glowed, beacons every-where. There were so many women, so many faces, so many voices raised in chorus and hope.

This was the story of Nisha Jayakody, as I understood it:

> Nisha was a mother of two children, who lived in
> different worlds.
> Nisha's child in Sri Lanka has curly hair, so soft it
> feels like the down of an owl.
> Nisha's other child is my child.
> Nisha had lost her first love.
> Nisha knew how to love.
> Nisha filled my daughter's heart with stars.
> I owe Nisha more than I could ever repay her.

That night, when I came in to kiss Aliki goodnight, she was sitting up in bed, looking out of the window. I followed her gaze to Monkey, who was outside and pawing at the window-panes, trying to get in.

'Look, Mum, it is our cat!' Aliki said. She began to laugh and then, quite suddenly, she exhaled and gave in to a mighty exhaustion and began to cry. She scrunched her face and her tears flowed out. They flowed like they would never stop this time and amongst her sobs she said, 'I'm so tired,' and, 'I miss Nisha so much.' I sat down beside her and held her in my arms. I held her in a way that I never had, like I should have all those years gone, like Nisha had always wanted me to. I felt my daughter crying on me, I felt her tears soaking into the skin of my neck, into my veins, right through to my heart.

I rubbed her back and rocked her. 'Tell me what's in your heart,' I said.

'I want Nisha, Mum,' she said into my neck, with shaky breath and tears. 'I want Nisha to come back. I want to sit in our boat. I want her to tell me stories and get me ready for school and . . . and . . .'

'And?'

'And do the stupid times tables with me and . . . and . . . and . . .'

'And?'

'And I wake up at night and I'm so scared because Nisha is not there. Sometimes I wake up and knock on her door and wait for her to open it, but she never opens it. She never opens it anymore.'

My chest burned and my eyes burned until I too was crying, crying and rocking Aliki.

'I want Nisha to come back so much.'

'I know baby, so do I.'

Slowly she ceased crying. Now and then she whimpered and then her breathing slowed. We remained there in silence. I stroked her hair and watched the cat jump down, glancing at us one last time before it skulked off into the dark.

28

Yiannis

IT WAS DAWN WHEN I finally slept, haunted by images of the red lake and memories of Nisha. When I finally woke up, late in the afternoon, there was a cacophony in the street below. I went out onto the balcony as hundreds of protestors filled every inch of the road, and flowed along it like a river. People marched with banners, passing the trees where Nisha's flyers hung, away from the border and into the city, to find the root of the problem and stand before it, defiant and strong.

Here we are, they were saying. *We do not simply appear from nowhere in a taxi with a suitcase and disappear once more to nowhere.*

We are human.

We love.

We hate.

We have pasts.

We have futures.

We are citizens of countries, in our own right.

We have voices.

We have families.

Here we are.

The little bird was on the table beside me and it fluttered up to the nearest tree and watched the crowd below with black eyes. Then it flicked its head back to me. Something came over me. I felt such a sadness. Such a painful despair.

'Go,' I said to it, though I wanted to hold onto the bird and all that it meant, forever. 'Go. Go fly. Go.'

In that moment, as if it understood, it opened its wings and took off into the sky.

Watching the bird leave, knowing it would probably never come back, suddenly woke me up. I dressed myself with purpose and went out onto the street. I caught a glimpse of Mrs Hadjikyriacou at her front door, watching with those observant but cloudy eyes.

I allowed myself to be taken by the current. I could hardly see for tears. I allowed myself to be taken until eventually we reached the presidential palace and I sat down on a bench, unable to stand any more. I had no strength in my legs.

I sat there and watched the women, their faces lit up by the candles they held in their hands. There was pain in those faces, and real fear, and, in the light, an anger that allowed them to stand straight and say *Here we are*.

There was a reporter beside me, and a cameraman. They were interviewing one of the women. She was probably in her twenties, with a round milky face and a French plait that hung over her right shoulder. She stood there looking straight into the camera and because she was so close, I heard her voice above the crowd: 'I am one of lucky ones,' she said. 'I have a great employer, a good woman, she treats me well. My sister, she was sexually abused by her sir. She went to the police and they did nothing to help so she left her job. Now she has just three more months to find work or she will have to return to Nepal. We need to send money to my parents, they are very sick. But when I think about the women in the lake, and the children . . .' She paused and took a deep breath.

'Where does it end?' A taller, darker woman standing beside her said. 'Are we the "lucky ones" because we have not been *killed?'*

A strong wind blew and some of the candles went out. I saw Ruba amongst the crowd, and the two maids from Theo's without their rice hats, their hair long and dark. Ruba relit her candle from the flame of a woman standing beside her. She then passed her flame to a child. The sun set further into the earth.

Where was Nisha to tell her story? What would I do without her? What would Kumari do without her mother? And Aliki?

I could barely breathe. I felt like I was in the middle of a burning world. But in this moment, I imagined that it burned with gold.

It was certain. Nisha had vanished and turned to gold.

She turned to gold in the setting of this winter sun. Now, for a brief moment, I caught a glimpse of her, and I think I heard her, in the burning faces and voices of the women that surrounded me.

This is where Nisha exists.

Here.

And, in the moment, she kissed me, high up in the mountains, when she had been partly with me and partly in the world from which she had come.

The red lake at Mitsero reflects a sunset, captures it, holds it, even when the sun has died. Red lake, toxic lake, copper lake. Mothers and fathers tell their children stories about it, tales of deep passages underground, where men crawled like animals and died in darkness.

Never go near the red lake at Mitsero!

The sunset holds the expectation of the hush and darkness of the night, that time when we close our eyes and meet our true selves. The lake is at the verge of this darkness, always.

It holds all the sunsets from the beginning of time.

A helicopter hovers above like a dragonfly. Four orange rescue crafts glide on the water. Divers enter. There are three, secured to the boats with bright yellow ropes.

They will not get lost down there; they have their colleagues at the ready to pull them out.

They slide in, and once again the lake is still.

In the village, the widow stands in her front garden holding a lit candle. To protect the flame from the breeze she cradles it in her palm.

The barley fields and wheat fields are gold beneath the setting sun. The woods are alight. A hare runs out of a bush and tentatively approaches the crater, keeping its distance.

After a while, a diver emerges from the water. He signals to the people in the boat and they throw down some ropes with hooks at the end. He goes down again and when he comes back up, he raises a thumb and the people in the boat pull until a suitcase is dragged to the surface.

29

Petra

ALIKI WANTED ME TO HELP her get ready. At first, she took her time choosing what she would wear, then she stood still while I pulled the jumper over her head – Nisha's orange jumper with the sunflower. I put her feet into her jeans, pulling them up. She stared out of the glass doors at the boat in the garden, at the orange tree, at the chickens that roamed out of their pen. Then I took the bracelet out of my pocket.

'Look at this,' I said.

She turned to me now, caught my eye for a second and there I saw a depth of sadness as vast as the sea.

'That was a present from me.' She smiled, sadly.

'Yes. You know she never took it off. She wore it every single day.'

I secured the bracelet onto her wrist and she twisted her

hand around so that the bracelet glimmered in the late afternoon sun that streaked through the glass doors.

We went outside to sit in the boat and wait for the others. First, Mrs Hadjikyriacou came with Ruba, then Soneeya and Binsa, then Nilmini, followed by Muyia, who arrived as the sun was setting.

Apart from brief greetings, nobody spoke. We all knew why we were there – to say goodbye to Nisha. I wondered where Yiannis was. His kitchen window was shut and dark. I helped Aliki pass the candles around and when I looked again, he was standing at the foot of the stairs with his hands empty at his sides. Face pale, lids heavy, shirt buttoned up to his neck.

He stood there and watched us light the candles, hold them in front of us to light the darkness on our faces. A hush enveloped us all; the boat was empty and I imagined Nisha sitting in it.

'Nisha is going away,' Aliki said suddenly, and for a moment all eyes rose from the ground and rested on her face. 'She is drifting away on the soft waves of the faraway sea above the sky.'

I put my hand on Aliki's shoulder and I felt her body shake. It wasn't a cold night, but she trembled as if an icy wind was blowing.

Then the wind did pick up and we moved back into the protection of the house, Aliki leading everyone into the warmth.

'Give me a second,' I said to her.

I walked over to the stairs where Yiannis was still standing. 'Are you coming in?'

He nodded. 'I've booked a flight to Sri Lanka. I'm leaving tomorrow.

I caught his eye, inhaling deeply, not knowing what to say.

'I'm going to see Kumari,' he said.

I squeezed his hand and he began to cry. With his chin down and his eyes scrunched up, and his chest shaking, he cried, and I held onto his hand as Nisha drifted away on the sea above the sky.

Later, I sat in the garden with Aliki and Nilmini. She opened her friend's journal and began to read. We sat there for hours, listening to Nisha's words. Tomorrow I would be giving Yiannis the journal to take to Kumari – its rightful owner.

Nisha's true story began to unfold. I heard the story of Kiyoma's death and the owl. I heard about how she travelled to Rathnapura, how she met her husband and the day he died in the mines. I heard about how she'd worked day and night at the market in Galle, how she had made the difficult decision to leave, and how she had felt that first year away from home, unable to hold her beautiful daughter, Kumari.

There was so much more I wished I could know. These letters were merely a handful of stars in the entire universe of her heart. But it was too late. If only I could have understood before it was too late.

Dear Kumari,

When I held you as a baby, close to my skin, and looked down into your eyes, I saw everything I loved and everything I feared. Within them, I saw the sunset over the Sri Pada (there's a story about this! Keep reading and you'll find out!). I saw rivers and waterfalls at dusk (this too!). I saw my own mother's eyes, and myself, walking beside her through the rice plantations at the end of the day. I saw peppers laid out in rows to dry in the sun, and steaming meals with lemon-grass and cardamoms and cinnamon. I saw my sister's eyes, all those years ago, when she would laugh with so much glee (you remind me of her, Kumari). I saw the dress I wore on my wedding day and your father's smile and his arms around me as we danced.

I also saw your future. This made me afraid.

In the house where I now live there is a garden and in that garden there is a small wooden boat. The boat is from far away, because there is no sea nearby. We are in the city, a very old city, with four old gates that are so big they look like they were made for giants.

I look after a baby girl called Aliki, who is two years younger than you.

Kumari, the garden is such a special place. A place that reminds me of who I am. It has an orange tree (like the ones back home, except sweeter), a cactus with prickly pears, lots of flowers, and a chicken pen. I wish you were here to see it. I've drawn pictures for you in this journal! You would love the chickens. They are so funny. One of the hens always manages to get out of the pen. She comes into the living room when we forget to close the door. She sits under the coffee table and watches TV with us. I make sure my boss doesn't see her so that she doesn't throw her out. Sometimes the hen comes up to bed with me, crawls under the duvet as if it's a paper bag, and talks to herself. She has feathers that grow over her eyes so she can't see much, but she doesn't seem to mind.

By the time you are old enough to read this you will probably know all this stuff already, but I need to write it down so that I can feel close to you when I'm alone.

When I first arrived here, I could hear you crying. You might find it hard to believe, but it was you that I heard, I know that now. I thought it was a young child in another house, but then I realised that the sound was coming from the earth, the trees and the sky, that you were sending it to me as a gift. Kumari, somehow, you found a way to send me your tears. So, I sat in the little boat in the garden and sent you stories and love through the night sky.

You didn't get to know your father. I am sure you would have loved him as much as I did. I will tell you about him – although I'm sure your acci will tell you plenty as you grow up.

Your acci won't mention this because she doesn't like to talk about it, but life can change in a second. From sunlight to sudden rain, just like the weather during the monsoon when the rain comes down like the sea. But one thing your father always said was that rain doesn't last for ever, and when the sun shines again everything will gleam. He was an optimist.

Your father should have been an actor. He did impressions of people and animals, flicked his hand when he spoke, had a twinkle in his eye. In real life, he worked in the gem mines, that's where we met! He went down into the dark while I cleaned the gravel in the reservoir to find the gems.

I have so much to tell you. But be patient. Reality and truth need time to unravel.

Acknowledgements

I have so many people to thank for helping me to understand more deeply the sensitive issues I was researching in order to create this novel.

Thank you, firstly and especially, to Menaka Nishanthe Ramanayaka for all the work you did over the years, for all your strength, for becoming a friend, for making me lovely Sri Lankan tea, for sharing your feelings and memories with me, for listening to me and for being such a beautiful and caring person. It is because of you that I wanted to write this novel in the first place.

Thank you so much to Marissa Begonia for being such an inspiration with your insight and determination and for inviting me to visit the Voice of Domestic Workers in Holborn. You are extraordinary and the work you have done, what you have achieved, is honestly phenomenal. I'd like to thank all the women at the centre who welcomed me with so much love, for sharing your delicious food with me and allowing me to hear your stories. I'd also like to thank Loucas Koutroukides in Limassol, Cyprus, for all the wonderful humanitarian work you have done to help domestic workers on the island, for speaking with me for so many hours and for introducing me to so many wonderful people. Thank you too for all the interesting, informative and courageous articles you wrote and shared with me, for being brave enough to seek the truth and speak the truth when so many others turned a blind eye or remined silent. Thank you also to all the women at the Blue Elephant, who spoke to me, who trusted me with their stories, who shared their emotions and fears with me – thank you, I learnt so much.

Thank you to George Konstantinou at NGO Protection of the Natural Heritage and Biodiversity of Cyprus; thank you so much for answering all of my questions, for all your help and advice, and for the wonderful photographs you took and sent to me. I wish I could have attended one of your wildlife tours if we hadn't been in lockdown, but speaking to you nonetheless was so informative. Thank you also for the wonderful and important work you are doing to protect the forests and the animals on the island.

Thank you Eva Spanou for helping me to progress with my research. Thank you so much Nicolas and Sotiroulla Simou for sharing so much information with me about poaching.

Thank you to Peter Louizou and Tassos Louizou, for talking to me for so long last Christmas about hunting, for sharing all your knowledge with me about the poaching of songbirds and the very specific technique of making limesticks. Thank you to my lovely brother, Mario Lefteri, for giving me so much advice and information about Cyprus and about poaching locations, for being one of the first to read my novel, as you always are, and for all your help and suggestions. Thank you to Angela Stella Monaghan for your help and for introducing me to your parents. Equally, thank you to Panayiotis and Andriana Michael for spending so long talking to me about poaching and for all the useful information you shared with me.

Thank you to Nishan Weeratunge and Sajeewa Dissanayake for all the information you gave me about Sri Lanka, Sri Lankan food and culture and Sri Lankan history. It was immensely helpful and so great that I made new and wonderful friends from it. Thank you to Maryvonne and Antony for inspiring me with all of your stories and for introducing me to Nishan.

Thank you to my beautiful friend, Anna Petsas, who I should have thanked last time, for encouraging me to volunteer, to take thoughtful risks, and for sending me the article about domestic workers in the first place and alerting me to what was happening. You are so inspirational; I have often found myself taking huge steps in my life after just talking to you!

I would like to thank my friend Paul Lewis for all the inspirational writing chats. I would also like to thank Conway Road Writing Group – it means the world to me to be part of this group. Thank you all for being such great, supportive and talented and lovely people!

Thank you to Mehr at Salt and Sage Books for your thoughtful and insightful authenticity read; it was a real privilege to receive your helpful feedback on the manuscript.

Thank you to my agent, Marianne Gunn O'Connor – you are my guiding star. Thank you for your love, care, support, encouragement, vision, for being such a beautiful, inspirational person, for caring so much about the world and for also being a friend. I would never have been able to do this without you.

Thank you to my foreign rights agent at MGOC, Vicki Satlow, for being so amazing, and for everything you have done for me over the years.

Thank you so so much to my publishers at Manilla Press. Thank you Kate Parkin for your constant and unwavering support and for everything you have done, for being so caring, insightful and passionate. Margaret Stead – you have been absolutely amazing – all those conversations we had over the phone during lockdown, your insight, your suggestions, your imagination and creativity, and absolutely everything you have done to help make this novel happen.

Thank you to Perminder Mann for all of your support. Thank you Clare Kelly, Felice McKeown and Katie Lumsden – you are all so great to work with; thank you for all the hard work you have put into bringing this novel out.

Thank you to all my friends and family for your love and support over the years. Thank you to my brother, Kyri, and his wife for always encouraging me and being there for me. Thank you to Maria and Antony for being the best friends anyone can ask for. Thank you to Stellios Arseniyadis for listening to all my ideas during the editing process, and for being so helpful and supportive. Thank you to Claire and Sam Afhim for your friendship and support. Thank you to Louis Evangelou for your advice, for being so helpful, caring and endlessly patient. Thank you to the whole Evangelou family – Katerina, Tina and Chris – for all your support and help and lovely food and love, always.

Thank you especially to my dad and Yiota for always being there for me, encouraging me never to give up and for all your love and help. Thank you to my mum, though you are no longer with us – thank you for the love you gave me, the belief you had in me and for how funny and creative you were. I have those things with me, every step I take.

Every time I write a novel, I learn so much, and I'd really like to thank everybody who helped me to know, to understand, and to see things in a new way.

Dear Reader,

Around ten years ago, I became friends with a domestic worker in Cyprus who worked for a close family member. K was from Sri Lanka and had not seen her two daughters for eight years. She used to speak to them on her tablet; she was a mother to them through a screen. She introduced me to her daughters, she showed me her house and the streets of her hometown through the iPad. On screen, she showed me the trees, the flowers, the sky, the food – she wanted me to know what home meant to her, what it smelt like and tasted like and how it felt. We went on virtual walks together through the town with her daughters and mother-in-law. Sometimes, like any parent, she would need to tell her daughters off, or remind them to do their homework; often she told them she loved them – always through a screen. She told me the story of how she was widowed when her husband, the love of her life, died in a farming accident. Subsequently, she had to make the difficult decision to work abroad as a domestic worker, in order to provide for her children. Since then, she has not been able to be present for her daughters as they grow up. She sends them clothes and money, but she cannot be there with them, as they grow into young adults. I could see the strength, resilience and immense love that K had within her, but I also came to see the immense suffering of her sacrifice. In the meantime, I could see how the other women, in all the households along that street, went about their duties, often unseen and misunderstood. 'Ah,' one of the neighbours said to me once, 'these women don't care about their families, they drift around the world.'

While I was on tour for *The Beekeeper of Aleppo*, I was often asked: 'How can we get people to understand that refugees are not like migrants, that they have come because they do not have a choice?' This question saddened me. Migrants are often forced to leave their homes for less obvious reasons than war – but they still leave because they feel that they have no choice.

Songbirds was influenced both by this question and by a recent tragedy in Cyprus, in which five migrant women domestic workers and two of their children disappeared. When the women were reported missing, the authorities did not investigate their disappearance or search for them, because they were foreign – it was assumed that they had simply moved on. Later, however, it was discovered that the women and children had been murdered. In reality, almost two years had passed before a couple of tourists discovered the first victim in an abandoned mine shaft after a heavy rainfall. This was a woman who had been reported missing and whose disappearance had been completely dismissed.

I followed the events as they unfolded. With a broken heart, I read newspapers and watched the Cypriot news, spoke to friends. But I was not surprised at all that nobody had searched for these women and their children. I was not surprised that an investigation had not been launched, that the police had dismissed them as runaways. I felt anger, such anger, because over the years I had witnessed the reality of what had led to such gross negligence.

Most of my family live in Cyprus. I was born in the UK because my parents came as refugees after the war in 1974.

Most of the middle-class families in Cyprus – just as they do all over the world – hire domestic workers. In Cyprus, you do not have to be rich to have a domestic worker, just reasonably comfortable. So, the presence of these women, who run the households, look after children, walk the dogs, clean the restaurants/shops or whatever other businesses or properties their employers might own, is commonplace. Migrant domestic workers are a part of the fabric of Cypriot life.

This story is not an attempt to represent the voices of migrant workers or to speak for them, it is an exploration of the ideologies, prejudices, circumstances and underlying belief systems that can lead to very sad and often catastrophic events. It is an exploration of the way in which a flawed system can trap people. It is also a story about all forms of entrapment – the way we can all trap ourselves into certain ways of seeing and being.

And so, the idea of *Songbirds* began to grow.

I decided to visit Cyprus, to speak to as many women as I could, so that I could understand things more deeply. I went to visit a man who is the head of a human rights organisation aimed at caring for domestic workers; he also owned a café where the men and women would meet on Sundays. It was he who family members and employers had turned to when the police would not investigate the disappearances of these women and children. At one point, he admitted, he was the only person in Cyprus looking for what he believed to be a murderer – he turned out to be right.

I became very moved by the stories I heard. He arranged

for me to speak to many of the domestic workers who came into his café on Sundays. The stories I heard opened my eyes to the difficulties and suffering that migrant domestic workers experience. When I returned to the UK, I contacted Justice for Domestic Workers, and helped to edit some stories written by the women who visit the centre. I wanted to learn more about the problems and hardships that domestic workers face around the world, because I felt that the failure of the authorities in this particular situation was not an isolated incident, it was a result of our deeply flawed society and civilisation.

It became clear to me that although some of the women were leaving their countries in order to be able to earn more and support family members, others were searching for their freedom. Many of these women ended up finding themselves more trapped than they had been before, with no way of returning home.

I had learnt so much just by listening and opening my eyes; I understood so much more than I had before. This is why I wanted to write a story from the perspective of the people who had to learn about Nisha themselves – her employer and her lover. I struggled to write the ending. I found it so hard because I knew that Nisha had to die. She had to die because the women in reality had lost their lives, so cruelly snatched away. Although my novel isn't based on the true story, it is inspired by the essence of it, by the way in which ideologies exist like powerful undercurrents. We hear Nisha's story through the mouths of others; we have to piece together her existence through the memories of others

– this is what I often saw and felt on the streets of Cyprus. But when we listen and look carefully, we see that each person has as much beauty and depth and hope and fear and history and aspiration and courage as we do ourselves. The reader must discover this. Until the end, when Nisha finally speaks. I hope there is an echo after the last page – her voice continuing out into the silence of the ending.

Songbirds is a story about migration and crossing borders: it is about searching for freedom, for a better life, only to find oneself trapped. It is a story about the way in which systemic racism exists often unquestioned, relying upon prejudice and nationalistic ideals to survive. It is a story about learning to see each and every human being in the same way as we see ourselves.

Christy Lefteri

Reading Group Questions

1. How does *Songbirds* explore the theme of motherhood?

2. What does this novel tell us about the lives of female migrant workers?

3. How do racism and classism operate within the world of the novel?

4. Both Petra and Yiannis are complex characters. Did you like them? How did that change as you read the book?

5. What did you make of Seraphim as a character?

6. What role do animals play in this novel? What do you think the songbirds and the mouflon ovis represent?

7. What do you think Nisha really felt for Yiannis?

8. What role do you see Aliki playing in the novel – is she key to helping Petra come to realise she has to find out what has happened to Nisha?

9. Why do you think Petra struggles to connect with her daughter?

10. We never hear Nisha's voice until the end, but we see her through the other characters' eyes. What did you make of Nisha, and how did your image of her develop across the novel?

11. At the end of the book, Yiannis is going to find Kumari and her grandmother, and give them Nisha's journal and the money he has made. Do you see hope for their future, despite the fact that they have lost Nisha?

12. If you've read the author's letter, how did it affect your understanding of the novel?